SEDUCING SELENA

UNDERGROUND OMEGA SYNDICATE

DEVYN SINCLAIR

To those of us who fantasize about giving up control...

There's nothing wrong with you.

Promise.

AUTHOR'S NOTE

Dear Readers,

If you've read my Slate City Omegaverse, this book is **_NOT_** **_THAT_**.

Though the Alphas in this book are good men, the situations our characters are forced into are rough, and they have to make difficult choices. Consent is often dubious, and there are things which may make some readers uncomfortable.

This book is undeniably darker than my other Omegaverse books, so please proceed with caution.

Please check the content warnings available on my website, as they will guide you to know whether the content of this book is right for you, and allow you to protect your mental health if necessary.

www.devynsinclair.com

A NOTE ABOUT BDSM:

Seducing Selena features intense power dynamics and BDSM scenes.

As an author, I cannot stress this enough: This book is not meant to be either a realistic or fully healthy version of BDSM. Consent is the cornerstone of the kink community, and because of the nature of this plot, the consent of the characters is admittedly murky for a portion of the book.

In my personal life, I am a member of my local kink community, and an educator in kink spaces. I do understand the nature of power dynamics enough to feel comfortable portraying them, even in a manner that is not realistic, because this is fiction. Additionally, this book is not meant to provide any instruction about scenes, negotiation, or BDSM as a lifestyle or community.

If BDSM is something you're interested in, seek out kinksters at your local coffee or munch. Most people love sharing and helping people new to the lifestyle! All I ask is that you go in with your eyes open. BDSM is inherently risky, and you have to acknowledge that in order to play safely.

So go play—And be careful! But in the meantime, come join the Warwick Alphas as they teach their Omega what it means to submit, and they work on Seducing Selena so they can keep her forever.

CHAPTER ONE

SELENA

The cup of beer slammed down on the table. "Oh my god, I am *exhausted*." Gloria slumped into the chair across from me. Kyle and I were already puddles in our chairs, ignoring most of the noise in the surrounding bar. None of us had even bothered to change out of our scrubs, because it had been *that* kind of Friday.

"I don't even really know what I'm doing here," I said. "I should just go home and sleep."

Kyle shook his head. "You're going to get plenty of sleep this week. You can stay for a little while."

I looked at him and raised an eyebrow. "Is that what you think a heat is like? That I just get to *nap* for a week?"

"Napping and masturbating," he sighed. "Such a hard life."

Rolling my eyes, I took a sip of my beer. It was too sour for my taste, but I was beyond caring. I wasn't joking when I said I was ready to pass out.

"I'd kill for a whole week off," Gloria said. "I know it's not going to be all sunshine and roses, but still."

My two best friends were Betas, and therefore didn't know what having a heat was like. Especially a heat that I'd put off since last year at this time. "Don't even start with that. You get just as much vacation as I do, *and* you don't have to spend a week of it on a heat."

"Touché," Kyle said, and lifted his beer.

Gloria tipped her head back. "If we get any more nights like tonight, next week is going to be a nightmare. What's that now? The fifth?"

"Yeah," I said. "I think so. There were some a couple of months ago, but we didn't have any idea. Did we lose her?"

1

Gloria nodded without saying anything.

What was there to say to that? Losing a patient was always devastating, even if there was nothing you could do. It hit differently for nurses. We spent more time with the patients than the doctors, and this week had been particularly brutal.

Five patients, all Betas, all with the same symptoms, but only after they were admitted. Some kind of overdose, but we had no idea what, and there was no way to treat it. Their systems just… overloaded. It was a painful way to die, and Gloria had the Beta who came in today.

"I overheard the med director talking," she said. "Some of the tests on the autopsies came back, and it's like they're Omegas. Literal heat hormones where they shouldn't be. And they're not synthesized. They're real. Which begs the question, what the *fuck?*"

It was strange. None of the Betas came in presenting the same symptoms at first. A general feeling of unwellness. The first one we sent home. When they rushed back and died in the waiting room, we paid attention.

We kept hormones in the hospital for various treatments, but we would never use Omega hormones on Betas. It would be a disaster. Which was exactly why we were in this mess.

"I hope next week isn't too bad," I said.

"This is what happens when a new drug hits the streets," Kyle said. "Everyone rushes to try it and they end up in trouble."

"But it's not drugs, it's *hormones.*" I shook my head. "Take it from an Omega. No heat is worth dying for."

Gloria made a face. "Not like we would know."

I sighed, wishing even more that I was on my way home. My friends meant well most of the time, but it wasn't a secret that Gloria wanted to be an Omega. Her bitterness about it soaked into conversations like this. "Gloria, you know if I could trade places with you this week, I would."

Being locked in my apartment, wracked with pain unless I was exhausted or using toys on myself, in order to take the edge off the *feral* need for an Alpha knot, honestly wasn't my idea of a good time. Not like I had any actual Alphas banging down my door to fuck me through it, and I wasn't one of those people who could just have a heat with total strangers.

No fucking way.

"Yeah, well, we both know that can't happen."

Kyle just sipped his beer. When she got like this, it was impossible to get her out of it. And it had nothing to do with me. Losing a patient fucked with you in ways it was hard to describe. Gloria just needed space to breathe, a few more beers, and a good night's rest.

"Topic change," Kyle announced. "Are you sure you can't come with me tomorrow?"

I frowned. "Where?"

He smirked. "That new club. *Remember?*"

Suddenly, I did. It was *not* a club or bar like this one. He thought it would be fun to go to a sex club. And this one, *Catena*, was more than that. I'd spent some time on their website after he mentioned it.

Chains and handcuffs and other, darker things which I would never admit to anyone I was curious about. Going to a club where people were just… doing that? There was no way. I couldn't.

"I'll pass."

"Selena," Kyle said. "The way you're blushing tells me you want to go."

I shook my head. "I'm not saying never, but not this weekend. I need rest before the heat, anyway."

He shrugged. "Well, I'll be going. I cannot wait."

"Have fun."

"You know I will." He waggled his eyebrows. "Gonna find an Alpha who will—"

I held out a hand. "Kyle, you know I love you, but I do not need to hear what kind of kinky sex you're looking for."

Kyle laughed. "Fine. But I know you'd like it."

I made a face. "And what, exactly, makes you think I'd enjoy a sex club?"

"I don't know about a sex club, but I know that every time Dr. Avila gives you an order, you blush like crazy and do what he says without any questions."

"Oh my god," Gloria gasped. "You totally do."

I tossed back a big swig of my beer. "Being good at my job doesn't mean… whatever you're saying it means."

It didn't matter that they were right. Dr. Avila and the way he said things *did* something to my insides, but it didn't mean anything. They teased me about it all the time, but it was nothing.

"Sure," Kyle said. "Whatever you say."

"I'm going to go to the bathroom," I said. "Watch my bag."

"Sure."

The bathroom was so much quieter than the rest of the bar, highlighting my exhaustion. The *relief* of the silence? Yeah, I needed to go home and get the fuck out of here. A bath and bed were calling my name. I probably wouldn't start my heat until Monday, so I would have a couple nice days to relax first.

I washed my hands and made my way back to the table. My purse was still there, and Gloria had tossed her wallet inside. I grabbed it and gave it back to her. "I'm gonna go home. Sorry, guys, I'm just not feeling it tonight. But I'll check in with you when I can and see you next week."

Kyle nodded. He pushed me to stay before, but we all knew each other well enough now to know when *not* to push. "Have a good heat."

I forced a smile. "I'll try. Keep an eye on Anna for me?"

"Of course. I'll text you updates." Gloria stood up and hugged me. "Call me if you need anything else, okay?"

"Okay." I hugged her back.

Of course, I needed more than either of them could give me. What I really needed was someone to make me feel not so fucking lonely this entire week.

Curse of being a nurse. You could love your job or love your family. It was hard to do both, and my friends would agree.

Tonight? I was so tired I didn't even think I could manage the bath. Not the long kind of bath I liked. That could be tomorrow. A rinse off shower was all I could make it through.

I tossed my bag on the kitchen counter, and of course it fell over, spilling everything. Why was it that things made themselves messy whenever you were least in the mood for it? Sighing, I started shoving everything back in the bag... what the hell?

Groaning, I let my head fall back. Gloria's keycard was here. It must have fallen into my bag when she tossed her wallet in. She was going to need it this week. The cards tracked anyone with access to the medications. Doors opening, time stamps, the whole nine yards.

Bending down, I rested my head on the counter.

Fuck it. I would call her in the morning to come get it. She would get it before Monday and everything would be fine.

Stripping off my scrubs, I left them on the floor as I got into the shower and rinsed off the day, barely bothering to throw on a big t-shirt and underwear before climbing under the comforter.

Sometimes there were just days like this. Exhaustion creeped into your bones and settled there until you gave in and slept.

Tomorrow I would get everything together and ready. Right now? I was already fading down into the blissful dark velvet of a well-earned sleep.

5

The sound of movement woke me. I sighed, rolling over on the bed. It was just the birds outside. Whenever I was close to my heat and my sleep was lighter, I always woke up like this. God, just go back to sleep.

A *creak* sounded loudly in my hallway. That wasn't birds.

What the fuck?

The hairs on the back of my neck prickled.

I rolled back over toward my bedroom door, every sense on high alert. Was I imagining things?

The door burst open, a shadow moving so quickly I couldn't move. Someone on top of me, cloth shoved to my face. I screamed and struggled, the sound going nowhere with the cloth they were able to hold so tightly. Their body was heavy on mine.

How could this be happening?

I pushed against my attacker and arched my back, trying to throw them off, but my strength was fading. I'd inhaled too much of whatever was soaked in the cloth, gross, sickly smelling, and heady. It made everything fuzzy. My body was falling unconscious again, and this time I didn't want to go.

CHAPTER TWO

NICHOLAS

*T*he club was busy. It was a Saturday night, so it was always busy. On both sides of the business.

Standing on the balcony, looking at the busy floor, I craved something I couldn't have. All the people in *Catena* right now, having fun, sexy scenes filled with joy and not thinking about anything but their own pleasure.

I wanted that again.

"Feeling sorry for yourself again?" Sebastian asked, joining me at the railing.

"No," I lied.

He sighed. "It's fine, Nick. I am too."

Three years into this, and we were close to being done. Every day now felt like it lasted a thousand years. Because catering to some of the world's most evil people would do that to you. "Is everything ready?"

"Yeah," he said. "Everyone is backstage, making sure they smell thoroughly enticing. And Delano is just getting settled."

I growled, grateful the thumping bass of the music covered the sound. "I don't want him here."

"Neither do I. Too bad it's not an option."

Christopher Delano was one of the world's biggest pieces of shit. Even bigger than me and my pack mates. And we were lucky enough to be hosting him for two weeks at the club as our honored guest. Because *he* was bringing other 'honored guests,' and we needed him to get to them. Not to mention he wanted to observe our operation before we hammered out what was sure to be a very lucrative deal.

But that didn't mean I liked having him under our roof.

"Two more weeks," Seb said. "Three at most, and we're done."

"Are you ever really done with this?" I asked.

In the last three years, we tried to minimize the damage of the operation, using countless willing Betas and Omegas trying to help us take down these evil men.

Too many of them had paid the price.

"Done with it? Yes. Done with the effects? Probably not."

"Yeah."

He clapped me on the shoulder. "Get it together, man. We're almost there."

"Where's Derek?"

"Already working the crowd. Oiling the gears, like we should be."

Point taken.

I turned away from the view of the public club and went through the hidden door to the very *un*-public side of *Catena*. Smaller and more intimate. With a few bedrooms for our guests, a stage and a theatre for the auctions, and our own private quarters. Among other things, like a section of the club for our less legal clients.

Backstage was *flooded* with the scent of Omega. Twenty women wearing almost nothing but skin, and scents that made my mouth water out of instinct, but not desire. The only thing was, they weren't Omegas at all. The hormones they painted on their skin made them seem like it and enticed our auction buyers to purchase them.

Once they were sold, they went on their way and did the lion's share of what we needed, tracking and tracing the lines and men who purchased Omegas for their own pleasure and used them until they dried up. When that time came, these Betas had a capsule under their skin to break. The Beta hormones inside would make them hibernate and activate a tracker. So close to death it would be assumed they were. They would then be retrieved from wherever they were dumped. After all, these Omegas were dispensable in the eyes of our clients.

Everyone was already in character. They never came out of character here, and they were in it before they arrived.

The scents were overwhelming, and to my nose, cloying. Nothing like what I wanted in the scent of an Omega.

Derek swept backstage and leaned on one of the cages. "Time to go. You will serve until it is time for the auction. Your eyes will remain on the ground, and the only words you are permitted to speak are 'yes, Master,' or 'thank you, Master.' Am I clear?"

Soft murmurs of yes, and all eyes looking at the ground.

I hated it.

I loved the sight of an Omega on her knees, but only if she wanted to be there. What these Betas were about to do—

Derek came over to me as the women filed out to where the waiting trays of champagne and appetizers were. "I'm going to need you to fix your face, Nick."

"He's in a mood."

"Yes, I'm in a fucking mood."

Derek looked behind him, where the last of them disappeared. "They're well trained. They'll be okay."

They were trained, but not by us, as all our clients believed. It was the one relieving thing. The women now going into the lion's den were stronger than we'd ever be, and they volunteered, knowing the risk and the pain, hoping to save lives.

"Let's just get this over with, I muttered."

"That's the spirit," Seb said. "But bring out the smile, please."

"I'll do my best," I said with a growl.

Derek chuckled. "Very convincing."

They headed out to meet our guests, and I glanced over the shadowy room and all the cages in it. There was a hint of scent in the air. Like roses and oranges. Lovely, but it wasn't real. None of this was real.

Taking a long breath, I pasted an easy smile on my face and took on the role of Nicholas. Me, and not me. We were almost there, and the end couldn't come soon enough.

CHAPTER THREE

SELENA

*M*y head felt like there was a railroad spike going through it.

What the hell?

I groaned. God, I didn't drink nearly enough to make my head pound like this. Was this some kind of new heat symptom because I skipped one? Whatever it was, I needed some pain meds, and fast.

Opening my eyes, I wasn't in my bedroom. It was dark, and there were metal bars inches from my face.

Everything came slamming back into my head. The sounds, and my attacker. Fading into unconsciousness. Oh, fuck, where was I?

I sat up, looking down at myself. A deep green baby doll nightgown was on my body, and I hadn't been the one to put it there. Now it wasn't just my head that was in pain. Nausea clawed at my stomach. I was in a cage.

A fucking cage.

A curtain draped around one side, shrouding me in shadows, but I heard murmurs of other voices. I couldn't make this reality fit into my brain. This was something that happened to other people in books and movies. It didn't happen to *you*.

On the other side of the curtain, a man's voice cut through the air. "Time to go. You will serve until it is time for the auction. Your eyes will remain on the ground, and the only words you are permitted to speak are 'yes, Master,' or 'thank you, Master.' Am I clear?"

There was a tiny break in the curtain where I could see

him. In a suit, built and handsome, as were the men standing next to him. Why were evil people all so beautiful?

I heard people—*women*—say yes, followed by the padding of feet.

If they were all being ushered somewhere, why was I still in a cage? More importantly, how could that scare me more than being in the cage itself? Why was I singled out?

Vibration startled me.

I whipped around, eyes locking on a phone in the corner of the cage behind me. The screen lit up, and there was a message on it.

What the actual *fuck* was happening?

Hello **Selena Martin,**

Welcome to the Underground Omega Syndicate.

You've been selected for a task of great importance, given your profession, skills, and crimes. You have been relocated to the criminal portion of the Catena *club, which will be your new home, and the starting point for your new role within our organization.*

There are three rules you must abide by:

1. Maintain access to this phone. Given your assignment, this will be difficult. But you will find a loose floorboard within your cage where you can hide it. It is your sole point of contact with The Syndicate.

2. Follow any orders we give you, or you are given within your role. If an issue arises, reach out to this number immediately.

3. Never discuss the Syndicate or your affiliation with the Syndicate.

Follow these instructions, and you will be able to earn your freedom. Ignore or deviate from these rules, and the penalties will be swift and severe. Any attempt to expose our organization will immediately activate **Termination Protocol** *which includes (but is not limited to): revoking and permanently canceling all treatment for* **Anna Martin**. *There will be no reinstatement or other avenues available anywhere in the world. While you remain on assignment and in good standing, her care will continue. Other consequences may be immediate termination of funding, available resources, and execution.*

Due to the nature of your assignment, all instructions must be given now. It is your task to find the manufacturer and distributor of Omega hormones. The same ones you have been using to cause overdoses in Betas.

The harvesting of Omega hormones is not only harmful, but using them to cause death is inexcusable, which is why you are here now.

Once you discover the origin and party responsible, respond to this message. You will be retrieved and returned to your life. In the meantime, actions have been taken to make sure your absence is appropriate and does not alarm anyone.

You have one month.

Remember, we are always watching... for your safety and ours.

We appreciate you helping to further our cause: putting omegas in positions of power globally, and equality and prosperity for all designations.

U.O.S.

I stared at the words on the screen.

What?

What crimes were they talking about?

The Betas that died? Why would they think I had anything to do with that? My heart jumped into my throat. The threat against Anna was the thing that gripped me harder than a boa constrictor.

My little sister needed the treatments she was getting. Continually. If she didn't, she would die within a week. Let alone looking *globally* for a place to take care of her. It wouldn't matter. The rare auto-immune disorder she had required constant battling. Even a day without the medication and care she had at the hospital would leave her body wrecked and make it that much harder to keep her alive.

I just…

This had to be a dream, right?

The person who broke into my house and drugged me, all of this. It had to be a heat dream. It *had* to be.

Moving, I tested the boards under me. The heavy metal cage was bolted to the floor. Sure enough, one of the planks was loose. I lifted it and slid the phone inside. Dread slid down my spine.

Please be a dream.

Please be a dream.

But if it wasn't, how was I supposed to find out who was making the hormones? Why was I at a sex club and in a cage?

Oh god, was I about to be sold? I had so many questions that didn't have answers. How would they explain my absence for a month? Who the hell did I talk to about this? Why the *fuck* did they think I was a murderer?

If they put me here… was the cage open?

I pushed on the door, and sure enough, it swung open. I carefully crawled out and closed the door to the cage behind me. They said I needed access to the phone, so I made very sure not to lock it. Who knew if I was going to get put back in the cage as soon as I stepped out from behind this curtain?

Slowly, I peeked out around it and found the entire room empty. It was full of cages just like this one, but they were empty too. The room was a riot of different scents.

Now out from behind the curtain, I heard the low murmur of a crowd. This was a club, right? But the message had said the *criminal* portion of the club. What the hell would I be walking into?

I wanted to turn around and hide, but on the off-chance I was either dreaming or hallucinating, seeing what was out there would tell me either way. And if it was real, there was no way to get out of this without doing what they wanted.

Anna came first.

It was the rule I lived my life by. So I would try to find what they wanted, even if it made no sense and it had nothing to do with me.

I tiptoed in the direction I heard all the people moving and found a dark hallway leading to brightness. This was definitely where I needed to be, then.

I blinked, adjusting to the contrasting brightness as I stepped up to the door. This was… a theatre? To my right, a brightly lit stage stood empty. Or mostly empty. A chain hung ominously in the middle of it, not attached to anything.

In the audience, people were mingling. Men in suits and women—Omegas—dressed in lingerie like mine, or skimpier. They held trays of glasses and food and circulated among all the men. In one corner, an Omega was on her knees and a man's fingers were in her mouth.

I saw the three men from the backstage area speaking with each other and a couple of others.

What the fuck did I do here? Were there more trays I missed? What was it the man had said? Yes, Master, and thank you, Master.

In spite of myself, I shuddered. Kyle was more on the nose than I would ever tell him about my fantasies. But that's what they were. Fantasies to get me off. Not something I suddenly wanted to live full time.

"Well, well. Aren't you a pretty thing."

A man stood at the bottom of the few steps in front of me, smiling. He had a glass of champagne in his hand and drank from it lazily. He smelled stale. Like bread that had been left out on the counter for far too long. "I don't think you're supposed to look at me."

I dropped my eyes to the floor. The backstage man *had* said that.

"Better." Something about the way he said it made me shiver. Not in a good way. His tone sounded oily and smooth, like someone hiding something. "Though I must say I like your eyes. I might like to see the fear in them while I break you."

Terror ripped me in half. I couldn't breathe. "What's your name?"

What did I say? I didn't want to talk to him. I didn't want to be here. Emotion started to overwhelm me, and I fought the whine in my throat.

"You won't get any words out of her," a new voice said. My eyes snapped up, and I found myself face to face with the Alpha from backstage.

Up close, his eyes were a piercing blue, and he was even more handsome up close. But beyond that, his *scent*. Crisp and cold, like mountain air. An intangible sweetness like I was on a brisk and beautiful winter walk. It was one of the most incredible things I'd ever smelled in my life, and my Omega body reacted. Perfume whirled out of me and toward him.

I saw him stiffen, pupils going wide and dark as he caught my scent. Did he like mine too? What was he going to say to this man? Was he going to save me? Was he my enemy?

16

With his scent wrapped around me, I felt dizzy.

He recovered after a moment. "She's not allowed to speak without permission. Isn't that right, *gattina*?"

CHAPTER FOUR

DEREK

The pre-auction drinking was in full swing. "See?" I said to Nick. "Everything is fine."

Anger burned in his eyes. I felt it too, but I was better at hiding it than my pack mate. "Nick," I said. "Get through it and beat the hell out of the punching bag later."

He nodded sharply, nodding to someone as they walked by. The cameras in the corners were panning around as those clients who weren't here in person observed the merchandise.

I didn't like to call them that, but it helped to keep my mind on the part I was playing.

"When can we start this?" Seb asked.

"Give it a few minutes," I said. "Some of them need time to call their bosses." Which was important, if we wanted to track them. We needed them to buy and be hooked. So we would let these people drink and ogle the beautiful women before we sprang the trap.

A few clients stopped to chat and ask questions. Nick turned on the charm, and absolutely nothing was amiss. I understood the mental strain. After so long trying to get to this point? All of our nerves were frayed.

"Who the fuck is that?" Seb asked.

I followed his gaze to the edge of the stage, where a woman was standing like she was terrified. She was fucking *gorgeous*. Curvy and tan with long black hair that shone even across the room. The smoothness of it made me want to fist my hand in it while I did naughty, naughty things to her.

But none of that mattered because she wasn't supposed to be here. Every one of the women in this room we knew. We knew their names and training and what they planned to do once we inserted them with the clients.

This woman was a stranger, which meant danger.

Delano approached her, and Nick swore. "This isn't good."

"I'll take care of it," I said. "Seb, as soon as we take care of this, go ahead and start. If there's something wrong, we can't delay."

"Agreed."

I put my hands in my pockets as I approached, putting on a casual air. Like nothing bothered me, despite my instincts going absolutely fucking crazy. The closer I got, the more my Alpha told me there was something about her. I wanted to reach out and hold her so that scared curve in her shoulders would disappear.

But first, I needed to get her away from Christopher fucking Delano.

I was about to open my mouth when her scent slammed into me. Roses on the wind mixed with the delicious, sweet sharpness of oranges. It made me want to bury my face in her neck and breathe it for a thousand years.

Mine.

My hair stood on end. She was an Omega. A *real* Omega. I didn't know why she was here—if she were a plant from the very people we were trying to trap, or something else. But this little, beautiful Omega was mine, and no one in this room was going to touch her.

"You won't get any words out of her," I said to Delano, clinging to the character I'd developed. "She's not allowed to speak without permission. Isn't that right, *gattina?*"

Her dark eyes went wide as she stared at me, but she nodded, the relief there plain.

Delano turned to me. "She's yours? If she's yours, then why is she here with the merchandise? You shouldn't let your pets run around without a leash."

"No, I shouldn't," I said softly. "She'll be punished for it later. But then again, she likes that." The smirk I allowed frightened her, the orange in her scent turning bitter. Good. Whoever she was should be terrified. This was a place she should never be, even if she was right where I wanted her.

"Were you looking for us, *gattina*?" I asked. "It must be important for you to disobey. You may answer me."

She licked her lips, and I prayed allowing her to speak wouldn't put her at risk. Delano was watching, and more than anyone else, we couldn't fuck this up with him. I didn't want him anywhere near her.

"Yes, Master. I'm sorry."

Hearing *Master* from those pretty lips did things to me I couldn't show right now. But I also needed to make sure everyone in this room didn't question who she was, or who we were. The regret in my chest was strong, but neither of us had a choice. "Strip," I told her. "You've lost the privilege of clothing for the night. Go kneel with your other Masters and wait for me. We will decide your punishment together."

There was hurt and betrayal in her gaze, and it deserved to be there. But being naked and embarrassed was better than being bought, beaten, and raped. Which is what it would be with her.

With shaking hands, she stripped the baby doll night-gown over her head, and I held out my hand for it. She gave it to me, and turned away, slowly and deliberately going where I'd told her.

Thank fuck she'd noticed enough, and both Nick and Seb didn't bat an eye as she knelt at their feet. If anything, they looked at her with enough disdain to sell the bit.

"I'll pay whatever you want for her," Delano said. "She still has some life in her eyes. Breaking her would be fun."

"I apologize for my slave," I said. "She's brand new. Still being trained and should have known not to tempt our clients. She will be disciplined, but she is not for sale."

His eyes narrowed. "Interesting."

I smirked. "You know perfectly well I don't sell untrained slaves, Delano. Once her training is complete, we will make a decision about whether to keep her. If we don't, you'll be my first call."

This fucker wasn't getting anywhere near her, but he didn't have to know that right now.

"Then I look forward to observing her training while I'm here."

Fuck. I walked right into that one. And now I'd put the Omega into an impossible position. Then again, she was here, and she'd caught Delano's vile eye. It didn't matter who she really was, she was fucked one way or another. Better it be us.

I threw on my laziest, most arrogant smile. "I'm sure you will. Enjoy the auction."

Turning, I made my way back to where the little Omega now knelt by my pack mates, shivering. I sat in my chair and pulled her roughly between my legs, forcing her to look up at me. The roughness was mainly for show, knowing Delano's eyes were still on me.

"You're not supposed to be here," I said.

She didn't say anything, just stared through me like she was dazed. Beside me, I felt the tension in both Nick and Sebastian. Were they reacting as strongly to her scent as I was? Because if so, this changed everything at the worst fucking time. In our line of work, surprises were the enemy.

An unclaimed Omega who was a scent match?

That was the ultimate surprise.

"Who are you?"

She licked her lips, eyes looking anywhere but at me, trying to figure out an escape. No matter how she ended up here, there wasn't one now. If we let her go and she wasn't seen with us, Delano would ask questions and our story would fall apart. Or if she went into the world and he had her followed, she could be taken and never heard from again. He would do it. He'd done it before.

Fuck, he probably had people out there doing it right now.

"Selena," she finally whispered. "My name is Selena."

"How did you get here, Selena?"

She was shaking, and the cruel, sadistic part of me liked it. I savored her fear. I wanted to shape it into pain and pleasure for the both of us. I wanted to lean in and inhale the heavenly scent coming off her skin and knot her until she surrendered. And she would. Because she was my match. Glancing at Nick, I confirmed with one look.

She was *our* match.

There was a reason we were chosen for this assignment, and it wasn't only because we were smart and ruthless. We also enjoyed a willing Omega tied open for the taking.

"I was just in the club," she said. "Someone mentioned something about an auction. I thought they meant an auction like… for members of the club to play with each other. So I asked and came here."

That was a lie. None of the staff of the club would ever send a patron to this room. They would be fired immediately, and they knew it. "Try again."

"I don't know."

"You don't *know*?" Sebastian asked.

Weaving my fingers into her hair, I pulled her head back, nearly to the point of pain. "I'm not going to ask you again. How did you get here?"

"I swear," she gasped. "I woke up back there. I don't know how I got here or why I'm here. I went to sleep in my bed last night." Big tears gathered in her eyes. "I'm not even sure where I am. All I know is the name of the club."

Interesting. It had to be a lie, too. Because no one could get into this club without us knowing. But it was closer, at least. It felt like she was telling the truth.

It was possible she didn't fully know or remember, and this was a different kind of attack on us. Maybe whoever sent her drugged her as a part of the act. The question was, what was she here to find? Who sent her? Questions we'd have to discuss later after the auction was over.

I tightened my fingers in her hair and rose-scented perfume enveloped me in a cloud. So she was affected by this too. Excellent.

"Please let me go," she whispered.

"You see, I can't do that. The man I pulled you away from is a very bad Alpha. And if I let you go, he's going to take you. Even if you go back to wherever you came from, he'll find you. So you'll stay here."

"You're selling Omegas." She gritted her teeth. "Are you saying you're a *good* Alpha?"

I laughed. "No. But I promise you'd rather us than him. And you don't want to find out the hard way."

She looked at me and glanced at my pack mates, terror clear. "So you're going to punish me?"

Sebastian crouched down beside her and gripped her neck. It looked far harsher than it was. "Yes. Punish you, train you, and own you."

"Own—"

"You are now a slave," I told her. "Our slave. I already told you we can't let you go, and even if I could, I wouldn't. Not without knowing the truth about who you are, why you're here, and who sent you."

She opened her mouth, and Nick interrupted. "There's no point in begging. You won't win. Whether you came here yourself or someone sent you to attack us, you're ours now. You can accept what is required of you, or we can force it on you. It will happen either way. But it will be much more enjoyable for you if you agree."

The idea of forcing anything on this beautiful, curvy Omega made me sick to my stomach, but it was the truth. In

24

order to take down evil—true evil—you had to become evil yourself. And as intoxicating as she was, one Omega couldn't be worth more than the lives of all the Omegas and everyone else being sold across the world.

Even if I wanted her to be.

Her cheeks were flushed, chest rising and falling almost too quickly. "What will I have to do?"

"You're our slave, Omega." Sebastian's voice had deep notes of Alpha command threaded through, and her body wilted in the face of it. "You will do what we say when we say it. Or you will be punished. And trust me, we'll enjoy that just as much as your obedience."

"Now, *gattina*," I said, reaching down and unbuckling my pants. "You will suck my cock while the auction proceeds. After that, you'll be punished. And later?" I shrugged. "Later, we'll figure out what to do with you."

My cock was already hard as I pulled it out, and in the corner of my eye I found Delano smiling. Bastard.

Selena was flushed bright pink, glassy eyes staring at my length. She was hesitating too long. I wished this could go differently.

"Now, slave. Hands behind your back, put your mouth on me before I have to make you."

She was shaking, but she did it, leaning in and brushing me with her mouth. And as soon as her lips closed around my head, I realized what a fucking terrible idea this was. Her scent and the hesitant earnestness of her lips made me want to spill into her mouth right now.

But I couldn't do that, and had no plans to.

I would never come in front of this crowd. As strange as it was, they would take it as a sign of weakness.

"Sebastian?" I asked.

There wasn't any way I could announce the start of the auction while I was getting blown.

He headed to the stage, and the lights in the theatre

25

dimmed twice. Sebastian stood on the stage with a glass of champagne, and I could barely focus on him. Selena timidly licked the head of my cock, not daring to go further.

I couldn't let her do that for long, but because I'd said she was brand new, she would get some leniency. I wanted to take my time and gently teach her how to bring me pleasure. At the same time I wanted to drive myself so far down her throat there was no cock left for her to take.

It had been far too long since any of us had had someone to play with in this way. It was too much of a risk. Whoever sent this Omega ensured we didn't have a choice, and I was fucking grateful even if she was a spy. No way anyone could have known she was a scent match.

"I told you to suck it," I told her. "Not to treat it like a lollipop. Put it in your mouth, Omega."

An intoxicating mixture of anger and helpless arousal filled her gaze. Big green eyes I wanted to sink into. She obeyed, wrapping her full lips around the head of my cock and sucking lightly.

I gripped the arms of my chair so hard they creaked. *Fuck me*, this was going to be exquisite torture. She would get plenty of the same soon enough.

"Welcome," Sebastian said. "Most of you are already familiar with our format. For those that aren't, the merchandise will be displayed one at a time. You are allowed one private bid per lot, and one only. Once the auction concludes, the bids will be counted, and you will be informed which, if any, lots you have won. After payment has cleared, we will arrange for the delivery of your merchandise where you choose. Enjoy."

The lights in the theatre dimmed, and one of our men brought out the first Beta to be auctioned. All the people bidding thought she was an Omega. Beautiful, but didn't compare to the woman on her knees in front of me.

Her hands were lifted over her head and attached to the

chain, lifted over her head until she was on her toes as her stats were displayed to the bidders. No more clothing was to be found.

I closed my eyes. The last thing I wanted was to see anyone else while Selena's tongue did *that*. Following my instinct, I reached out and fisted her hair, pulling her further onto my shaft. "I like it when you use your tongue," I said. "But I need you to *suck my cock*, Omega. Do it, and do it like you mean it before I fuck your mouth the way it was meant to be."

A cloud of perfume wafted from her. My little Omega was aroused in spite of herself. I should calm her down. The perfume could attract questions from more than just Delano. Yet I was greedy. I wanted the intensity of her scent wrapped around me the way her lips were wrapped around my dick.

The woman on stage changed, but nothing changed for me. My eyes were on Selena in the dim light of the theatre. Her eyes were closed as she moved her head up and down, sucking my cock like I'd ordered her to.

For the moment, she looked calm and at peace. It was natural as a scent match. I would taste like fucking candy to her, and I was going to struggle not to haul her up to our apartments, spread her on the kitchen counter and consume her.

I wanted those thighs locked around my ears while she screamed and drenched my face with her perfect pussy. There was no need to see it. I already knew it was perfect. Because she was perfect. I'd pretended to be disinterested in her body for Delano's sake, but the glimpse I got, and the little I could see now? It made me want to sink my teeth in and take a bite.

A claiming bite.

God, I'd heard about this. Being scent bonded with someone you didn't even know. Holy shit, it was so different from I'd imagined. I was ready to throw everything away for

27

this Omega even when it was more than probably she was here to try to take me down and betray me.

"That's it, *gattina*," I whispered. "Take me deeper."

The softest whine reached my ears, and another wave of perfume. At this rate, there was going to be a puddle on the floor and a pack of hungry Alphas coming for her.

Leaning forward, I pulled her off my cock and made her look at me. Selena's eyes were glazed and overwhelmed with arousal. "Why are you here?"

"I don't know."

"Mmm." I leaned in even further, inhaling the scent of her pulse. "You're awfully aroused for someone who doesn't know why they're here. Maybe I was wrong. Maybe you did want to be in an auction."

Her eyes cleared in a flash. "No. Not like that. *Please*."

"Shh," I kept her quiet as the next Beta was brought to the stage and chained. "Do I smell good to you, *gattina*? And don't you dare fucking lie to me. I will know."

She shuddered. "Yes."

"You smell good to us as well. I still want to know why you're here and who sent you. But you need to understand that being our slave means no one touches you but us." I traced a finger along her neck. It would look gorgeous in a collar. A permanent one. Maybe cuffs for her wrists and ankles, too. Always available so she could be restrained.

If I wasn't already hard as granite, that thought would have done the trick. I couldn't fucking wait to tie her down.

Putting my cock back inside my pants and zipping them up while so hard was easily the hardest thing I'd ever done. "Come here," I said, shifting her around to the side of my chair and letting her lean against my knee. "Stay still and stay quiet," I whispered. "Don't draw attention to yourself. When you kneel at your Master's feet, it is your job to be invisible unless he decides otherwise."

She stiffened, and I stroked my hand down her hair, all

the way to her shoulders. I was instructing her and, at the same time, testing her reactions. Most people couldn't hide their first instincts. It took years of practice and training to show *nothing*. This little Omega clearly didn't have that.

Interesting.

The auction continued, and I continued stroking Selena's skin, keeping her connected to me. What were we going to do with this little trespasser?

CHAPTER FIVE

—————————

SELENA

My tongue tasted like him.

I desperately wished I could say I didn't like it, but the flavor of him was just like his scent. Elusive and delicious, and I'd found myself sinking into the act of that blow job like I wasn't in this position. Like I hadn't just been kidnapped and forced into whatever hell this was.

What was wrong with me?

The two other Alphas with him smelled just as intoxicating. Warm, baked apples with spices like cinnamon, and a sharp peppermint that felt like it had a citrus undertone. Maybe lime? It didn't matter. All I wanted was to stay in this vortex of scent.

In spite of the awful things happening in this room, I *felt* safe within their scents, even if I wasn't.

The man kept brushing his knuckles along the back of my shoulder, and I knew I shouldn't take comfort in the touch, but I did. What else was I supposed to take comfort in? If I closed my eyes, I could pretend none of it was real. That I was just in a club meant for kinky people, and I was *choosing* to kneel at this man's feet.

I wasn't sure how long I knelt there. My legs were numb, and I was cold. But I would take being cold if it meant I could stay right here and not be on that fucking stage.

How could people do this? How could they buy *people* like it was nothing? Omegas…

Finally, the lights rose, and gentle music started to play. The men began to stand and mingle once more. What happened now?

"Stand, Selena." One of them said.

If I stood up right now, I would fall over. My legs were entirely numb from the knee down. "I don't think I can."

"What was that?"

A little louder. "I said I don't think I can."

Fingers tilted my chin up. The biggest of them. Dark hair and dark eyes. The richness and warmth of his scent contrasted with the harshness of his gaze. "Did you forget who I am, little one? Because the next time you say something without my title, I'll have to punish you. And I believe you already have one of those coming."

I swallowed, knowing now what he expected and not quite believing I was going to do it. "I don't think I can stand, Master."

A hint of a smile reached his eyes. "Better. Why can't you stand?"

"I'm not used to kneeling like this for so long, Master," I added the word just in case. "My legs are numb. If I stand, I might fall over."

He looked down at me and observed how I knelt. "I won't let you fall." Taking one arm, he pulled me up, and just like I thought, my legs, without sensation, couldn't hold weight. I would have collapsed had one big arm not come around me and held me to his body.

"Very affectionate with a slave," an already familiar voice said. The man from the stairs earlier. He looked at me with what could only be described as *hunger*. It slithered over my skin and made me sick.

The man holding me laughed, but even as he did it, his hand tightened around my waist, like he was making sure no one could pull me away from him. "Sometimes you need a handful of softness, Delano. It makes a good contrast to when you're making them scream."

Chills ran down my spine, and I kept my gaze on the floor. He didn't say what kind of screaming he meant, if it were the fun kind or the horrific kind.

"Is she a screamer?" Delano asked. "That's interesting."

"She's so new, I haven't had time to truly find out," my Master said. "But I'm sure we'll know soon enough."

"Have I told you my favorite way, Sebastian?"

Sebastian. That was the man's name. Sebastian stiffened beside me, and it sounded like he was speaking through his teeth. "To make someone scream? No, I don't believe you have."

Delano shrugged. "I find a scalpel usually works the best if you want the finest cuts and the smallest pieces. What I carve depends on the day, and what the slave hates the most."

I didn't move. What the actual fuck. That's what he did to people? I already knew the men in this room were evil, but that? Was this a serial killer convention?

"While you're fucking them, of course," Sebastian said.

"Of course," Delano inclined his head. "Nothing feels quite as good as pussy squeezing you so hard it's trying to eject you from their body. Except maybe forcing your way back in." He laughed, and I turned closer to Sebastian, my mind going blank with horror. The other man had been right. They might not be good Alphas, but they weren't *that*.

"You always did have… unique tastes, Christopher."

"You should join me sometime. Maybe your new slave would enjoy being taken by the two of us together."

Sebastian's grip on me now was painful, and I liked it, because it meant he wasn't letting me go. "As Derek told you, she's not for sale. But thank you for the offer."

"Everything is for sale once you find the price. Over the next couple of weeks, I'll be sure to find it."

Delano walked away, and I heard Sebastian mutter, "Over my dead body."

I squeezed my eyes shut, turning further into Sebastian's suit. His scent was intoxicating. Just like the one he called Derek and the third, nameless Master. It was electrifying and terrifying, because I knew what it meant. Everyone knew what it meant.

A scent-match. Rare enough that finding your match was a thing to be celebrated under different circumstances. They made me *perfume*. If I'd stumbled into these three men at the bar last night, on the verge of my heat, I'd be over the fucking moon.

As of now? I didn't even know how long I would survive.

"Will your legs hold you now, Omega?"

The low shiver of his voice rolled across my skin and gave me chills. I nodded yes. "Good," he said. "I can't hold you like this while we walk, but you will follow me, and I expect you to stay close. Understood?"

"Yes, Master." The words slipped out nearly automatically.

His arm slowly came out from around me, but it lingered on my skin. "Let's go."

We walked back down toward the front of the theatre again, toward the stairs where I'd entered in the first place. We came close to a group of men, and one of them turned toward us. "Seems like you're hiding some of the goods for yourself, Sebastian."

He laughed, lighter than before. "Gotta have some perks of the job, right?"

When he stepped back, I went up the stairs first. Through a door and into a dark hallway, followed by an elevator with a keypad. He entered a code, and we *flew* upward. How tall was this building? I didn't realize *Catena* was in one of the downtown skyscrapers, but it seemed that way right now.

The elevator opened directly into an apartment. A *gorgeous* apartment. It seemed strange that there was daylight pouring through the windows. There weren't any down-stairs, and it still felt like night. But the sun was setting, painting the place in orange and gold.

Sebastian walked over to the sunken, lush living room

and pulled a giant pillow from beside one of the couches and plopped it on the floor. He pointed at it. "I want you on that pillow. And when I come back, I expect you to still be there."

I walked to the pillow and sat down, sinking into it. It was big enough and fluffy enough I felt like I was falling into a cloud. As soon as I was on the pillow, Sebastian turned and left.

Of course I wanted to get up and explore and figure out what the hell the Syndicate wanted, maybe from *these* men. But I also didn't know who I was dealing with, and the potential consequences of being caught snooping didn't seem worth it.

Instead, I let myself curl up on my side and close my eyes. Despite being drugged and unconscious for almost a day, I was exhausted. Part of it was the intense emotions and fear, and the other part was my coming heat. My hormones were close to the surface, begging me to give in to them.

And fuck, did my body want to give in to the three men who now held me captive. Scent matched. I must be the unluckiest Omega in the world to find my scent-matches after getting fucking kidnapped.

The air was cold in here, colder than the theatre. I didn't move, just burrowed myself deeper into the pillow, trying to create a little pocket of warmth for myself as I let myself drift.

I must have fallen asleep, curled up in a ball. Because it was dark outside when I heard the *ding* of the elevator opening once more. My eyes were still shut, and I left them that way. If they thought I was asleep, what would they say?

"You left her up here alone?"

"What, you wanted her downstairs with the rest of them? We have the cameras. It's fine. Besides, it looks like she barely moved."

Heavy footsteps approached me. "Selena."

I blinked my eyes open, not needing to fake exhaustion. Derek stood over me. "Did you move from this spot?"

Lowering my gaze, I shook my head.

He sighed and ran a hand through his hair. "Okay. Come here. We need to have a chat."

Slowly, I extricated myself from the pillow and followed him out of the living room. We went down a hallway and into a big office. Sebastian and the third man were already there, sitting in chairs. A big desk sat in front of the large window, but the three chairs were on this side of the desk.

"There," Derek pointed to the floor. "Kneel."

I couldn't stop the small whimper in my throat. My knees still hurt from earlier.

The nameless Alpha snapped his eyes to me. "Part of your training, slave. You better get used to being on your knees, because you're going to spend a lot of time that way."

My mind shut down at his words. I still couldn't believe this was really happening. I'd been... sold. Ripped from my home and sold, sent on a mission, all because of some crime I didn't commit.

Derek sat in the empty chair. "How did you get here, Selena?"

"I told you that. I don't know. I woke up backstage."

"Nope," he said. "Try again."

Looking up, I got my first *real* look at all of their faces. The unfairness of all of it hit me once again. Because they were handsome. In the real world? This would be a no-brainer. Too bad being beautiful didn't mean anything when it came to being a good person. "There's not another answer," I said.

"We know everyone who comes in and out of our club, Omega. So to get in here without us knowing, someone had to help you. Tell us who it was, and we can protect you." The nameless Alpha said. "You don't seem like someone who wants to hurt anyone, so if they sent you to spy, just tell us."

He was right. They had sent me, but I didn't know who, and if I opened my mouth, I put Anna at risk. I couldn't do that, no matter how much. Aside from that, these Alphas were *selling* Omegas. They weren't good. I had zero confidence that they wouldn't hurt me if I told them the truth.

I wasn't an idiot. This wasn't a situation where I had a white knight about to ride in and save the day. People who disappeared usually didn't come back, and the best I could do right now was keep myself, and my sister, alive.

Sebastian looked over at the man. "Seems like she's made her choice, Nick."

Nick.

Derek sighed. "It seems so." He locked his blue eyes on me again. "As I told you before, we can't let you go without knowing why you're here or how you got here. I'm sure you understand why. Even if I could let you go free and are completely innocent, you've been seen and would be in danger. I'm not in the habit of letting a perfectly good product walk out the door that someone could have for free when we can make a profit, but we're still going to offer you a choice."

I looked up hopefully.

"Be sold or stay here."

Dread slid down my spine. "What?"

"There are plenty of people who would buy you outright. So it's your choice whether to stay or go."

"That's not a choice."

He shrugged and spread his hands open. "It's all you have."

My mind was still shuttered. I knew what was happening, but I didn't know how to react. Was I pushed so far beyond the edges of my mind that I couldn't react?

I lowered my eyes to the floor.

It was… okay. If my mind was trying to protect me by not letting all of this in, I would let it.

"Here," I whispered.

Sebastian nodded. "Good choice."

"I think it's already clear," Derek cleared his throat, "but I'm going to lay some things out for you. You are now a slave. You are our property, and you have no rights. You may do nothing without permission. We are going to train you to be the best slave you can be, and when your training is complete, we will decide what to do with you."

Nick stood and walked out of the room, but Derek kept talking.

"As our property, we can use you however we please, at any time of day. Your holes will always be available for our pleasure, without resistance. Any pleasure you receive is our choice, and if we allow you to come, you will always say thank you."

My head snapped up, and Derek smirked. "You heard me right, *gattina*. Even your pleasure belongs to us now. You may not come without permission. If you disobey, you will be punished. And that doesn't merely apply to orgasms, we expect obedience in all things."

Steps sounded behind me, and Nick appeared at my side. "Give me your hands."

I obeyed.

Quickly, he wrapped a measuring tape around different parts of me. Wrists, ankles, neck, bust, waist, and hips. I supposed they needed to know what kind of chic *slave* clothing to put me in.

Then he had something I recognized from the hospital—a mechanical inserter, used for forcing things under the skin quickly. I jerked away from him. "What the fuck is that for?"

He held my arm still, pressing the machine to the inside of my forearm and pressing the trigger. Fierce pain pierced my skin, and I gasped. When I raised my other hand to touch, there was a small flat disc I could feel beneath my skin.

"A tracker," Nick said. "Because we don't let merchandise out of our sight without knowing we can find them."

I felt sick.

Taking my right hand, he wrapped leather around it. When he let it go, and I lowered it, I saw what he'd put there. A leather cuff that was familiar, because I saw it on the covers of some of the books I read and in the porn I watched, unsure if I'd ever take the step to experience a fantasy.

Black leather and a blood red stripe. Metal hardware buckled it onto my wrist, with rings to hook it to things.

"Stand up," he said, after attaching the second cuff, and more went on my ankles.

"These will mark you as ours," Sebastian said. "So there will be no more repeats or questions about who you belong to. As for a collar, you'll have to earn that."

Somehow, I managed to keep my face in check. Like a collar was something deserving of being *earned*.

"Finally," Derek said, "you will address us as Master, without exception. You may use our names with it if you need to. Do you have any questions? This is the only time you'll freely be able to ask them, and consider it a gift, given the fact that you won't tell us why you're here, infiltrating our club."

I shuddered as Nick put his hand on my shoulder, pushing down. Not a lot of pressure, but I knew what he wanted. I went to my knees. "I do... have some questions."

"Ask them," Nick said.

"What does *gattina* mean?"

Derek looked surprised at the question, and arguably, it was the least important. But I needed to know. "It means *'kitten'* in Italian. Not something I say often, but it suits you."

I nodded once. "Okay. We're... we're scent matched?"

"Yes," Sebastian leaned forward, his elbows on his knees. "We are, little one."

My breath caught in my throat, a sob that I forced down.

How many times had I imagined meeting my scent matches? When it was in my imagination, it was nothing but gorgeous pleasure and love. Not… this.

"Does that matter at all?"

I glanced up in time to see what I thought was regret in Derek's eyes. There and gone so quickly, I probably imagined what I wanted to see.

"Any other questions?"

"Yes. When will I be trained? Like when is that process finished?"

Sebastian smirked. "When you obey every command we give you without thinking. When you know exactly what we mean when we tell you to get on your knees and suck. When you know your Masters' pleasure better than your own."

He leaned a little closer, voice lowering. "When you can take a ten inch cock in every hole and *love it*. When you crave the taste of your Alpha's cum more than food. When you beg for the pain only he or they can bring you. When you finally understand that your pleasure isn't yours, and you're not allowed to come without permission. Ever. Even if I chain you to a fucking machine and leave you there for hours."

I scoffed. "I'll never do those things. I can't."

"Oh, *gattina*." Derek moved, coming to crouch in front of me and brushing a piece of hair off my face. "Yes, you will."

"And you're so sure about that?"

"Yes."

"Why?"

He smiled, the expression razor sharp and sinister. "Because every slave I've ever sold has said the same when they started. And within a month, they were perfect."

"Not me."

"Yes. You." He bent, dropping his lips to my skin and sucking one nipple into his mouth. I gasped, and the way the pleasure of that simple motion hit me made me so fucking confused. Perfume swirled around me, giving away how much I liked it.

But I didn't.

How could I?

His hand pinched my other nipple, simply and clearly illustrating what they'd laid out. They could do whatever

"I think you may be more than perfect, *gattina*. I think you might be the end of me."

"Good."

He just laughed and tucked a finger under my chin. "I think you'll find it's not all bad," he said. "You will want for nothing. Protected and cared for. And if you're good, you will earn the occasional pleasure."

"How gracious of you."

His eyes went hard. "Careful, Selena. We're being gentle with you for the moment. But a tone like that would have you over my knee and your ass bright red. Remember that you chose to stay, and be grateful we're lenient."

I flushed, because imagining being so close to him, flush with his body after I already knew how good he tasted, was arousing in spite of everything.

"Our little slave is aroused," he said quietly. "Poor Omega, going to be turned out without pleasure most of the time, aren't you?"

Glaring at him, I let my annoyance cover up my fear. I didn't know how I was going to make it through a heat without any orgasms, but I would. For Anna, I would.

He retreated, and I took my chance. "I have one more question."

"Yes?"

My hands clenched into fists. "Are you going to cut me open?"

"What the *fuck?*" Derek reacted instantly, which made me feel better.

"Delano made some of his… particular interests known to Selena," Sebastian said.

Nick swore under his breath. "No, Selena, we're not going to cut you open. Even if it was something we were interested in, which it isn't, we wouldn't damage merchandise in that way."

My mouth tasted sour. "Thank god for that."

"Time to start your training," Derek said, turning to face me once more. "And now that we don't have an audience, I don't have to hold back." He began to unbuckle his belt. "Time to finish what you started."

Nick stood, and before I even knew what was happening, my arms were behind my back, cuffs clipped together so I couldn't move them.

I hung my head. I knew this was my choice, given the options I had, but I felt…

Conflicted. Because the base part of me *wanted* to finish it. I wanted more of the way he tasted and smelled. I craved it beyond any reasonable desire. But the thought of doing it now just made me want to curl up.

"On second thought," Derek said. "I think a clean start tomorrow will be better."

I looked up, shock rolling through me. His hands were nowhere near his belt, and I couldn't interpret the look on his face. Nick lifted me to my feet. "Then it's time to put you away."

CHAPTER SIX

_____

SEBASTIAN

he relief in the Omega's eyes made my chest ache. I knew exactly why Derek had changed his mind, and it was going to be the hardest part of this. The charade we had to play between our instincts and the reality of what was happening.

The roles we were playing to save a lot of fucking people, and not knowing if we could trust this beautiful woman with that information. If we assumed she was trustworthy based on scent alone, and she wasn't? Three years of work could disappear overnight.

Since she wouldn't tell us the truth about it, we didn't have a choice, and I was losing my mind. Because this Omega drove my instincts crazy, and we'd only known her for a few hours. I could have torn Delano's head off earlier for even _suggesting_ his vile desires were meant for Selena.

But as soon as he'd said it was time to finish the job, her scent turned so bitter it made me choke. She was terrified and had every right to be. We weren't going to hurt her, but there were plenty of people who would. I just hoped when we were able to tell her the truth that she would forgive the deception and understand what we needed to do in order to keep her and other Omegas safe from monsters like Delano.

Which was why we gave her a tracker. Because we didn't know who she was, but she was our scent match and we would protect her regardlesss, until she gave us a reason not to.

Nick had her by the arm, her hands cuffed behind her back, and now that we were in our own home, I had a chance to really look at her. Curvy and soft, with thighs and ass that

I wanted to dig my fingers into and bite. Fuck, I wanted to spank her and watch her skin turn pink. I knew I would, but just the thought of it had me hard.

And once again, we came back to the crux of the problem. We gave her as much of a choice as we could, given the situation, because we wouldn't force her hand in the way our guests downstairs would. And if we'd discovered her where she said she woke up, before everyone saw her, we wouldn't have to do anything but lock her away until this was over.

But Christopher *fucking* Delano was here, and now we had to train her. If he didn't see us doing it, and if he thought for even a fraction of a second that we weren't who we said we were, everything could come tumbling down like a house of cards.

With everything in my body, I wished we hadn't agreed to let him stay here for the next two weeks. We needed to because the apartment he was staying with was packed to the gills with state-of-the-art surveillance equipment. Virtually undetectable, so while he purchased our Betas and arranged for the transfer of merchandise, we could have direct proof of his crimes.

That was the heart of what we discovered. There were tentacles and arms of this operation, but the biggest piece was masterminded by Delano. Once we took him down, seventy percent of the country's Omega trafficking would crumble into dust, and a greater world network would be severely damaged. And as much as I loathed having to put the mission above myself and my pack, so many Omega lives couldn't be ignored.

"Let's go," Nick said. He was being gentle with her, but I doubted she would feel it. She would also think that what Derek said—that every slave we'd ever *sold* had completed the training—meant that we trained them.

We didn't. The Betas trained with each other. We knew

44

the methods, but again, we weren't slavers. Until now, I supposed.

He led her into the depths of our apartment, to a room that was for show and had never been used until her. A large room. One side was a big fireplace with comfy armchairs and a bar. The other side was a cage.

Floor to ceiling steel bars and various things inside the enclosure. A bed surrounded with a steel frame someone could be bound to. A spanking bench with so many adjustable bits I hesitated to call it a bench, and a fucking machine.

I would be a damn liar if I said the things inside the cage didn't interest me. We were who we were, and all three of us were kinky fuckers. But we wanted the woman we tied down eager to be there.

Selena gasped when we entered the room, automatically cringing away from the cage. Nick pointed to the side of the room and unhooked the cuffs from each other. "The bathroom is in there. Go ahead."

She didn't hesitate. The three of us waited in silence, though I knew we were all dying to say something. Once she was taken care of, we would talk.

Derek went to the fireplace and lit it. The person we had come clean the apartment—also an agent—kept the fireplace ready to light. We had to keep up appearances in case we needed to bring someone in at a moment's notice. Like this.

When Selena came out, she glanced at the fire and the chairs. I saw something in her eyes I couldn't identify before Nick extended an arm toward the open door of the cage. Her head dropped, but she went.

"On the bed," he said.

Selena looked at the bed for a few seconds before she moved, and Nick followed her, quickly taking her cuffs and attaching them to the chains at the corners of the steel frame. These would allow her a little movement, but keep her where we wanted her. The padlocks weren't something she could get out of, and neither were the cuffs.

They clinked together as she settled in the middle of the mattress, arms around her knees. "Master?"

I loved hearing that word from her lips even as I hated the resignation in her voice. "Yes?" I asked.

She wasn't looking at any of us. "I'm—" Her whole body tightened into a smaller ball. "I get cold easily."

Derek lit the fire, but this was a large room. The thought of her shivering and in chains wasn't one I could stomach. The only shivering I wanted Selena to do was shivers of anticipation before I showed her exactly how beautiful submission could be. How pain could bring both of us pleasure beyond imagining.

I strode out of the cage and over to the armchair where a soft throw rested. It was a deep green like that confection she'd been wearing before Derek took it from her. The color suited her.

Taking the blanket back into the cage, I did what I knew I shouldn't. Because there was no way my Alpha could let this go. I crouched down and spread the blanket around her shoulders. She shuddered at the touch. Not pulling away, the kind of shudder that made me want to pull her closer.

I reached out and cupped her cheek. "Don't be afraid, little one," I said quietly.

"No?"

"No."

She didn't believe me. And I didn't blame her one bit.

Retreating, the others were already outside of the cage, and Derek was the one to close the cage door and enter the code on the lock. The code changed as soon as the door locked, and we only had access to it. Even if she figured it out, she couldn't open it.

We lowered the lights so that the fire was the only source,

and I watched her turn and move, curling herself under the blanket before I shut the door behind me.

"Wait," Derek said. "Until we're back in the living room."

I did, and the three of us all felt the same. The bar we used the most was in here, and after that, I needed a fucking drink. "I don't know if I can do this," I said, pouring myself a drink that was probably too large.

"We don't have a choice," Derek said.

"There's always a choice," Nick said. "We can't just pass it off like there are no options."

"Oh? What options would you like, Nick?" Derek's voice echoed through the apartment. "The one where we let three years of fucking torture evaporate because we let our guard down, and let god knows how many Omegas be stolen, sold, raped, and killed? Or the option where we die and she dies because we make the mistake of showing our hand by being kind? Or the one where we protect her as best we can, and try to protect everyone else. You think I want to do this?"

"Derek," I said.

He spun to me, eyes wild, and I wasn't even sure he'd been fully conscious of what he'd been saying. He was so far gone, trying to reconcile the beautiful Omega and his instincts. I understood. I was there with him. Instead, I handed him the drink I'd poured and went to make another one.

"Sorry," he said.

Nicholas sighed. "No need. I get it. I don't want to do it either. But I also don't think any good comes from pretending our hand is being forced. It is, and yet it's not. Because when we tell her the truth—and I don't fucking care, we *will* tell her the truth eventually—the reasoning 'we didn't have a choice,' isn't going to fly.

"We are making the best choice out of a list of absolutely *shitty* choices. And we need to own it."

He was right, even if I hated it. "What are the odds we

could do only non-sexual training in public?" I asked. "We've never been open in front of the clients. Maybe we can lean into that."

Nick sighed. "And if someone asks her what we've been doing with her in private?"

"She's a slave," I said, throat burning on the word. "She doesn't speak to anyone else without permission."

What none of us were saying was that it wouldn't fly with the most important client of all of them. His preferences were far more violent and deadly, but he still expected us to back up our claims of being the premiere slave trainers in the country. He'd said as much multiple times. Until Selena came out from behind the stage, our plan had simply been to shrug and tell him we were in the middle of acquiring new merchandise, since everyone had been sold at the auction.

"We are fucked from absolutely every angle," Derek said. "Like... every single one. If any one thing tonight had gone differently, we'd have options. And of course, she's—" he dropped his face into his hands. "She's our fucking scent match. Did someone find a way to predict that and send her to fuck with us? Or are we just the unluckiest bastards of all time?"

I didn't know. "If she's faking it, she's one hell of an actress."

"Anyone who has the balls to come after us would absolutely make sure they had the best of the best. As far as the scent match... are we sure it's real? We use fake hormones. She could be using them, too."

"I've never heard of the hormones being able to fabricate a scent match," I said. "But if that's true, we'll know soon enough. She obviously won't have access to them, and they'll fade in a few days."

"Yeah..."

I knocked back my drink until the glass was empty. "Do we have a plan? As far as training her?"

"She's clearly new," Derek said. "Even if she's faking it. It's obvious enough she's never had any kind of slave training. Her kneeling alone is enough to tell that."

That was true. If you were used to kneeling, your knees would eventually get used to it. Hers weren't.

"So we can take it slow at first," Nick said. "Use the logic that we make sure the basics are down first before anything else. That might buy us a little time. The rest of it? We'll have to do what we've been doing this whole time. Playing it by ear."

He was right. So close to the end, and we were in the worst position we'd ever been. We might have to do this, but that didn't mean I had to like it.

CHAPTER SEVEN

SELENA

*E*verything hurt.

My heat was coming like a freight train. If I'd only been unconscious for a day, it was Sunday morning. I hadn't expected everything to start until tomorrow, but being around scent matches would do that to you.

And now I wasn't going to have anything I needed. What would they do when they found out I was on the verge? Would they leave me in this cage?

Morning light streamed through the windows, and I'd turned to stare out at the sky through the bars instead of at the rest of the things in the cage with me. I didn't really want to think about those.

We were high up. I could see the tops of a couple other buildings, but mostly I was looking at the sky. A pale gray morning with a few clouds. Had anyone noticed I was missing yet?

They wouldn't, would they. The Syndicate said they took care of it. I didn't know what they would have said, but clearly they had the power to put me here. I didn't doubt they had the power to make my disappearance seem normal as well.

It was like I'd simply been erased from my own life.

There was something about the three Alphas who now owned me. I didn't feel like they were all bad. I had no evidence to prove it, and maybe it was my own mind desperately trying to cling to something. Or maybe it was us being scent matched that made me want to believe they weren't like the other Alphas in that room.

I didn't know, but the way Sebastian looked at me last

night as he gave me the blanket, it was like he saw me. And not as a woman he was going to train to be a fucktoy before selling me for money. Like he saw *me*.

Don't be afraid, little one.

Little one.

I liked it, though I was far from little. I had curves. My body was soft and round and it didn't help that half the time on my nursing shifts I was so busy I was left eating junk food from the vending machine.

But again, it didn't feel like they cared. They looked at me like I was…

It probably didn't matter, and it probably wasn't me. It was probably the fact that they owned me and could do whatever they wanted to me that turned them on. That would be enough for people like them, right? Was it the power or the helplessness?

I shuddered. I couldn't even say that was a thing exclusive to bad men. That was the fantasy, right? Being helpless? This wasn't what people meant, though. I didn't think anyone meant being an *actual* slave.

The scrape of the lock alerted me that someone was entering the room. I didn't move. My body ached too much —full of both desire and hormones—for me to move. Being completely still was the only solution.

At least being beneath the blanket was cozy. I supposed I would have to take joy in the little things now.

"Holy shit," the quiet words came. It sounded like Derek.

He came into view, silhouetted against the bright morning windows and crouched in front of me. I'd moved close to the edge of the bed, to see more of the sky, pillowing some of the blanket beneath my head.

"You're going into heat?" He asked.

"Yes, Master."

He frowned, reaching out to put his knuckles against my forehead. "Why didn't you say anything?"

"I didn't think it would matter," I said honestly. "Why would you care about a slave's heat?"

Nor did it matter that I'd taken off the week from work for it. It's not like it would prove to them that I wasn't a spy.

"I'll get the suppressants," I heard Nick say.

"They won't work," I whispered.

Derek's hand was still on my skin. "Why not?"

"I skipped my spring heat."

He closed his eyes. "Fuck."

"It's fine, Master. Leave me here. Let me go to the bathroom every once in a while and I'll get through it. I won't orgasm." My voice sounded dead, even to my ears. But it was the only way to get through this. If I let in real emotion, I wouldn't be able to do it, and I wasn't going to risk Anna's life for some discomfort. There would be plenty of heats for me in the future if I could just make it through this.

Both anger and heat flared in Derek's gaze. "We'll be right back."

He disappeared from view, and I still didn't move. The clouds were moving in a way that was soothing. If I stayed just like this, maybe it wouldn't be that bad.

The footsteps came back sooner than I expected, and Nick placed a glass full of pink liquid on the steel frame of the bed. "You need to eat something."

I stared at the glass. Was that a smoothie? "I get food?"

"Did you think we were going to starve you?"

An answer didn't come to mind. Food and bathroom use weren't exactly things you thought about when it came to being kidnapped and enslaved. Getting to drink a smoothie certainly wouldn't have been in any mental picture I had.

"Drink it," he said. "Half of it needs to be gone when we come back."

That meant moving. But my stomach growled. I hadn't eaten anything since the day before yesterday. I was *hungry*. Slowly, I pushed myself up to sitting, fighting the aches and pains. The flashes of pure lust I couldn't escape. The traces of scent they left behind made my mind glaze over, salivating for Alpha knot.

At home, I had different sizes of knotting toys, and if I was still there, I'd probably have already used them at least once. That was why there was pain. Because just *sitting* through a heat wasn't what Omegas were made for. We were made to fuck anything and everything while our heat lasted.

I supposed I was grateful I hadn't fully gone into heat yesterday while in that theatre. Would they have been able to stop an Alpha free-for-all trying to claim me? Would I be bonded to some nightmare of an Alpha right now?

The smoothie was strawberry and *delicious*. Like my body suddenly remembered food existed, I was ravenous. Granted, this hungry pretty much anything would taste good, but I still allowed myself to enjoy it. Keeping the blanket around me, I tried to move as little as possible. My fever was rising, and my mind became more and more detached from the real world.

It wasn't hard to obey Nick's command. The smoothie was almost entirely gone. I could probably drink another whole one. But that would be uncomfortable. I wasn't sure how much they were going to let me out of the cage for this.

I did feel better. Now that my stomach was content, I could even go back to sleep if they let me.

The door opened, and the three of them entered, coming toward me with determination. They unlocked the cage and came inside, watching me carefully. Nick saw the empty cup where I set it on the frame, and a fraction of a smile flickered across his face.

Sebastian was the one who lowered himself this time so he could look me directly in the eye. "Give me your hand, Selena."

I obeyed, putting my wrist in his hand. He didn't bother to unlock the chains attached to the cuff, instead unbuckling the cuff itself from my wrist. He did the other one, and my ankles too. I wasn't about to ask him why the hell he was unchaining me, because it wasn't something to complain about.

"How long do your heats normally last?"

"It depends. Three or four days, but I've never skipped one before, so I'm not sure. But I'll be fine. You don't have to worry about me."

His gaze hardened. "Heats are much longer if you're not helped through them, yes?"

In theory, yes. But for myself, I didn't know. I'd never been helped through one. That wasn't to say I was innocent —I definitely wasn't. There just wasn't anyone in my life who I wanted to spend four days fucking.

Maybe in another life, I would be helped through my heats by three handsome Alphas who bore a shocking resemblance to these men.

"Stand up."

A whine came out of me. Standing would hurt. It would be so much easier if I didn't have to move. He knew, and he didn't hesitate to lean forward and scoop me into his arms like I was one of those tiny Omegas from last night.

"What—"

"We will be helping you through your heat," Sebastian said, tone allowing no room for argument. "We cannot train you while your mind and body are in heat, nor can we take you into the club while perfuming like you are. So we will help you. This apartment is equipped with a nest, and while it lasts, you are excused from calling us master."

We walked through the room I'd been left in last night and down a different hallway. "You likely won't remember anyway, and though we are strict masters, we would rather not punish you for things your instincts will not allow."

Derek slipped in front of us and opened a door. The room was small and dim, with black cushions lining the floor and walls. It wasn't what I would choose for a nest, but my mind instantly eased, recognizing the small, the soft, and the dark.

"We still have business to take care of, but we will do our best to take care of it while you are sleeping."

My Omega didn't like that. My instincts wanted all my Alphas close so they could be there to knot and comfort. But they weren't *my* Alphas, were they?

"Selena?" Sebastian asked.

I looked up at him. "Yes?"

He smirked briefly. I missed something. "A heat is one of the few things we do not interfere with. If you don't want us to help you, we can leave you in the other room."

Blinking, I looked at him and then at the others. "You're letting me choose?"

"Yes," Nick said.

My mind told me I should tell them to fuck off and leave me alone. It would probably be the smarter thing to do. But they were my *scent matches*. Even if this was the only time I ever got to be with them in this way, and even if it would be more painful later, when they chained me up again, I couldn't say no.

I wanted the kind of passion everyone talked about with scent matched heats. Just once. So I chose to be selfish and foolish.

"I choose you."

CHAPTER EIGHT

DEREK

*A*s soon as the door closed behind us, I looked at my pack mates. "Are you fucking kidding me? Seriously?"

Walking into the room was like walking into heaven. Heaven that was made of roses and oranges and the sweetest, most delicious perfume I'd ever experienced in my life. Ten times the little taste I got in the theatre. The whole room was *soaked* with it.

And just like everything else about this situation, it was absolutely fucked. We didn't have time to take four days away from our duties and responsibilities to fuck an Omega through her heat, no matter how much I wanted to.

Yet, I wasn't going to leave her in that cage and in pain. No part of me was capable of that.

"Do we train her through the heat?" Nick asked. "She'll certainly be more receptive to things."

"If we're helping her through it, there's no fucking way I'm going to let an Omega—*Our* Omega—go through a heat while asking to come. It's more than cruel. And given that in any other situation we'd be head over heels and courting her by now, I'm not going to fuck her as a slave during her heat. I *can't*. If that makes me weak, I don't care."

Seb put his hand on my shoulder. "No, it doesn't. And I agree with you. Her heat will go faster if she's helped through it. We can keep up appearances when she's sleeping, or take breaks if needed. It isn't a normal situation, and we have to deal with it. But I'd like to help her through it, and not as a slave. I don't even care how we look to her. I'd rather her choose whether she wants us to help."

"She will," Nick said. "We're scent bonded. I'm barely hanging on as it is from going back in there and fucking her into the floor. I'm sorry, Derek, I didn't—"

I waved a hand. "I know." He hadn't meant to minimize anything or imply we should use her. We were all trying to make the best of a bad situation. A fucking awful situation.

"We just do the best we can," Sebastian said. "The place has a nest."

A startled laugh burst out of me. I forgot about it. The apartment we now occupied belonged to the government. Before it was our base of operations for *Catena*, it was a place used by visiting dignitaries, and sometimes those dignitaries required a nest. "For once we have a little luck."

"Let's show her the nest," Nick said. "Make it clear that we want to help, and not as masters to a slave, and let her choose. Everything else aside, we can do that."

I agreed. "Okay."

We went back inside, and I was beside myself, my instincts right at the surface. She smelled so fucking good my instincts were screaming at me to *knot* and *bite* and *claim*.

I barely heard the words Seb spoke to her as he unlocked her chains. Instead, I was looking at her body. The rich tan of her skin and the slightly darker shade of her nipples peeking out from underneath the blanket. The glossy shine of her dark hair and the generous curves of her ass as Seb picked her up.

The way his fingers dug into her skin, I couldn't wait to feel her underneath me, and I hoped she chose us. Because I'd already chosen her. We had to make it through this mission, because this fucking gorgeous Omega belonged to us in every way, and I wanted her to be ours by choice. Not because of this... mess.

And if she didn't choose us after we told her the truth, at least we would have these few days with her. Because I already knew on scent alone, she was the one. The blessing and curse of these instincts we had. They could be the source of such incredible beauty and an entire world of pain all at the same time.

I ducked in front of where Sebastian carried her and opened the door to the nest and flicked the lights on. Not exactly the world's prettiest nest. All the cushions were dark and utilitarian, but it would be so much better than fucking her in that cage on a tiny bed. My Alpha wouldn't let me. It would be fucking unacceptable.

If she chose us.

"Selena?" Sebastian asked. He'd asked her the question, but she was still staring at the nest, bewildered.

She looked up at him suddenly. "Yes?"

I caught the way he squeezed her a bit tighter. I sure as hell wasn't the only one of us affected by the little Omega. "A heat is one of the few things we do not interfere with. If you don't want us to help you, we can leave you in the other room."

Her mouth dropped open as she looked at him, and then at Nick, and finally at me. The hope in her gaze broke my heart. "You're letting me choose?"

"Yes," Nick said.

Selena didn't speak right away. She just stared into the middle distance, and we waited. She was already going into heat, and her mind probably wasn't working as quickly as she was used to. Not to mention this was all going to be a bit of a mind fuck.

There wasn't much we could do about it, but it didn't mean I wasn't sorry.

"I choose you."

Everything in my soul filled with relief. For a few days at least, we could pretend that the outside world didn't exist, and while we were in the nest, we didn't have to keep up appearances. We could simply treasure her like an Omega was meant to be treasured.

How I had wanted to the second I caught her scent.

I sensed all of us felt the same relief. "Are you fully in heat yet?" I asked.

"Not yet," she said, blushing. "But I'm close. It was meant to start tomorrow, but I think... being around the three of you made it come a little early."

Her wording wasn't lost on me, and I wished we could fully trust her. It seemed obvious that someone who was planning their heat wouldn't be a spy. But in these last years, I'd seen stranger things than someone waiting until the brink of heat to take action. We needed to be careful. If someone wanted us involved in a heat and out of the way?

Still, I was going to relish every second I could be in this nest with her.

"What triggers it?"

Her face and body turned a deeper shade of her blush. "Time. And sex."

"That won't be a problem," Sebastian said. "Trust me."

Nick stepped closer on the cushions and looked at our Omega. She looked up at him too, chest rising and falling more quickly. So fucking stunning. I couldn't believe we were in this position.

I'd never been a person to blame things on being unfair, but it felt like it this time.

"We still are who we are, sweetheart," Nick said. "Any objections to us using some things on you in here? Tying you up?"

There was conflict in her eyes. Not because of the question. We all scented the wild burst of perfume now swirling around us at the idea. I knew why it was there. Because if she said yes, then did that mean she accepted the treatment she would get once she returned to being a slave?

"We won't use it against you," I said quietly. "I told you before. We're certainly not good Alphas. But we're not as bad as some."

"Okay," she said. "Then that's fine with me. What i—" she bit her lip, and fuck if I didn't want it to be me biting her lip.

Sebastian lowered her to the cushions. "You can speak."

"We're probably overwhelming," I said. "Right?"

Selena nodded.

I looked at Seb and Nick. "Give us a minute."

He set her down.

Shrugging off my suit jacket, I pulled my shirt over my head and tossed it to the side of the nest. Selena was naked. At the very least, I could make her a little more comfortable by not letting her be the only one exposed.

But I kept my pants on. We weren't there yet. I sat down on the cushions in front of her, noting how her eyes traced my body, just like mine traced hers.

Her perfume bathed me in roses and orange, and a purr sprang to life in my chest before I could stop it. She stared at me for a moment, blushing and ducking her head.

"What were you going to say?"

"You know it's fucked up that I'm confiding in the person keeping me prisoner."

I smiled. "Sorry, *gattina*. I don't have a therapist on speed dial."

"I'm going to need one after this," she muttered.

The smile dropped from my face, and I almost told her the truth right then and there. Finally, she looked back at me. "Are we just supposed to pretend that the last day didn't happen? Am I just going to pretend that I *don't* know as soon as my heat is over I'll go back to being a sex toy for you? A fucking object that you can use whenever you want?"

"Is that what you think training will be?"

She made a face. "If you're about to go off on some speech trying to explain to me that fucking *slavery* isn't that bad, you can save it."

Scooting closer so our knees pressed against each other, I

slipped one hand around her neck and pulled her closer. "You asked last night if being scent matched mattered at all."

"And you said nothing, which tells me enough."

"Or it was because I didn't have an answer I could give. The short answer is that yes, it does. And all three of us are going to enjoy the hell out of this heat with you. But remember, especially in our world, not everything is as it seems."

She tried to pull away, and I didn't let her go. "What the hell kind of fortune cookie nonsense is that?"

"It's all I have for the moment. I just want you to remember that, okay?"

"Sure."

Her tone didn't make me think she would try, but I hoped she did. "As for pretending? Yes, I guess so. You can still change your mind and suffer through it if you want. But I think this is better for everyone, don't you?"

Selena's eyes turned glassy. "It's a stretch to say any of this is good for me."

"I understand that."

"But," she looked at me. "You said it matters?"

"*Gattina*, I don't think you quite understand the amount of self-control it has taken us to hold ourselves back. You smell fucking divine. I want to consume you."

A shudder ran through her. "I don't know how to just forget about it. I need it to kick in already, so I don't have to think. Once that happens, it will be okay."

"Let me help," I said.

She swallowed. "How?"

"Lie back."

As long as I lived, once all of this was over, I would make it my life's mission to make sure my Omega never had that kind of doubt in her eyes ever again. But she did as I asked, and I couldn't hesitate anymore. I gave in to my instincts, pushed her thighs apart, and devoured her.

CHAPTER NINE

_____

SELENA

*D*erek's tongue met my skin, and the inferno beneath it erupted. Pure fire fell through me, meeting his mouth and doing exactly what he said he wanted to do: consume me.

"Oh, fuck," I managed the words.

The low hum in Derek's throat just made me wetter. "You taste even better than you smell, *gattina*."

My mind was still fighting it. Because I didn't know how to let go with these men who were somehow made for me, and yet were only allowing me freedom so I could get through the heat.

Sealing his mouth over me, Derek rolled his tongue under my clit. I writhed beneath the pleasure, but it wasn't enough. They weren't going to stop me from coming, but I didn't know if I could, with my mind like this.

The door to the nest opened, the other two Alphas staring at the scene in front of them. "Guess you got a head start."

Kind of.

Sebastian and Nick stripped, showing me bodies that were gorgeous. Perfect. As if they came from a catalogue where I picked out what I liked and wanted. Like they were made for me.

Nick handed something to Derek, and he tossed it into his mouth and swallowed. Derek smiled, and I realized it was the birth control Alphas could take for the heat. There was little to counteract the Omega's biology in that way. For Alphas, it was easier. A wink at me, and he dove back between my legs.

Seb was the one that laid down beside me and turned my

face to his, kissing me slowly. Between my thighs, Derek lifted his mouth from my skin briefly. "You're allowed to come, *gattina*."

I whined. "I *can't*." Sebastian was looking right into my eyes, searching for what was wrong. "It's not real," I whispered.

"It is real, little one. It is."

A tear slipped out. "No, it's not. I need it to be real."

One hand wove itself into my hair, making sure I kept looking at him and his dark eyes. "This nest is a different world. In here, nothing exists but the four of us. You're not a slave and we're not masters. We're just three Alphas who are going to help you enjoy the heat the way it's meant to be enjoyed. And introduce you to exactly what being a scent match means. Because you were made for us, little one. You'll like what we like."

"I—"

Derek's tongue pushed inside me, and I moaned.

"You see, Derek," Sebastian said. "Loves pleasure. We have to stop him sometimes from giving too much. But he also loves seeing a pretty Omega like you tied up and at his mercy. He loves bondage, and he loves fucking a throat so deep you don't even get to taste his cum when he fills you with it."

My whole body shuddered, and Nick slid in on the other side of me, mouth dropping to my skin and kissing down my shoulder toward my breasts. But Sebastian wasn't done.

"Nicholas likes to push limits. Teaching you to like things you never knew you could. Making you crawl across the floor to him, and just enough degradation to make your cunt soaking wet while you do. He'll make you beg to be called a slut. Fuck you while you're sleeping, so when you wake up you're already coming all over his cock."

The way he spoke into my ear like a caress, my body was

finally relaxing, sinking into the pleasure of Derek's mouth and Nick exploring my skin. "What about you?" I breathed.

"Me? I'll fuck you while taking your air, so you pass out for Nick. I like predicaments where you have to choose between pleasure and pain. I want to spank your pussy until it's swollen and then make you come. Back and forth until you don't know whether it's pain or pleasure, you're just coming. Fire and wax. So many other things I can't even think of because I'm so overwhelmed by your scent right now."

Nick closed his mouth over my nipple, and I arched my back. Pleasure was building now, fever rising, and Sebastian ducked away for a second and came back with his belt.

Before I could react, the leather was wrapped around my wrists and buckled, my arms pushed over my head. His hands pinned my wrists to the cushions, and it was his strength that made it feel different.

"Do you like his tongue in your cunt, princess?" Seb asked. "Tasting just how wet you are for us?"

He sent me over the edge. I moaned, the orgasm washing over me quick and fast. It was the doorway to more.

"I'm going to fucking knot her," Derek growled. "Can't wait to feel this Omega pussy hug my dick like it was meant to. And have her love every second."

Derek slid into me, all the way to the hilt, body coming down on mine. Our faces were close, those blue eyes staring into mine. "There you are," he said quietly. "No one but you and me, *gattina*. Nothing else matters. I've got you. Promise."

Something about those words allowed me to let go of the rest of it. I melted into the cushions, closing my eyes and surrendering to the feeling of him inside me. The *rightness* of being with the Alphas who were my match, no matter what.

Later, I would dive deep and ask what it said about me that I was matched with men who were capable of such crimes. Right now, the heat was knocking at my door, and I couldn't hold it closed forever.

With a sigh, I wrapped my arms around his neck and pulled him closer, awkward with the way my hands were bound. I kissed him with everything I had, tasting myself on his lips, reveling in the feeling of his cock. He was long and curved, hitting places inside me a toy could never. And I knew in that second, I would never be the same.

A heat alone would never live up to this, and it was only the first few minutes.

"Good girl, *gattina*," Derek whispered before kissing me again. "Such a brave Omega."

I didn't feel brave. I felt desperate and hot and needy. He thrust deep, and light flared behind my eyes. "Focus on me," he whispered. "The way my cock is fucking you and driving you higher and higher. Every bit of friction? That feels good for me, too."

It did feel good. And still, my Omega was resisting full submission. I couldn't quite get there, no matter if I wanted to. "Help me," I whispered. "Please. I can't—"

The quickly hidden torment in Derek's eyes was relieving. At least this wasn't just hard for me. "Seb," he ground out, still fucking me.

Sebastian was beside me again, hand skimming across my skin to land around my throat. Nothing but the threat of pressure. The gentle tension in his grip that told every piece of me how much strength he was holding back. He pressed his lips to my ear, the words such a quiet whisper I was the only one who could hear them, and yet they held every once of Alpha power. I was helpless to do anything but obey, and that was what I needed.

"You want me to help you, Omega?"

"Yes." A single, strangled word.

His fingers tightened on my skin. "The three of us promise we're not going to harm you in this nest. We will fuck you through this heat as equals. Nothing outside matters. So *stop resisting your heat, Omega*."

The growl shredded through me, tearing down my resistance. "Yes."

What I'd thought was heat before? Wasn't. My whole body was an inferno, begging for more. None of my heats had ever felt like this—intense and fiery and likely to consume me.

Derek drove into me, and I came, the orgasm a new explosion swirling around us together and comforting every fear and every hesitation. *Mine.*

Mine. Mine. Mine. Every thrust made my heart sing with it, and Derek's knot locking into place made me see stars. His lips on mine, my chest vibrated with something between a growl and a purr. "You feel incredible, Selena."

He did too. A fake knot was *nothing* in comparison to a real one pressing into all the places I needed and couldn't force a toy to reach. Someone released my hands from the belt.

Leaning down, Derek kissed my forehead. My heart tumbled into something, because there was an aching truth to the movement I couldn't explain and wasn't going to question.

His knot eased quickly. They did in the heat, responding to an Omega's desire to be rutted and fucked and knotted over and over again. Already, the heat was building under my skin again, and my fear was gone.

"Come here, sweetheart." Nick lifted me up onto my knees, slipping into me from behind. His back lined up with mine, my mind holding onto the beautiful, chilly scent of peppermint with the barest hint of something tropical. Like a lime.

One arm wrapped around my waist and held me to him as he took me. Gently at first, and then not at all gently. My body was prepared, ready to come, and falling over into the golden, emerald bliss that was an orgasm so beautiful I couldn't even breathe.

Derek's cock appeared in front of me, and *yes,* I wanted to taste him again. That intangible clear fragrance and taste I couldn't describe but was so fucking sweet, mixed with *me.* My whole body shuddered, wanting more of this. All of this.

Forever.

I shoved the thought out of my head. If this was the only heat I would have with them, I was going to make it the best fucking heat I ever had.

With his hand in my hair, and Nick fucking me like the world depended on it, Derek guided my mouth lower. To his balls. His moan when my mouth connected with his skin was enough to send me over again into another bright and quaking orgasm.

Nick swore, driving deep and unleashing himself before his knot swelled and sent stars shooting across my vision. I couldn't do anything with my fucking mouth when he was making me moan like this.

"Do you know how long it's been since I've had pussy this good?" Nick asked. "Fucking never."

He dragged his lips down my spine, leaving kisses on my skin and tracing his fingers down to my hips before pulling away from me.

I was on my back in seconds, Sebastian looking down at me with a gaze of dark fire. Everywhere. He was everywhere because he was the biggest of them physically. And not just his body. His cock was the biggest, and he knew it. The shadow of a smirk on his face told me that.

"That won't go in."

Sebastian chuckled and leaned down close, kissing my neck. "Yes, it will. And both of us are going to enjoy making it fit."

I whined, and he purred. The warm scent of baked apples

68

enveloped us as he eased in, even the first inches of him stretching me. "Fuck, Alpha."

A growl that had my body heating up and relaxing, taking more of him. "Breathe, princess," he whispered. "Your Omega body was made for this. You can take it."

It didn't feel like I could, and yet, with each thrust he pushed deeper and I loved it. Every one of them filled me differently. Sebastian filled me to the brim. So full it felt like pleasure was spilling over into different places in my body.

And still, there was more of him to fit. Pleasure on the very edge of pain, but not quite crossing over. Instead, it made it hotter and sweeter.

Sebastian braced himself above me, looking down to where we were connected. "Fuck me, Omega. Look at you. This greedy pussy wants everything I've got."

It did. It really did.

His hips met mine, pressing flush against my body. All the way inside me, I could barely keep my eyes open because of the full, delicious pressure. Feral need rose under my skin, begging to be fucked.

To be *knotted*.

My fingers dug into his hips, pulling him closer and urging him to move. Now that he was inside me, I wanted him to do something about it.

"Mmm," Seb said. "Bossy little Omega. I see that defiance."

"Get used to it," I said.

"Oh, I don't have to get used to it. I love it. It makes submission so much sweeter."

I opened my mouth to tell him it wasn't going to happen, and he proved me wrong. His hand came around my throat again, pinning me to the cushions while he fucked me.

Fireworks exploded across my vision and a cry ripped from my throat, echoing across the nest. Satisfaction so deep it set off another orgasm, and his next thrust brought another. Or maybe it was the same orgasm. It didn't matter, and I didn't care, it was all pleasure. Pleasure with Alphas who were made to give it to me.

And for the next few days, I was going to embrace it for the gift it was. It was that thought that had me smiling as my body surrendered to Sebastian's knot, and the power of pleasure took me down into darkness.

CHAPTER TEN

NICHOLAS

I leaned against the dark cushions of the nest, catching my breath and watching as Seb fucked our Omega until she passed out.

Her black hair mixed in with the inky darkness of the velvet cushions. It looked a little like she was a creature of the night. An exhausted goddess laid to rest for a while.

She was already asleep, but Seb leaned down and touched his forehead to hers reverently.

"That was fucking brutal," I said, shaking my head. "Fuck."

Seb moved gently, lifting her up so he, too, could move to rest against one of the cushioned walls while she was still knotted to him. The way he held her said everything about what I was feeling. He clutched her to his chest, wanting to hold her so tightly she melded into his being, and at the same time, he didn't want to hurt her.

My chest ached, both for her and for us.

"Are we sure we can't tell her?" I asked. "Because I don't know how to watch her struggle like that. She's *ours*."

Derek dropped his head in his hands. "She can be ours and still be someone sent to take us down. Pretty sure I can say neither of us expected a scent match. We don't know anything about her loyalty or why she's here. I'm with you, Nick. I want her to know. But…"

"I know," I said. "I know."

We couldn't risk the lives of thousands of Omegas for one, no matter how much we wanted to. Even if my instincts were screaming at me to take her and run. Hide her away from this vile world and protect her at all costs.

But I would burn myself to the ground instead. Because

71

this was what we agreed to. To turn ourselves into monsters, in order to stop bigger ones.

"She's fully in heat now," Seb said. "Let's be grateful for that."

I was. But fuck, I wasn't going to be able to unhear or unsee her misery at it not being real. Because it *was* real. She had no idea how real it was. I didn't even give a fuck where she came from or where her loyalties lay, because as far as I was concerned, our loyalty should be to her, and it was shredding me apart that it couldn't be.

"While she's sleeping, we'll have to take turns monitoring things," I said. "We can't just disappear. I'll go down to the office and make sure things are proceeding. Take care of anything outstanding. Text me when she wakes up."

Derek nodded. "Either shower or use some scent canceler. The last thing we want is Delano scenting heat perfume on you and knowing we're vulnerable."

Good fucking point.

I shook my head as I exited the nest. What kind of fucking world was it where we had to hide our Omega's heat for fear that someone who wanted to kill her, and kill us, didn't find out we were helping her through her most vulnerable moments?

Stepping into the shower to rinse Selena off me, I prayed to whatever gods might be listening that our mission ended fast. We'd been steadfast for three years and were almost there. But every hour we went with Selena in our lives was one where the four of us were ripping ourselves to shreds for no reason.

I shoved her out of my mind. The faster I got downstairs, the faster I could get back to her.

CHAPTER ELEVEN

SELENA

*M*y whole body was warm and swathed in softness. A rough purr rumbled against my back, but I didn't open my eyes. Not yet. I was in the nest with my Alphas, and while my eyes were closed, I wanted to revel in the peace it brought me.

Clearly, they'd found a blanket and wrapped me up in it, which I appreciated. Even in the middle of heat, when I slept, I got cold.

"Do you know your breathing changes when you wake up, little one?" Sebastian was the source of the purr behind me. We weren't locked together, but he'd still stayed with me.

Without opening my eyes, I turned over. It was like cuddling with an apple pie straight from the oven. He smelled incredible, size dwarfing me as his arm came around my back to hold me to him.

"Why are you suddenly shy?"

I finally opened my eyes and found myself staring at his chest. "I'm not shy," I whispered.

"No?" A smile hid in his voice. "Pretending to be asleep seems like it."

"Maybe I just wasn't ready to wake up."

"The perfume rolling off you says otherwise," Derek said behind me.

Just the mention of it, drawing attention to the need in my gut, ignited it like dropping a lighter onto gasoline. I shuddered and stretched, the desperate warmth of lust grabbing me with claws that had no intention of letting go.

"Will you let us play with you?" Sebastian asked.

I looked up at him. There were no tricks in his eyes, and no lies. Just genuine curiosity.

"Play?"

A hand on my shoulder turned me to where I could see Derek, and Nick was standing near the door, shirtless but back in his pants. I must have been sleeping for a while.

Derek draped something over me. I sat up and wrestled my hands out of the blankets to see what it was. Soft and silky, deep green and...

Rope.

He smirked at my expression. "We did ask to tie you up."

"With this?"

"With this, *gattina*. You'll look beautiful."

Seb's fingers trailed down my arm. "The first round of the heat was about getting your desperation out of the way. And it's still there, but now you can have fun."

"And how do you know I think this is fun?"

Leaning forward, Derek dropped his mouth to my shoulder. "Because it's fun for me," he said. "And you're my match."

I'd never been tied up before. I didn't count being chained in the cage. "What do you like about it?"

"It's like wrapping myself a present," he said. "Not only can I make the person I'm tying feel incredible and beautiful, but many people enjoy the feeling of bondage."

Not like I could deny that after I came with their hands around my throat and a belt around my hands. I'd seen pictures of beautiful women twisted into impossible positions with ropes like these. I was neither that small nor that flexible.

"Am I too big for that?"

A choking noise drew my eyes to Nick. "I swear to god, if you just called yourself fat—"

"No," I said. I knew I wasn't. But there was a big gray area between being the skin and bones blonde girls you saw tied up and delicate, and being what the rest of the world consid-

74

ered fat. I didn't give a shit, as long as people were healthy. Which was why I looked the way I did. "But I have hips. And an ass. I'm soft. I've never seen anyone like me tied up like this."

Derek's eyebrows rose. "So you've seen pictures?"

My face and chest flushed. "Of course. Everyone has."

"Mhmm." He sounded like he didn't buy it. "Well, the answer is *fuck* no. You're not too big, and anyone who says someone is too big for bondage doesn't have enough of an imagination. You want to try it?"

"Okay."

The hesitation in my voice made him pause. "If you don't like it, we'll get you out." He touched the cushions beside him, where I hadn't seen a little pair of dull scissors. "Promise, *gattina*."

"Okay," I said again.

Derek pulled me to my knees on the cushions, and just him entering my space was enough to make me close my eyes. That sweetness and mountain air scent—I wanted to collapse onto the cushions in front of me and *present*. Maybe lilacs? No, that was too floral for what he smelled like. And it was too rich for jasmine or honeysuckle. It was just so *sweet* and delicious.

The first touch of the rope on my skin made me gasp, because it was nothing like I imagined. It was soft, but it wasn't just that, it was the *way* he laid it against me. Directly and intentionally, skimming his hands over it as he placed it. It was slow, sensual, and so much more intimate than I imagined it would be.

He wrapped the rope around me under my breasts and then over them before ensnaring my arms behind me. They rested against each other, tight but not uncomfortable. Rather than discomfort, this felt... cozy. Was that something you were allowed to say about being tied up? Every pass with the rope somehow made me feel safer and more compressed.

I supposed it was all a part of the nesting instinct. Omegas needed the small and the dark. The cozy. Enclosed spaces and defined boundaries in order to feel safe. The irony of feeling safe while an Alpha was deliberately making it so I couldn't move wasn't lost on me.

When my arms and torso were secure, Derek leaned in, wrapping himself around me. "I'm going to lay you down so I can work on your legs."

He tilted me, and the shift in weight was different from when you laid yourself down. No control and total reliance on the other person. And the way he gently placed me on the cushions, no part of me doubted that he would catch me.

One by one, he folded my legs, challenging my flexibility and looping the ropes until my ankle pressed into my ass, and I *loved* the feeling. As turned on as I was, I could fall asleep like this. I was like being held without being held.

"Someone likes this," Derek said, rolling me over to work on my other leg and exposing my pussy to the air. No chance of denying it. I was soaking wet, slick coating my thighs and the rope near them.

"I do," I admitted. "It feels like a hug."

My head was light, floating and falling in a space that was nothing but clouds and bliss.

"Hey, little one." I looked to my right, and hadn't noticed when Sebastian came so close. He was right there, smiling. He had a pretty smile. "Do you remember what I told you about what I like?"

"A little." I was too floaty to remember things. Derek's hands on my skin tightening the last of the ropes felt so good I was going to beg them to fuck me.

"Derek has you tied open," he said, just as I was rolled on my back. My arms were beneath me, but they felt fine, and he was right. I was open and ready. Any one of them could take me and I couldn't stop them. But I'd *chosen* this, and that was what made white hot spirals of lust burst through me. "And I'm going to play with you. Let's see if you remember."

Suddenly, his mouth was between my legs, and I couldn't see or breathe. There was no where to go with the rope holding me like this, and my inability to move made the pleasure that much more. "Oh my god."

Soft laughter from around the room. A hand smoothed my hair off my forehead. Nick was there, kissing me. Tilting my face to his. "You feel good?"

Sebastian did something fucking divine with his tongue, swirling it around my clit before lowering it down and fucking me with it. I tried to lift my hips for more, and I couldn't. All my leverage was gone. There was absolutely no way for me to move.

Heat swept through me. "I feel so good."

"Good." He kissed me again, long and slow, mimicking the way I was being kissed elsewhere, my mind nothing but a golden fog of molten pleasure.

Between my legs, Seb pulled away, and I moaned, wanting the clever strokes of his tongue back when I'd been so close.

Fiery pain surged through my clit, his hand coming down on me hard. Almost instantly, it transformed into a blaze of desire so bright I thought it would burn the ropes off me. I cried out, and it got lost in Nick's mouth. And then Derek's when he came and pulled me into another kiss. A tongue was on my clit again, the stinging ache of my spanked pussy making every suck and stroke feel more intense.

That was what he meant.

I want to spank your pussy until it's swollen and then make you come. Back and forth until you don't know whether it's pain or pleasure, you're just coming.

"Oooh," I moaned into Derek's mouth. "I remember."

"Do you?" Another spank stole my breath. The pain was so swift and sharp it was like a knife that melted into sugar and butter and all the good things in life. Why the fuck was I craving more of this?

A gush of wetness gave me away.

"Fuck, princess." Sebastian's voice was a growl. "Give me more of that."

His hand came down on my clit again, sending tingles of fire and stars whirling through my brain. Nick and Derek moved together, dragging their mouths over my skin and sucking my nipples into peaks.

The next time Sebastian spanked my pussy, I ruptured. Golden fire cascaded over me, my ragged scream loud in the nest. Somewhere I heard them praising me, and the long, sensual strokes of Sebastian's tongue kept me going through the orgasm and further, until I was shaking.

"I want to drink you," he murmured against my clit. "So fucking good, little one. I need you to give me more."

My pussy clamped down, wanting a knot. "Knot," I begged. "I need one."

"Oh, we'll give you one, sweetheart," Nick said, drawing lazy circles around my clit with his tongue. "More than one. After you give us another orgasm like that."

I didn't know how.

My head was only glitter and glass. Fractured into stars of pleasure like constellations in my vision.

Fire like a nova bursting, nothing but pleasure and pain. Sebastian's hand on me, perfectly placed, coming down with a force I should have hated, but loved. Every time his fingers connected with my skin, I was pulled further into this galaxy of gorgeous bliss.

The wet heat of his mouth and all their tongues touching me. It was too much. Too much to contain in one body.

"That's it, princess. Enjoy it."

A scrape of teeth on my skin, and it wasn't pain or pleasure, it was simply *fire*. Exactly like he'd said, there was no telling the difference. They turned my body into a furnace, and every touch was fuel.

I sagged in the ropes, my body spent and dazed and already wanting more. A heat by myself was never this intense. But then, when I was alone, I didn't have three scent-matched Alphas driving my instincts fucking crazy.

The ropes on my legs loosened one by one, Sebastian pulling me onto his body and lowering me onto his cock. Derek held me from behind. "We're going to take you together, *gattina*, all right?"

"*Yes*."

More.

Faster.

All of it.

My arms were still bound, and I didn't care. I felt Derek's skin with my fingers. The only experience I had with something in my ass was an experimental plug years ago, but I was too far gone for it to matter. He was gentle, and all I felt was the perfect bliss of being full and shared. Treasured and cared for.

Nick stepped in front of me, and I reached for him with my mouth, accepting him like the peppermint lollipop he was. One hand in my hair, he guided me deeper, and I let him. My mind was a starry field of glittering snow. I didn't want to do anything except *experience*.

And they gave me everything.

There was no beginning or end to the pleasure, just waves of it coming from different directions and carrying me away. How could I have ever thought this was a bad thing? Every moment and every breath was the best I'd ever experienced. So much pleasure and so much joy. I needed more and more and more.

Sebastian came first, locking me to him, and Derek came a second later. Their knots pressed against each other, stealing my sight and what was left of my conscious thoughts.

Nick came last, the candy-cane flavor of him the perfect end of pleasure even as his knot swelled in my mouth and locked me against him.

My arms came loose, Derek massaging them in the quick minutes before their knots released me, and I collapsed onto the cushions. It was impossible my body wanted more after that, right?

Right?

Pain and fire surged, driving me up onto my knees and bending me forward so I was presenting for them, begging for their knots and everything else.

"Alphas," I whimpered.

Hands landed on my ass. I didn't even know who they belonged to as he entered me. "Don't worry, baby. We've got you."

CHAPTER TWELVE

SELENA

I sat on Sebastian again. He was too big to go anywhere else inside me. Or at least I was too nervous to try that yet. All I wanted was pleasure, and him filling my pussy was more than enough.

Except it wasn't.

Seb's hands cupped my face. "Look at me, princess."

I *was* looking at him. His face all sharp angles and planes, the darkness of his eyes pulling you down so deep you'd never come out, and I didn't want to.

How many days had we been in here? I didn't know. But every hour with them erased the idea that there could be nothing between us. I was addicted to them. Breathing in their scent and tasting them until their flavor was the only flavor. The heady mixture of the three of them together.

"Breathe," Sebastian said.

Was I not breathing? I was breathing.

I felt untethered from myself, lost in the fever of heat, which was the highest it had ever been. Spinning in a world of fire all my own, and sometimes they joined me inside of it with lips and hands and gentle words.

Was there a time when I thought they weren't gentle?

Seb pulled my face down to his, our lips brushing. "Stay with me, princess. We have you."

I gasped, the feeling of someone behind me and the scent of peppermint and fresh, sharp limes. Nick. The feeling of them together was a comfort now. They anchored me to the earth through shattering pleasure. "Ohh." My eyes fell closed.

And then something else. Another—

My eyes flew open, trying to find where to look. "What?"

"Keep your eyes on me, Omega," Sebastian ordered. "Relax."

I did, the third cock slipping inside me. Not fully. But enough to make me come apart. I was no longer in control of my body, shaking, novas of pleasure firing everywhere, and through all of it, Sebastian kept me with him and kissed me, though they fucked me together.

The true molten core of the heat was here. Diving into the heart of the volcano. There was no way for me to come out of this. I would perish within the wild storm of sparks and flame. Everything burned up.

The three of them surged into me a final time, throwing me off the cliff into bright oblivion. I screamed, collapsing onto Sebastian's chest. Two knots locked me into place, and I didn't know where the third one was, but I knew that the fire burning inside me extinguished with that orgasm.

Everything was suddenly cold. My body still shook, exhausted and spent, I heaved in breath, trying to catch it and unable to.

My mind cleared, and everything came crashing down on me at once. It was over, and that meant—

I couldn't bear it.

When their knots eased the final time, I curled onto my side on the cushions, burying my face in them, unwilling to look at them or anything else.

"Selena," Sebastian asked. "What's going on? Are you all right?"

I curled my body tighter, and he came with me, surrounding me with his giant body and making me feel protected even though I wasn't.

The rough rumble of his purr had me relaxing into him. He brushed my hair back from my face. I kept my eyes closed and imagined what this would be like if we were far from here. In a nest I designed, all greens and blues and purples, with a window where you could raise the blinds and see a view, with sunshine for plants and flowers when the nest wasn't in use.

I imagined the two of us just like this, him brushing my hair back and purring. Nothing for any of us to do but lie here and breathe and enjoy the feeling of each other.

"Selena?" He asked quietly.

Unsuccessfully, I tried to keep the emotion out of my voice. "Just a few more minutes," I begged. "Please. Let me believe it."

His whole body went stiff, the backs of his fingers touching my forehead, but his purr didn't stop, and he relaxed against me again, saying nothing.

I wasn't sure how long it was before he turned me over, stretching me out from my curled up position. I stared at the ceiling. "I guess it's over."

"Not yet." He ran his knuckles down my cheek. "Derek's going to take you for a bath, and we'll sleep for a while."

It was still over. They knew that as well as I did. Coming down from a heat was always hard. The surge of hormones and the sudden absence… the intensity of this hadn't even hit me yet.

"Okay," was all I said out loud.

He tugged me toward him and kissed my temple. "Thank you for letting me spend your heat with you, little one."

I nodded, and he purred before releasing me. Nick knelt and pressed his forehead to mine. He said nothing, but I felt things I wasn't allowed to feel. Finally, Derek picked me up off the cushions and carried me from the nest into one of the giant bathrooms in the apartment.

Nick ran the water in the bath, and Derek carried me into it once it was full. It was big enough for all of us, but Nick and Seb excused themselves to check some things down in the club. After all, they still had a business to run. And I was part of that business.

Derek settled me against his side so I could lie across his

83

chest, his arm around me. Slowly, he dragged warm water up my side and back and stroked his hand back down. It was the perfect moment, and I wanted to stay here. Only I knew it wasn't going to happen, and it killed me.

It was impossible to hide my emotions now. Everything was at the surface, ready to burst. Tears welled in my eyes and spilled over, but I kept them quiet, trying to still enjoy the moment for as long as it lasted.

But my tears reached his skin, and I felt him startle, his hand pausing in its soothing motions. "Why are you crying, *gattina?*"

"You know why."

"It's going to be all right, Selena."

I turned my face into his chest, perversely seeking comfort from the Alpha who was going to be my captor once again, once we were out of this bath and the cuffs went back on. "How can you say that? I'm still a slave. You're still taking everything from me."

He turned us together so my back pressed against the cool porcelain. "You chose to stay," he said gently.

Closing my eyes, I leaned my head back against the tub. "You know I used to dream about being scent matched? It used to get me through bad days, thinking about building a nest with them, how they might spoil me." I shook my head, unable to make myself open my eyes and look at him. If there was hardness in his gaze, I couldn't bear it. "Now I don't even know if my scent matches are going to sell me to someone who will enjoy fucking me while they murder me."

"That's not going to happen."

"No? Your words, Derek." I took advantage of the last moments I could call him by his name. "That you would decide after my training whether to sell me."

"Look at me."

I shook my head. "No."

"*Look at me.*" The Alpha command in his voice forced my

eyes open. There wasn't harshness in his gaze, there was pure intensity. "If you think we could sell you after this, you're wrong."

"But I'm still a slave."

He inclined his head. "Yes, *gattina*, you are. I hope you'll see it's not as bad as you think."

A whine came out of me, panic and terror overcoming me. "Not as bad? I—"

"Shhh." He covered my lips with his, kissing me like we were still in the nest. "Breathe, Omega. Don't worry about it tonight." He brushed away some of my tears. "You will be okay, Selena. I promise."

I wished I could believe him.

"Come here." The words were gentle as he turned us so I laid against him again, and I cried. He didn't tell me not to, nor did he admonish me for it. Simply held me and stroked my skin, occasionally whispering that I would be all right.

But how could I be all right?

How?

The water started to cool. "Sit up for me."

I did, and he washed me, making sure the last remnants of the heat were gone before wrapping me in a towel and carrying me to a bedroom. His bedroom. "You'll stay with me tonight."

There was a hesitation in his voice. "But?"

"Give me your wrist, *gattina*."

I closed my eyes and obeyed. The leather cuff wrapped around my wrist, and then the other one. A heavy, clinking weight attached to my hands, and he laid them on the bed before climbing in on the other side and pulling me against his chest.

"I promise," he whispered again. "I promise everything will be all right."

Closing my eyes, I let myself rest and believe it was the truth.

CHAPTER THIRTEEN

SEBASTIAN

I scrubbed my hands over my face and shoved into the office. The need to hit something was rising, but I couldn't do that without raising suspicions from everyone around us. But I was coming apart at the seams.

Selena's face broke my heart, and I worried we weren't going to be able to bring her back.

"Have we heard from the Denver Coalition?" I asked Nick when he stepped in behind me. It was what we called the agency we worked for, and he was the last one to check in. I hoped to god we had, because there was only so long I could do this before I was going to drag Selena out of here and make her mine, damn the consequences.

"No," he said. "Or at least nothing of substance. Continue as planned."

I swore, grabbing a statuette off my desk and catching myself just before I threw it against the fucking wall. Why did we even have this thing? Pretentious as fuck, having a bronze cast of some classical statue like the personas we played were supposed to be art connoisseurs while we were selling *people*.

"Seb," Nick said. "I know. I'm there too. I've been there for days. But there's nothing we can do."

"She wouldn't say anything," I hissed. "She wouldn't."

His mouth firmed into a line even as I saw grief enter his eyes. "We don't know that."

And of course, he was right. The women we 'sold' were some of the best actresses I'd ever seen, and they never broke character. Not once. I had every confidence that if they were somehow a scent match with one of the men that bought them, they would continue their mission and duty, regardless.

Which is what Selena would do if she were like them.

I turned and leaned both hands on the desk, everything suddenly pressing down on me like a weight I couldn't bear.

What we were doing was good. Undeniably. It would save lives and end a whole hell of a lot of evil. But at what cost?

Squeezing my eyes shut, I gripped the desk so hard the wood creaked. Four lives were worth the thousands of Omegas that were stolen and sold every year. They were. But *fuck*, I didn't want to be the hero right now. I wanted to burn it down. Burn everything fucking down to make the hurt and despair on my Omega's face disappear.

And she *was* my Omega.

Body and soul.

There would never be anyone else for me. Not after the four days I'd spent steeped in her beauty and her scent. The brave and delicate trust she surrendered to us, even though she thought we were monsters.

"We should make an appearance," he said. "We've been absent enough as it is."

"Fine," I said. Because if I was going to hell anyway, I might as well throw myself into the fucking flames.

I followed Nick out into the club, my body falling into years of muscle memory. An easy stride and a *don't fuck with me* face that had people scrambling to get out of my way.

Until the man I wanted to see least in the world stepped into my path.

"And here I thought I was going to see a display of training from the best of the best. I've barely seen your shadows. Some people might think you're ignoring more important things."

His tone was casual, but the threat was there. He needed to see us take control, and he needed to see us train Selena. No part of me wanted to subject her to that.

Too bad what I wanted didn't fucking matter.

"Not all training is suited to the public eye," I said. "But we'll be introducing her to public training tomorrow."

"Is that so?"

"It is," Nick said. "I'm sure you'll enjoy it."

"And how will you train her?"

I smirked. "Wouldn't want to ruin the surprise. But this week you'll see more than enough."

"Good." He lowered his voice. "Because it's easy to take my money and merchandise elsewhere."

"You asked for a show and you'll get one," I snapped. "The insinuation we wouldn't honor our agreement? That can fuck off. We have a process, and you'll see how it works. If you're no longer interested, feel free to leave."

Instinctively, I felt Nick tense, but he was good enough that he didn't look at me in shock. Just stood with me, silently backing my play.

Christopher Delano wasn't a man who responded to weakness and acquiescence. He wanted to watch us dominate and harm. Assuring him wasn't going to do the trick.

A muscle ticked in his cheek, and he smirked. "Fair enough. I look forward to your... display."

He walked past me, just barely missing knocking into my shoulder, and disappeared into the depths of the club. Delano knew that none of the paying patrons were to be touched. The second he did the deal was off, because if we didn't have a place to conduct business, it affected his. That was one boundary I knew he wouldn't cross, thankfully.

"Fucking risky, Seb," Nick said under his breath.

"Strength with strength," I said. "It's the only way we're going to get through this."

He nodded. "Yeah. And now we have to bring her down here."

"We were going to have to do that anyway." I sighed and

fought the instinct to hang my head. "Just promise me this is worth it."

"It is," Nick said.

But as I walked away, I heard him speak again to himself.

"It has to be."

CHAPTER FOURTEEN

SELENA

"*K*eep your eyes on the ground," Derek said. His voice was quiet and even, but firm. "You don't have permission to speak unless the three of us give it to you. You do not respond to anyone else unless we say you can. Follow behind us, and when we stop, you kneel. If we're settled somewhere, you can sit to the side. And if any of us allow you to do anything, you will thank us."

My eyes were on the floor, and I kept them there. I was a little dazed. Once again, the world didn't seem real. From the fever dream of a heat to this reality and the truth of the Syndicate, part of me wondered if I'd fallen into the deepest dream ever.

I wasn't naked, and for that I was grateful, but it was a barely there thing. Less fabric than the green concoction I'd been put in for the cage. It was pretty, and in other circumstances, I might feel sexy. Burnt orange at the straps flared through the brighter color and into a pale yellow around my hips.

Thin, sheer fabric around my breasts and gathered beneath them, with no underwear. So it was a fraction of a step up from being naked, but it still felt like a bit of protection.

"Selena?"

My eyes jerked up to Derek's, and I dropped them to the floor again. One of the first things he told me was to respond to all commands with, *yes, Master*. I'd already forgotten.

"Yes, Master," I whispered.

When I woke up this morning, Derek was still wrapped around me. Not just that, he was holding me so tightly to him it felt like he was trying to keep me with him. As if I were being pulled away, or *he* was being pulled away and I was his anchor.

He moved as soon as I did, and there were imprints of his fingers where he held me. I didn't know what to make of the look on his face. A mixture of fear, horror, and devastation, before he shook it off and got me this scrap of a dress. It was already evening, my heat having taken us to strange hours.

"Let's go," he said.

I followed him into the elevator. It was better this way, the floating. Because if I wasn't truly aware of what was going on around me, it wouldn't matter. I would simply listen and hope I heard something that could give me the answer the Syndicate wanted. Then I could get back to Anna, and my life.

Grief struck me, and I pushed it aside.

No.

I couldn't deal with the complexity of my feelings for these men right now.

The elevator doors opened to pulsing music and sound. It was so loud compared to the last few days. I kept my eyes on Derek's feet, following him as he strode through the darkness and pulsing lights. He stopped briefly, and I stopped. Not long enough to kneel.

"There you are." Nick's voice reached me over the music. "It's about time."

We were by a black leather couch. His hand came down on my shoulder, and I knelt on the floor, shifting to the side to sit on my hip next to him. Nick's hand rested on the back of my neck, rubbing gently.

From the outside, I realized it would look possessive, with my head bowed, hair curtained around my face, and his hand gripping my neck. But in his touch I felt only tenderness which twisted into longing in my gut, and I didn't know what to do with that.

"Good to see you follow through on your word."

The familiar voice sent chills across my skin, but I didn't look up. Derek's shoes were still beside me, noticeably blocking the stranger from getting closer to me and Nick. It was the man from the theatre. The one who wanted to buy me and cut me into pieces.

"Of course," Derek said. "As they told you, it's important for us to do some training in private first. As you can see, she is well in hand now."

"Is she? I don't know. What do you say, slave? Are you well in hand?"

I didn't move and didn't speak. They hadn't given me permission, and I didn't want to talk to this man. Where was Sebastian? He was the one who made sure he… Christopher? Was that the name he used? That he didn't take me after the auction.

Nick lifted his hand from my skin as if to illustrate he didn't need to touch me in order for me to obey.

A dark chuckle. "Are you sure she's awake?"

"Slave, look at me," Derek said.

I instantly lifted my face to lock eyes with him. Pride and relief rested in his gaze. "Stand."

Without any help, I rose to my feet.

"Offer your wrists to me."

I held them out, and he grabbed them, pulling me against his body. The motion looked rough but felt smooth. One hand came around my throat, tilting my head back.

My eyes were no longer trained on him, looking down as far as I could.

"If I turned you around right now and spanked you, what would you say?"

"Thank you, Master."

In the corner of my eye, I saw the smirk. "If I ordered you to your knees and fucked your throat?"

There was no resistance in me, because on some deep

level, I knew this was important. Making sure this man knew I didn't belong to him was a goal we both had. At the moment, we were aligned. So I took a risk. "I would thank you after you came down my throat, Master."

"You may return to Master Nick."

I hoped no one could see the way my knees shook as I turned and took the step back to him. He caught me before I could sink back to my knees, arranging me to straddle his lap. Putting my hands behind my back, he clipped my cuffs together and began to touch me.

I didn't react, allowing his hands to roam over my body. Heat rose beneath his fingers. But just like I knew I needed to show the man I didn't belong to him, I knew just as deeply I couldn't show him I would be aroused by anything they did.

Nick slapped the side of my breast through the night-gown. It stung, but no more than in the heat. He paused, and I realized I was supposed to speak. "Thank you, Master."

Another slap. "Thank you, Master."

He lifted me and placed me back on my knees without unclipping the cuffs. I returned to my previous position with my eyes on the floor and his hand on my neck.

"Satisfied, Delano?"

"It seems I stand corrected," the man said. *Delano*. I would remember it now. "My offer is still on the table. Name your price."

Nick's hand tightened on my skin, but he remained silent.

"We'll let you know," Derek said. There was a smile in his voice, but at least I knew it was a lie. I was choosing to believe what he said yesterday. They weren't going to sell me to a monster worse than they were. "Enjoy the exhibition."

The words seemed to be final because Delano walked away and Derek sat on my other side. "Well done, *gattina*. Good girl." His hand stroked my hair, and I shouldn't have loved the way it felt or his praise, but I did. For the few minutes we were aligned, we'd worked together, and made sure that asshole went away.

Derek stroked my hair a few times. "You have permission to watch as well, Selena."

Watch what?

I lifted my eyes from the floor, noticing the stage in front of us. A woman was strapped to big X, naked, gagged, and blindfolded. A table of things sat beside her from whips to candles, and a bare chested man in leather pants was looking over the things he could use.

Nick leaned forward and reached down behind me and unclipped my cuffs, relieving my shoulders. "She is a normal paying member of the club and chose to be here," he said so softly I barely heard it. But tension I hadn't even noticed creep into my body suddenly dissolved. He felt it.

Pulling me against him, Nick let me lean against his knee, hand still resting against my skin. We watched the woman in front of us be tortured into screaming pleasure with wax and whips, clamps, and floggers. And the whole time I wondered how it was possible that in the middle of this, I could feel safe kneeling at someone's feet.

That wasn't supposed to happen. Right?

CHAPTER FIFTEEN

SELENA

*T*here wouldn't be kneeling this time. I already knew that. The way Nick walked in front of me, with purpose and direction, I knew this would be different.

Last night he kept me by his knee as we watched people play, and then they put me in the cage. Almost nothing was said, but they fed me and let me shower, and put me back into the cage until it was time to come here.

This time, I was naked.

All I wanted was to raise my arms and cover myself, but I didn't dare.

I was grateful he didn't lead me onto a stage. We were in a dark corner of the club. There were still people, but they were on the periphery. "Sit here," Nick instructed.

I glanced up and froze. It was what looked like a medical exam table, stirrups and all. He saw the flash of fear in my eyes, and I also saw him glance behind me. So I stepped forward. "Yes, Master."

Pushing myself onto the table, I sat. He hadn't instructed me to lie down.

No, he did that for me, pressing me back onto the table and lifting my feet into the stirrups. Then there were the straps. Rubber straps that buckled me onto the reclined table. Shoulders, waist, hips, and arms included. My legs too, in the stirrups, and one across my forehead.

Held captive like this, I was immobile, and I flashed back to my deepest fantasies before all of this happened. Not in a medical chair, but I'd thought about something somewhat like this. Completely at the mercy of an Alpha—or Alphas—I could trust to bring me pleasure.

"Master?"

Nick focused on me, and both Derek and Sebastian stepped out of the shadows where I hadn't seen them. All three of them like a wall, blocking me from the sight of the rest of the club.

"You may speak," Seb told me.

"How am I being trained?"

Part of me didn't want to know, and was afraid they were tying me open in order to share me with the people of the club and let them have their way with me. But I needed to know.

"A lesson in how your Master's commands are above all else," Derek said. "Above everything, including your own body."

What did that mean? The other question was on the tip of my tongue, and I swallowed it back.

"You have another question?"

I didn't meet his eyes. "Are you going to give me to other people?"

A low growl that didn't quite make it above the music, but I *felt* it. "We only share with each other," Sebastian said, dark eyes pinning me with a stare I wasn't supposed to meet.

I tried to nod, and my head didn't move because of the strap. "Thank you."

In the dim light of the club, I saw his jaw flex, and he turned away.

Nick stepped into the shadows, and when he returned, rolling something, I couldn't not stare at it. I knew exactly what it was. Enough porn I watched used it for me to know, and also give me exactly an idea of what was about to happen.

Now, I didn't care. The pale plastic dildo on the end of the fucking machine didn't scare me. I was always curious what it was like to be taken by an actual machine. My mind piped up and told me during the heat I'd come close, but I pushed it away. I wasn't going to get fucked by strangers, and that was all that mattered.

Derek leaned over me. "You are not allowed to come, Selena."

I knew he would say it. Whether I could actually obey, I had no idea. But he wanted to train me to deny myself. *They* controlled my pleasure. *They* were the only ones who could allow me to orgasm.

Nick was working on the machine, attaching something to the top of it—oh my god. I knew that toy. I *owned* that toy. The bulbous head of the vibrator was attached above the dildo, and that would place it right on my clit.

"Master," I licked my lips. "I—"

"Be very careful, Selena."

"What happens if I can't obey?"

He considered me for a moment. "Because this is your first time, after we're finished, you'll be paddled every time you come without permission. At least the number of orgasms, but maybe more. By all three of us."

"Thank you, Master." I swallowed. A punishment I could handle.

Derek smiled, his eyes crinkling at the corners. "Good girl."

Shutting my eyes, I wished I could turn my head to look away. His smile did things to me I didn't like, because it only added to my ever-growing confusion.

"All right," Nick said, placing the machine in front of me. He reached between my legs, stroking my clit before sliding the dildo inside me. My body responded in spite of myself. Five days locked in a nest, and I was trained to surrender to his pleasure.

Between the straps holding me down and him knowing exactly how to touch me, I was wet. The dildo slid in easily, filling me up. Not even close to what they felt like, but it was more than enough.

"How long, Master?"

Nick looked at me, and the heated lust in his eyes further lit my arousal. He shrugged. "As long as we want. Don't bother begging, the answer is no. Feel free to scream as much as you want."

One flick of a switch, and the machine began to move. The vibrator sprang to life directly against my clit. *Fuck*.

What could I think about to make this not happen? Because my body *wanted* this. After a heat? Two full days without an orgasm? Unheard of. My pussy was desperate, and being tied down, I couldn't move to relieve the pressure.

The dildo slid in slowly. Out just as slowly. It felt good, but it was manageable like this. I didn't think it would stay this way, but for now, I was okay. I looked at the ceiling and focused on the lights. I could see ones that changed colors, pointing at the dance floor across the room.

Red, purple, green, orange, blue, white, white, white.

"Fuck," I said. The machine sped up, and the vibration changed to a wave pattern which rose in intensity and dropped.

"I said you could scream," Nick said, appearing at my side and looking down at me. "I didn't say you could curse. I control the machine, Selena." Heat still poured out of his eyes, igniting lust in my gut it was impossible to ignore. "Every time you speak a word that isn't 'Thank you for the pleasure, Master,' I will increase the intensity. And you still don't have permission."

A whimper came out of me. His eyes dropped to my lips, and I wondered if he was remembering the heat too. How they took me and let me come and we fell into bliss over and over again.

He disappeared into the shadows again. A light shone directly down on me like a spotlight, painting the rest of the club—other than the lights I saw—in silhouettes. I was alone in this, fighting for myself.

The part of me that wanted to tell them to fuck off and send the machines so high I was forced to orgasm until I passed out was matched with the part of me that desperately wanted to obey because they needed this. How I knew, I wasn't sure, but they needed to do this.

There was something they were hiding.

In the fog of fighting growing pleasure, the revelation came. They were hiding something. Of course they were hiding things. They were traffickers. The whole operation they ran was hidden within this club. Why was I shocked about that and why hadn't I thought about it before?

The familiar growth of pleasure in my gut came, and I forced my mind away from it. Ice. I would think about ice and rain. Going outside in the dead of winter without a coat. In the snow. With wind chill.

It managed to fade, and I breathed out a sigh of relief.

Another notch up, and another pattern. Short bursts of vibration and the rhythm of the machine changed to feel like one of the Alphas rolling their hips, striking deep at the spot that seemed impossible.

Starry pleasure shone in my vision, gathering in the club lights and spiraling through the air.

Mud. I needed to think about mud and dirt and grease. The least sexy things in the history of the universe. Creepy crawlies. Bats. Snakes. The taste of root beer. *Fuck*.

Like they knew I needed a breather and had mercy, the intensity backed off and I got hold of it just in time. One more second and I would have lost it. There was no way I would make it through this without coming, but I could minimize the punishment coming to me.

It rose again, and I squeezed my eyes shut. No.

No.

No.

No.

Maybe sheer will could get me through.

I was a nurse, dammit. I wrestled with patients three times my size when they tried to fight me and didn't break a sweat. I could handle fighting an orgasm by three Alphas who didn't deserve to see me break. If anything, they would be proud of me for making it through. If I could.

Stop it, Selena.

What they thought didn't matter. I would do this for myself. To prove that I was strong enough to survive this. I could. I could do it.

The vibrator sped up a notch, and I cried out, my voice echoing off the ceiling. Shit shit shit, maybe I couldn't do this. It was only a paddle, right? Sebastian had spanked my pussy and it had been fine. I could survive that.

But did I need to?

"Master." I barely mouthed the word, hoping they would see, and he did. Nick stood next to me in a moment, stance casual, hands in his pockets, staring down at me like he didn't care what I was going through.

The intensity in his eyes told me differently, but there was no way to prove it. Only desperation drove me to do this. "Closer?"

Whispers were the only way I could function. Anything louder, anything more to distract my mind from its singular mission and I would explode without intention.

Nick leaned down. "Speak, Selena."

"Do you need me to succeed or fail?"

The way his face went slack in shock told me I hit my mark. "What did you say?"

"Do you want me to do this? Or not?"

He stared at me, face unreadable. There was this intangible thing between us, the pull and the reality. I was theirs and didn't have a choice, but it was also *more*. I needed just one thing to tell me I wasn't nothing.

The toy between my legs slowed, the vibrations dropped to a rumble, and I gasped in relief, heaving breath. He pressed a hand to my forehead, like he would stroke my hair if the rubber strap wasn't in the way. "I *want* you to succeed," he said. "To be a good fucking girl, Selena."

But, I answered in my mind.

"But I need you to fail."

My stomach plummeted and my heart rejoiced. It wasn't much, but it was something. A singular admission to what Derek had told me—not everything was what it seemed like.

"Put up a fight," he said. "Try. Because you're my slave and I'm ordering you not to come. But you will, sweetheart. I'm not going to give you a choice. The ground underneath this table is going to be soaked with you by the time I'm done."

He didn't let me respond or ask me to, just stepped away. This time, in the corner of my eye, I saw them. Three shapes to my left, out of the sphere of light. Other shapes beyond them. I couldn't make them out, couldn't move my head, but they were there, and everything in my mind was easier.

I obeyed, and I fought.

The machine fucked me and the vibrator toyed with me, and I pushed myself to the edges, trying to resist the pleasure.

But Nick was right—it was too much.

I came. Screaming.

The build up was so much, and the machine didn't stop. He was right. I soaked the floor. The vibrations on my clit overloaded my body again and again, and I hoped they were keeping track of the times I came, because I certainly wasn't.

I didn't even notice the machine had stopped until Derek was unhooking the straps and folding my body over the table to expose my ass. They hooked my hands together, and I didn't resist it, because they needed this, and I would give it to them even if I didn't know why.

At the very least, maybe they would trust me more, and maybe I would find out what I needed to get back to Anna.

"You came four times," Sebastian said. "You're going to thank us for the discipline we offer after you don't obey."

What the hell was wrong with me right now? My body was languid and peaceful. I didn't care that my ass was about to get spanked. The pleasure I just experienced had me so blissed out, I wasn't even *worried*. Everything was calm because I knew they needed it.

Was it the nurse in me that put others before myself one hundred percent of the time? Was it the memories of us together in the nest? Or was it something deeper I was afraid to examine because it would tell me things about myself and the situation I wasn't ready to acknowledge?

Like the fact that obeying them made it easier to breathe. And that I trusted them not to truly hurt me while they punished me. Or the feeling of satisfaction in truly being able to let go.

Smack!

The pain burned in my ass, and I spoke the words they wanted me to. "Thank you, Master." It felt easy. Every time the pain spiked and faded into impossible warmth, I thanked them. Each of them punishing me for what I'd let happen.

Derek stood me on my feet. "Follow me. The rules still apply."

I shook, but obeyed. All the way back into the elevator and to the cage, where he locked me to the edges of the steel frame, and I fell into sleep before the cage was even closed.

My dreams weren't bad ones this time.

CHAPTER SIXTEEN

NICHOLAS

a chuckle rose behind me as I watched them take Selena back to our apartment. She was dragging, weak on her feet and I was amazed she was still standing. I wanted to follow her and make sure she was okay, but that wasn't the right call.

We had to look impassive.

Turning, I found Delano behind me. "Impressive. She seems to be on the edge of breaking."

"Possibly," I said. "But I'll leave the true breaking to Sebastian. He does enjoy it. Especially when there's punishment involved."

"Something we have in common," he said. "Though I prefer my implements to have a little more bite than he does."

I forced myself to smile. "You of all people know it would be unwise to permanently damage someone who could be merchandise."

"I suppose that's true." He slid his hands into his pockets. "Again, I'm willing to pay whatever you like for her. Have you whipped her yet? Her skin is so pure, it makes me want to create a masterpiece on her."

"Not yet. It will come soon, and I'll keep your offer in mind. You didn't bring any of your own slaves to keep you company?"

Delano's eyes scanned over the dance floor in front of us, leaning against the railing that separated this section of the club. "I try not to mix business with pleasure, though, for that Omega, I would make an exception."

Of course he fucking would. But he was getting close to Selena over my dead body. "And business?"

He glanced at me. "So far, everything is going well. Half of your auction lots have made it where they need to go. The other half are almost there."

"Excellent. I'm glad to hear it." It took time smuggling people.

Delano observed me, and the intentionality of it felt *too* casual. "I'll admit, I had my doubts. Your… caginess with this slave had my hackles up. But seeing the auction, and the three of you in action, it's better. I think we'll be able to have a healthy partnership."

"May I ask what doubts?" I tilted my head. If there were rumors about us beyond his own mind, we needed to squash them now, before they took root, even if he said they'd faded.

Delano shrugged, focusing on a couple near us. A man in a suit and a female submissive collared on a leash. Tame by his standards, but she was very pretty. He knew everyone on that side of the club was here and playing consensually. I wondered what he thought of them. "It just seemed… convenient. No one in the world had heard of you, and suddenly the three Warwick Alphas were the premiere slave trainers and suppliers in the world? I've only survived this long because of my suspicions. Don't be offended."

I laughed. "I'm not."

"Like I said, it's better. If I hadn't known anything about you, that might not have been enough, but I hope to see more. Regardless, you followed through. It's the way it should be. Put them in their place. It's the only way they learn. Though I might have only let her make the first mistake."

"Yes," I agreed. "You can't have any leniency. But the rest was for us. We wanted to punish her more."

My stomach churned. He was boxing us in and he didn't even know it. Because now we couldn't show any mercy to

Selena whatsoever. And I'd said something that could put her in danger because she was my Omega and I wanted her to be okay. I'd made a mistake, and there wasn't a way for me to take it back.

Except for me to actually put her in her place. My Alpha warred in me with the need to protect her and how to do it. Because by treating her like the slave she currently was, she *was* more protected from the piece of shit in front of me. But I didn't want to fucking do that.

My instincts were rising, and I needed to get the fuck out of this conversation. Scenting Selena, watching her come, having to punish her and not fuck her was pure torture. Now Delano was dangling the idea of her torture in front of me, and I could feel rut hovering around the edges of my vision.

I needed to contact headquarters and find out how much longer this was going to take. It had been a week of him staying here. Surely—*surely*—they had enough dirt on him now to pull the trigger.

"Once all the merchandise has been accepted, I'll have a proposition for you," he said. "I know you're the premiere in terms of sourcing that merchandise, but if you're willing to entertain a wider source, there are some available."

Matching his pose, I leaned against the railing. "I'm listening."

"Naturally, I can't give you all the details until I'm sure our business here is complete. But I will say that no one will miss these whores, and having... amply sampled the merchandise, they'll do just fine. Especially for clients like myself who prefer our purchases to be expendable."

Mother fucker.

The man was literally taunting me with the fact that he liked to buy women, fuck them, and kill them. Like hell was I going to find out if he liked doing it at the same time.

Though my stomach tangled into knots, I let an easy smirk slide onto my face. "Sounds intriguing. I look forward to discussing it more." Derek appeared across the room again, providing me with the excuse I needed. "Excuse me."

Delano nodded, and I went straight for Derek. "Where the fuck is she?"

"Upstairs, in the cage, already asleep."

"Good." He followed me, stopping me before we reached the elevator. "What the hell is going on? We weren't gone that long."

I pressed my mouth firmly closed and nodded to the elevator. Only in our private areas were we free to speak our minds. Really, the apartment was the only safe place. The office too, but I still preferred not to. I waited until the doors opened into the living room. "That man is a fucking piece of shit."

"Tell me something I don't know," Derek said. "What is it this time?"

It wasn't anything worse than we knew, but seeing the way he looked at Selena, and practically bragging about kidnapping and murder after watching us punish our Omega? My Alpha was seething. Raring to go.

"It was everything." I spat out a repeat of our conversation, and that we couldn't afford any slip-ups with Selena.

He sighed. "Yeah. I figured. I'll reach out and see what they're thinking. You're right, they have to be close."

"And I—" I shook my head. When I'd come back from her calling me over, I hadn't told them what she'd asked. "I fucked up," I said.

"How?"

All this time I was the one who said we weren't sure if she could be trusted, but I was the one who'd broken. "She asked me if we needed her to succeed or fail, Derek. And I... I told her I wanted her to succeed, but needed her to fail. I pulled it back and told her I wasn't going to give her a choice, but I fucked up."

I paced back and forth, everything rushing to the surface.

What I needed right now was to go into the cage and fuck my Omega. Get her ready for the next few days, even if it made her hate me. Because if she was alive to hate me, at least she was alive.

My pack mate said nothing. We both knew it had been a mistake, but Derek couldn't say he wouldn't have done the same. Finally, he looked at me and the way I paced like a feral animal. "She's asleep. Go do what you need to."

"Should I go in there like this?"

He snorted. "You're not going to hurt her, are you?"

"No," I snarled the word. Fuck the shit out of her? Yes. Make sure she understood her place for the next few days? Yes. But hurting her?

The thought of her hurting made me want to burn the world down. If I could, I would pummel Delano into the ground. But since I couldn't have that kind of release, I would find another one. One that allowed me to unleash myself in exactly the same way.

"I'll see if headquarters has anything, and let you know when you're finished," Derek said.

I said nothing. My mind was too unhinged with anger and desire, and my instincts were on the verge of rut. Stalking through the apartment to the cage room, I unlocked the door and stepped inside, the air filled with her scent calming me just enough to take the edge off.

But not entirely.

The fire burned, casting the room into flickering orange. Selena was chained to her bed, asleep, the cage already locked. Gorgeous.

Even if she wasn't our slave in this way forever, I wanted nights where she was bound to me. Maybe even a sleeping pill, so she could feel how hard I'd fucked her in the morning. In those instances, I'd have her full permission.

Technically I had it now, but it wasn't the same as clear and burning passion.

She didn't stir when I unlocked the cage, and I stripped at the door. Her hands were chained above her head, legs attached to either side of the steel frame. I wondered if Derek or Sebastian had known I would need this tonight, or simply wanted to train her to sleep in this position and feel the vulnerability of being stored for use.

Her shackled hands stretched over her head, and that luscious dark hair fell over her face.

I eased onto the bed, and she didn't move. Our Omega was exhausted from her time in the club earlier. As she should be. But my cock was hard, and I needed her cunt like I needed my next breath.

Pulling the blanket off, her pussy glistened in the dim light. She was wet, her body betraying her, poor thing. She was made to surrender and submit, no matter how hard she fought it. I wished we weren't in the position we were, so the three of us could show her what being owned meant in the way we loved.

Too bad it couldn't happen.

I leaned down and licked her, dipping my tongue inside and swirling it around her clit, savoring the intense, delicious flavor. If I had my choice, I would drink her for breakfast every day. Make one of her rules that she needed to sit on my face in the morning until I was satisfied.

Her satisfaction wouldn't be a factor.

Selena stirred, but didn't wake. Good. I didn't want her awake yet.

With aching slowness, I lined myself up with her pretty pink cunt and sank inside it. Balls deep. All the way. Her body hugged mine like no one I'd ever felt. Fuck, she was incredible.

I eased myself in and out of her slowly, enjoying the way she had no fucking idea that she was being used. It was the darkest part of my kinks, and one I'd never truly indulged in.

But *fuck*, I was close to coming just seeing her seeing face and bound body underneath mine.

But she wasn't drugged now, so it was time for her to wake up.

I began to fuck her, plunging my cock deep and taking exactly the pleasure I wanted from her. Hard. Every thrust drove my entire cock into her body, and her pussy took me like the greedy thing it was. God, I loved the wet sound of an Omega being fucked.

Selena jerked, eyes opening in confusion. It took her the space of three long breaths to fully wake up and realized I was above her, balls deep in her cunt, fucking her without mercy while she slept.

Sudden clarity snapped onto her face. "What are you doing?"

I wrapped my hand around her throat, holding her down and fucking her harder. "I'm fucking my slave. What does it feel like I'm doing?"

"Nick—"

"What did you call me?"

"Master," she gasped. "Please."

"Please what?"

She shook her head, and I wanted to see her eyes close again. I moved my hands, covering her nose and mouth and cutting off her air as I buried my cock in her. With her arms above her head, she couldn't fight, and the way she went limp as she nearly passed out had me gritting my teeth to keep from spilling myself.

I released her, and she coughed, heaving a breath. But it wasn't lost on me that her pussy was so much fucking wetter than it had been.

"You know what I love about Omega pussy?" I asked, leaning close.

Selena shook her head.

"You can't fucking hide anything, sweetheart. Hear that?"

I shoved deep, the sound of our bodies slapping together loud in the room. "You're so much fucking wetter than before I took away your breath. You *love* this."

"No. I—" She moaned and bit her lip.

I smirked. "Wet cunts don't lie, sweetheart."

Bracing myself over her, I fucked her harder.

CHAPTER SEVENTEEN

SELENA

*H*e moved, thrusting deep and causing heat and pleasure to fly through me. I pulled on my restraints, hands unable to move from where they were locked to the steel frame of the bed.

Nick dropped his mouth to my skin, moaning his pleasure. I'd already done the same. He knew how much he was affecting me, even if I denied it.

"We *own* you, Selena," he said into my neck. "Your body is our property, to be used whenever we *fucking*. Feel. Like. It." Every word was punctuated with a thrust of his cock. "That includes when you're sleeping, Omega."

I whined, the pleasure building, and I knew there wasn't anything I could do about it. If I came without permission he would punish me. And at the same time, he knew exactly how to force me over the edge. And he was doing exactly that. Just like earlier, driving my body into pleasure in spite of itself. Hitting the place which sent me to the stars, and as much as I could try, there was only so much I could hold back my own body.

"You're not used to this life yet, little slave, I know that. But the faster you accept it, the faster you'll find the beauty in it. Enjoy the pleasure we can give you."

"Beauty?" I choked on the word. "Are you fucking serious?"

After everything, he was going to say that?

He growled, but speaking was the only way I could obey him. If I kept silent my orgasm was going to overwhelm me, and my ass hadn't recovered from their last punishment. How long had I been asleep? "Where you keep me chained and silent, no choices, no voice, no say. Just a thing for you to use."

"Where we keep you protected and safe from others who would harm you for speaking. We give you pleasure when you've earned it and a purpose: to serve. We give you freedom others can't imagine because they don't have the strength to surrender."

"I didn't surrender. I was stolen."

"So you say."

"Normal people don't volunteer to be slaves," I snapped. "They don't give up their entire lives to be fuck dolls for entitled Alphas."

All he did was laugh. "Maybe I should bring Derek in here to gag you with his cock in your throat. You're mouthy tonight."

"I'm sure you'll punish me for it, *Master*. Of course. Punishment for being a normal person."

"I'm not going to punish you," he said mildly. "I didn't forbid you from speaking. But I am going to remind you of your place, little slave. I hope you can learn to find some happiness in it, because it *is* your life now."

"No. Never."

He stared at me, moving his hips slowly. "I'm sorry to hear that."

There was something different about Nick tonight. He was harder and more ruthless. Not the Alpha I was used to. Something had pissed him off, and I didn't think it was me. But I was paying the price.

Pulling out of me, he moved, sliding up my body to straddle my chest. My orgasm fled the second he stopped moving, leaving me heated and aching.

He leaned over and grabbed something I couldn't see, keeping it out of my line of sight. "I would have let you come again. After the beating you took, I felt you earned it. I guess I was wrong."

Tears of need flooded my eyes. "Please."

"No."

He stroked himself, closing his eyes and focusing, driving himself to the edge of his pleasure. There was no denying his beauty, the way the muscles in his stomach and arms contracted as he fisted the swollen head of his cock.

His free hand shot out, grabbing my jaw and forcing it open seconds before he fit his cock to my lips, filling my mouth with cum. He groaned, the raw noises of his orgasm filling the room as continued to come. So much. He hadn't ordered me to swallow, but it was about to overflow.

Keeping his hand hard on my jaw, he looked down at me. "This is your place," he said. "Naked, open, and filled with Alpha cum. Cherished because you give us everything, even if we have to take it from you. Remember who you *could* belong to and be grateful, Selena. Close your mouth and swallow."

I obeyed, fighting against the urge to savor him. It was so fucking delicious it made heat spread down between my legs again.

The screech of tape startled me, and I opened my eyes to find Nick ripping off a large piece of tape. He spread it over my closed mouth and patted it in place before adding two more pieces to make sure it wouldn't move.

"You'll view this as a punishment, little slave, but it isn't one. You're still in training, and you clearly haven't accepted what you are. You have lost the privilege of your mouth for the next day. If you want to eat, it will be from our cocks."

My eyes went wide, and he smiled. There was as much lust as there was pleasure in his gaze. He loved this. The sick bastard. I shook my head, trying not to admit that part of me loved it too. I was just as sick as he was.

"Oh yes. And the others will happily agree. You need to understand what it means to be owned. We've been lenient with you, but you *are* a slave. You *are* being trained. Being owned means everything. From the air you breathe to what you wear to what you eat. You never have to decide. It's all our responsibility. You have to trust us and accept what you are." His voice lowered. "I promise. I promise you will love it once you let go."

Something about that last made it seem like he was begging me to love it. To *please* let go and let them own me.

I shook my head again. Never. I would never accept this. Even if I wanted it. Even if the deepest part of me craved them and the strange relief they offered.

He sighed. "You will, but you give me no choice but to force you. If you're hungry, you know what to do." Standing, he folded off the tape and put it back where he found it.

Right. Like I couldn't go a day without food. I would never ask for that. I'd given them what they needed, and now I would rebel when I could.

"And don't think you can get out of it, Omega. You will feed on our cum, whether you like it or not. Accept it or not. Get some sleep."

The door closed behind him, and I sagged down onto the bed. I was spread open, wet, and horny. How the hell was I supposed to sleep now?

"Rise and shine, Selena."

Derek stood at the door of the cage, leaning against it like it was a normal thing to have a fucking walk-in cage in your house. Don't want a walk-in closet? A walk-in cage is the next best thing.

"Nick informed me about your little encounter last night. I'm here to serve you breakfast."

My eyes went wide, and I shook my head. Tape still bound my mouth, but I wasn't hungry. Not for that.

Derek was shirtless, sweatpants slung low on his hips,

showing off the lean body I loved so much. He sauntered over to me. "I admit, I thought it was a bit overkill. But seeing you like this? I think I'm on board."

He stripped off his pants and straddled my chest, gently pulling the tape off my mouth. "I'm not hungry."

Smiling, Derek ran his knuckles down my cheek. "When will you learn, *gattina*? What you want doesn't matter." His hand dropped to his cock. "Even if your training didn't require this, I do love the feeling of Omega throat in the morning. Now be a good slave and open your mouth."

My body responded to him, warming. If my legs hadn't been chained open, my thighs would be rubbing together. They knew how much I liked feeling like a toy, in spite of everything. My instincts made resisting impossible, and I opened my mouth for him, a whimper in my throat.

"Good girl," he praised, voice low. The tip of his cock brushed my lips, and he stretched himself out over me. "I'm going to fuck your throat like it's your pussy, Selena. But since this is breakfast, I'll make sure you get a taste."

Derek's hips moved, and I closed my eyes. He slipped straight into my throat, hips fucking me as he held himself above me. He was fucking my throat exactly like he would between my legs. Every time he thrust my nose pressed against his stomach.

His hands came down on my wrists, holding me further captive. I was wet. So wet I was dripping. After being denied last night, and the delicious dominance right now, my body was *begging* for release. Could I come from being throat fucked?

Right now? I thought I might be able to.

"Mmm," he groaned, pulling back so I could breathe. "I need one of the others in here fucking your cunt at the same time. You'd get two portions of breakfast."

I shuddered.

He plunged back into me, and it wouldn't take long. I

knew these Alphas now. The way they fucked, the way they tasted, the way they came. Derek moaned when he was close, and he was doing that right now, the sound sending heat straight south. If they unlocked my hands today, I was getting myself off. I didn't even care about the punishment.

"Oh, fuck," he groaned. "Oh, *fuck* yes."

His hips ground down into my face, cock stretching my throat. At the last second he pulled back, cum exploding across my tongue. I drank him down greedily. That I loved the taste of them would never leave my lips, but I enjoyed it every time they used me like this. Scent matching had its benefits.

Derek moved back, watching me swallow before he reached where Nick had last night. The tape. "*Wait.*"

He covered my mouth with it and pressed it down. "No. Like Nick said, you lost the privilege of your mouth unless it's being used as the fuckhole it is. Now, I need to go get ready for the day. One of us will be back soon."

Before he left, he glanced between my legs, smirking at the wetness there. "You can fight us all you want, *gattina*, but we know exactly what you like now. I promised we wouldn't use it against you, and I'm not. But let's not pretend you don't love being used. We both know you do."

Crouching down, he shoved two fingers into me and licked my juices from them. "Mmm. Maybe I'll eat cum today too. If you're a good girl and take your punishment well."

I moaned through the tape. My body was going to spontaneously combust. Derek laughed as he locked the cage and left the room, completely naked. The flavor of his cum still lingered in my mouth, and I closed my eyes.

My fucking body. He was right. I loved everything they did to me. Fucking hell, I was in so much trouble. Every day, my mind succumbed a little more. There was only so long I could hold on until I proved them right and gave in, and allowed myself to live and breathe with them, accepting this fate.

But today, I still had some fight in me.

Despite the delicious Alpha coating my tongue. Only my first meal of the day.

CHAPTER EIGHTEEN

SELENA

A formal dining room wasn't what you imagined being in the back of a sex club, but then again, I wasn't sure why I was surprised at this point.

Thankfully, I had a cushion as I sat next to Sebastian at the head of the table. My hands were cuffed behind my back, and the tape still rested over my mouth. My Alphas were eating lunch, and I was just here.

He allowed me to lean against his knee, and just like the other night, it was comforting. I closed my eyes and rested, savoring the inexplicable calm that sitting here afforded me. Seb occasionally reached down and pet my head or stroked my shoulder.

Last night, Nick—

In the clarity of daytime, I saw the signs. Something had been wrong. The urgency, and the tone of his voice. Something drove him into a panic last night, and he had come to me.

If someone asked me how I knew or how I sensed it, I couldn't answer. But this morning, Derek, the way he spoke, it seemed like a front. And the way they treated me now, with the same gentleness as always, things didn't add up.

Either all three of them were so inconsistent they liked giving me whiplash, or there was another factor I wasn't aware of.

The door of the dining room opened. On the ground as I was, I could only see feet.

"Alphas."

"Yes?" Sebastian asked, hand falling to my hair naturally.

"We received the latest shipment."

"What's in it?" Derek asked.

"Standard amounts of all the hard liquors and paper product replacement. The new glassware for the bar, three boxes of vials, and way, *way* too many straws."

They chuckled, and the man asked. "Do you want the vials taken to your office?"

Vials.

The Omega hormones at the hospital were stored in vials. That had to be it. *Please, universe.*

"No," Derek said. "Leave them in the storage room for now, along with everything else."

I didn't move, breathe, or do anything to make them think something was different.

"All right," the man said. "There's one more thing. Mr. Delano is here. He said you were expecting to eat lunch with him."

Sebastian swore under his breath. "Of course. Make sure a place setting is brought in for him and bring the food from the kitchen as soon as possible."

His hand landed on my shoulder, and I wasn't even sure he knew it was there. See gripped it harder than necessary, but released it the second the door opened again. "Greetings, Warwicks," Delano said. "Good of you to have me for lunch."

"Good of you to invite yourself," Sebastian said dryly.

The man circled the table until he could see me. "I don't trust staff. Nor do I trust whores like the one at your feet."

"Speak in a code if necessary, Christopher, but she remains."

The silence was tense. "*It* better keep its mouth shut."

My shoulders curled in on themselves, and I pressed my head harder into Sebastian's leg. He didn't touch me. Not until Delano retreated to the end of the table and sat. Then Seb stroked his hand over my hair. I shuddered.

Any punishment they would give me would be better than that.

"All the merchandise has been delivered, and everyone is very happy."

"Good to hear it," Nick said. "Thank you for orchestrating the delivery."

They went quiet as someone brought in Delano's food and plates. "Steve, bring a small plate back, please," Sebastian said.

"As I was saying." I heard the scrape of metal on china. "I have a new source of merchandise."

"Is that so?"

"It is."

There was a silence before Derek spoke. "Are you going to tell us or are you waiting for an invitation?"

Delano laughed. "I'll tell you enough, if you agree to the terms."

"What are they?"

"Forty percent of the profit, as I have to pay the supplier."

Seb snorted. "When we're taking the risk of hosting the auctions? I don't think so."

"Sixty, then. With the amount of product we'll be moving, it won't make much of a difference."

I sensed surprise in the air. "That will be fine," Nick said.

Across, beneath the table, I saw Delano's hands settle on his lap and smooth down to his pants pockets, and the movement was intentional. Smooth. It looked like he touched something before he began speaking.

"The system—"

Behind him, the door opened, and Delano ceased speaking as the one named Steven came and brought the plate Seb asked for. I took the chance, bumping my head into his leg a few times before looking up at him. He looked down casually, and I widened my eyes, shaking my head.

He looked back up as soon as the door opened, but touched me on the head. At least he knew there was something wrong. "Pardon the interruption. Before we continue, you will allow Steven to pat you down."

"Excuse me?"

"You don't trust our staff or our slave, but given what we're discussing, we can't be too careful."

I was glad I couldn't see Delano's face, but I heard the icy coldness in his voice. "Fine."

He stood, and Steve's feet approached him. I caught his face briefly as he patted Delano phone, pinpointing the pocket. A phone. I turned and looked up at Sebastian, whose head was tilted and looking at Delano.

"It's recording," Steve said.

Derek's voice. "Shut it off."

"Do you have a reason not to trust us, Christopher?"

"Can't be too careful."

"I suppose not," Seb said. "Leave the phone on the table where we can see it. You're dismissed, Steve."

The door opened and closed. Nick cleared his throat. "Continue."

There was a tense silence, but finally, he continued "As you know, the problem with the merchandise we use is making sure there aren't too many questions about where they come from. One of the largest untapped markets for this is the foster system. Not while they're in it, of course, but there are plenty of Omegas in the system, and once they're aged out and not tracked by the government, they're easy to procure before anyone has had a chance to notice them settle."

My stomach rolled. So young. He wanted to steal Omegas who were *so young*.

"Let me guess," Derek said. "You won't tell us where you get the information."

"Someone who's willing to pass on the names of those aging out. For a price. I won't tell you who, because then you wouldn't need me. But I assure you, this is a good plan. My other markets are dry at the moment, but as you well know, our clients are ravenous."

I closed my eyes and pretended I couldn't hear them. They were doing this over and over and over and the women who were sold probably went through things hundreds of times worse than me. If you looked at it objectively, I was lucky. They gave me a choice, and had been kind in ways I hadn't anticipated.

What happened to them that they would turn to doing this at all? It didn't make sense, given what I knew of them.

"Get us a shipment," Nick said. "We'll see if they're to the taste of our clientele. If they are, we can come to a more permanent agreement."

"Fine with me. What's the plate for?"

"Feeding the slave," Sebastian said automatically.

A sound of disbelief. "It eats from the table?"

"Hardly. She was mouthy last night after her punishment, so today she has lost the use of it, other than her meals, which are from us."

The sound of his low, vicious laugh sent chills skittering across my skin. "You plan to use her mouth, then?"

"No. She doesn't even deserve that." Sebastian's voice was colder than I'd ever heard it, and it felt wrong. "But she'll clean the plate."

I saw the way Delano's weight shifted back, like he was leaning and relaxing. It was clear beneath the table that his dick was hard, and I rolled my eyes. "I think I'd like to see that."

"Very well." Seb leaned back and unbuckled his belt. I didn't look up at him, because he hadn't told me to, and now we were being watched. This was different. Everything was different when this man was in the room, and not in a good way.

They talked about other things. I think Delano asked about the normal operations of the club, and they must have said something to answer him, but I couldn't hear them, because I was so close to Sebastian stroking his cock.

I watched him without lifting my eyes to his, but I felt him watching me. And something about being this close to an Alpha bringing himself pleasure had me squirming where I sat.

Because his eyes were on me. I was the thing he focused on while trying to come. If Delano wasn't here, I don't think it even would have taken as long. The way his fingers curled around his shaft, he knew exactly how to get himself off. I found myself wondering if I could memorize the motion and try it with my hands. Or if there was a way to mimic the motion with my tongue.

What are you doing, Selena?

Sebastian groaned, grabbing the plate and putting it beneath his cock a second before he came. And he kept stroking himself until there was nothing left, and it was all on that fucking plate.

With a shock, I realized that he was going to feed it to me.

I knew, but now I *knew*.

Between my legs I was growing wet, and I didn't understand why. I didn't like this. I didn't.

I didn't.

Maybe what Nick said last night was right. Wet cunts didn't lie. Not when no one was touching me. You could make someone wet, but no one was forcing my body to react this way. It simply was.

Sebastian leaned to the side, and I heard the soft clink of the plate being set on the floor. "Look at me," he commanded.

I did.

He pulled the tape from my mouth, the pulling of it making my mouth water.

"Eat your lunch," he said, glancing at the plate. I also saw him glance toward the uninvited guest. "All of it. I want the plate cleaner than when it came into the room."

A chair creaked, and heavy footsteps echoed in the room. Delano coming around the table to watch my humiliation. The embarrassment burned in my face, but at the same time, I couldn't be angry. Because if I had a choice in this moment, I would have let him come all over my tongue and savored the flavor of warm apple pie. Hell, in better circumstances, I would have made a joke about him being his own whipped cream.

I turned on my knees. With my arms still cuffed behind me, it was awkward, but I did it. There was no room for hesitation or fear right now. I did my best to balance and lowered my mouth to the plate, tasting him.

"You really do have her trained well," Delano said. "If she needs more, I'm happy to contribute."

"No," Sebastian said. "This will be fine."

"I want to see you beat her." Freezing, I had to make myself move and continue licking the plate like it was the best dessert I'd ever eaten. "If not to see the way she takes pain, for the way you work, Sebastian. I've heard you're a master of impact."

"I'm sure something can be arranged."

It wasn't a yes, but it wasn't a no, either.

They watched me as I cleaned Sebastian's cum from the plate. The burning embarrassment and humiliation somehow turned into arousal, and I prayed that Delano couldn't see behind where I was beneath the table and how wet I was.

If it was anyone but them and the damned scent matches, I wouldn't want this. But on my knees for them? Lapping up their cum like a cat with a bowl of cream? I couldn't explain why it made me want to arch my back and purr, if an Omega could purr.

Fuck, I wanted to lick it up while another one fucked me

from behind and came on the plate again, all of them rotating. If Delano weren't here? There was no doubt they could scent how wet I was, given our scent compatibility. They might do it.

But the plate was clean, and I struggled to sit up on my knees again, keeping my eyes on the ground.

Sebastian picked up the plate. "Pity, you did well. I was looking forward to further punishment."

Delano chuckled, and it was everything in my power not to react to the sound. "I'll have the details of that shipment in a couple of days, and I'll keep you posted. In the meantime, if you have anyone for me to play with, let me know. Your slave has given me a craving."

"You know the rules here," Derek said.

"I know, I know. But if you have anyone lying around."

The door shut behind him, and it felt like the very room itself let out a breath of relief. Sebastian lifted me like I was nothing and spread me to straddle his lap. "Good girl, Selena."

Fuck me. I didn't understand any of this. He unclipped my hands, and I found myself clinging to him, crying. Why was I crying right now? Why was I holding onto him like he was the only lifeline I had? Why was I still aroused and confused?

Every hour and every day was one headlong leap into further confusion and madness. And this was just part of it. The shift back and forth between the kindness of my Alphas and the harshness of my masters.

Tears leaked out of my eyes, and his big hands traveled up and down my spine. "You were perfect, Princess. Good girl. The punishment is over."

I sagged against his chest. The punishment was over, but nothing else was.

The real question was, how long could I bounce back and forth between these two realities until I broke? I couldn't live in two worlds forever, and as much as I was terrified of my mind shattering, it was getting harder to tell which was which.

For the moment, I chose to take the comfort offered me, and clung to the neck of my Alpha as he soothed me, imagining we were anywhere but here.

CHAPTER NINETEEN

DEREK

*T*he club was busy tonight. It always was on Fridays, the paying members gathering to have fun and experiment in a fun and kinky way.

I wished I could go back to the time when a club like *Catena* was a place of excitement for me and not a place of dread. I would always have my kinks, as would my pack mates. But I didn't know if I'd ever really be able to set foot in a place like this again with any kind of comfort.

Selena was behind me, and I wandered through our section of the club slowly. We did mingle with the normal, legal side of the club, but not always. Tonight, I wasn't sure what I would do with her, and so I kept walking so she didn't follow my order to kneel when we stopped.

My Omega had withdrawn into herself. It was clear something had shifted, and she was more like that first morning we found her in the cage going into heat. Like she was drifting in the sea of her own mind and not truly present.

We passed a display of toys used for breath play. Most of the time, if any of us wanted to restrict air flow, we used our hands. But there were any number of ways to do it, all with varying degrees of risk.

Depriving someone of oxygen was never safe.

But lowering the level of oxygen a little so her mind matched the spaciness she currently showed? That could be fun. We needed to do some sort of training exercise, and this would be something she could go through without it being too intense. Delano was watching closely, and after yesterday, the three of us didn't want to do it anymore. We were pretty much done.

Selena was perfect. Doing everything we asked and taking everything we gave, but we were losing her. And our increasingly frantic messages to headquarters were met with the same message: hold on.

If we had to hold on any longer, I was going to grab Delano by the neck and rip his head off. I would fucking enjoy it, too.

"Here," I said to her, gesturing to the space in front of the display. The gas mask would do what I needed. I could control the flow of oxygen to her. Tie her up and play with her while her head was in the clouds. She'd get some pleasure and wouldn't put up any resistance. Delano would see a slave we'd broken. It was a win for both of us.

"Kneel."

She did, her head bowed. The way her dark hair flowed over her shoulders made me want to shove my hands through it and pull her to me. So fucking beautiful.

Hold on, gattina. *You can make it. I believe in you.*

I pulled the gas mask off the wall and walked around her. "Look up, *gattina*."

She did, and her eyes landed on the gas mask. Rigid terror struck her, and she scrambled backwards away from me. "No."

I frowned. "What did you say?"

"No," she said. "No, I won't do that."

She never had this reaction to anything before. What the hell did the gas mask mean to her that she would react this way? More importantly, was anyone within sight of us right now that would cause a problem?

Delano was becoming obsessed with her. Not a day had passed without him offering to buy her, and today it was only a matter of time. And of course, when I turned, he was across the club, leaning against the wall, watching the entire interaction.

Fucking hell.

"I'm not sure what gave you the impression you had a choice in the matter," I said. "I told you to kneel."

"No," she shook her head. "*No.*"

Reaching into my pocket, I pulled out my cell and dialed Sebastian. He answered immediately. "Yeah?"

"I need you in the club. Right now."

"On my way."

Staring down at Selena, I kept my face neutral. There was nothing I could do while we were being watched except to look at her and hope she realized what she was doing. This wouldn't end well for her.

If this were currently a dynamic where we could talk about her fear, we would stop and sit and hash out the reaction and why she had it. We would decide together if it was something we needed to explore. Or, depending on the level of the dynamic, she would tell me, and I would decide how to proceed.

But here?

I couldn't ask.

Not even five minutes later, Sebastian approached and saw where Selena had crawled backwards against the wall and was still staring at us like we were venomous snakes. "What happened?"

"I was going to put the gas mask on her for some low oxygen play, and she told me no," I said with a sigh. "Fucking Delano is on the other side of the club, observing."

"Perfect." The word dripped with sarcasm.

I slid my hands into my pockets and kept staring at our Omega. "He's asked to see you do impact play with her multiple times, and while he's watching, we can't let something like this stand. Feel like getting out your toys?"

He considered it. Sebastian loved both impact play and

pain. There was a bit of a sadistic streak in him. But just like the rest of us, he preferred working on someone who agreed to it and actually enjoyed it. "Sure," he said. "Take her to one of the frames and I'll grab my bag."

I hung the gas mask back on the wall and hauled her to her feet. "I don't know what brought that on, but it wasn't a good idea, *gattina*. Whatever you were afraid of with that mask, it's nothing compared to the punishment you're getting for disobeying a direct order."

My hand was around her arm as I guided her through the club to one of the metal frames that allowed complete access in three hundred and sixty degrees. But I felt the change in her and the new relaxation. She didn't even care that she was being punished. Instead of conscious terror, she was far more relaxed.

Taking her hands in mine, I attached both of them to the metal loops above her head and left her standing. "If you think you're getting off easy for this, you're wrong, Selena. Disobedience cannot and will not be tolerated."

"Yes, Master."

Back to the vague and uninterested answer.

Seb reappeared, put his bag down on the nearby table, and began to unpack everything. He basically brought an entire kink store with him in the one bag.

"She's relieved to be punished," I told him. "This is deeper, so be careful, but we can't let it stand."

He looked at her, eyes scanning her back. "No, we can't. Put her hair up." Seb handed me a hair tie, and I twisted her hair into a knot so all the skin on her back was exposed with nothing in the way.

"Do you need me to stay?"

"Grab Nick," he said softly. "If I'm going to punish her like this, I want all of us close by. I'm not going to go too far, but you know why."

Because in spite of everything, we cared about this

woman. She took comfort in our presence because she belonged to us. This would be painful and if our presence made it one speck more bearable, we would do whatever the hell we could.

"I will."

Before I turned to get Nick, I saw him pull out a whip.

CHAPTER TWENTY

SELENA

Seb's face hovered in front of mine. "You disobeyed, princess."

Of course I did. He was going to put a gas mask on me. I was claustrophobic, and the idea of my face being fully enclosed like that nearly gave me a heart attack.

When they stole my breath it wasn't the same. There was still open space around me, nothing to run into and be trapped. Even the cage I woke up in had been all right because, though it was small, there was air and space between the bars.

This was entirely different. "Yes, Master," I said.

"Why?"

"Does it matter?"

A finger lifted my chin to look into his eyes. Sebastian frowned. "It could."

No. It couldn't.

The whip in his hand told me that. If they wouldn't listen to me, it didn't matter what I said. I was getting punished, end of story. My mind was done. There was a bleakness to the world today I couldn't combat. So I would stay here inside myself and let the world carry on without me. Maybe I could try again tomorrow.

"Just get it over with," I muttered.

"Watch your mouth," Seb snapped. "I guess I can't even have the option of going easy on you, can I?"

I said nothing.

Sebastian grabbed my chin. This time he took it fully in his hand, making sure I looked at him. "You think I want to do this?"

"You like pain, *Master*. I'm sure you'll enjoy it."

He sighed. "You like pain too, little one. But this won't be the kind either of us enjoys." Running his hands over my skin, he felt for something. I had no idea what. "I'm not going to break your skin, Selena. Even if it feels that way, I'm not doing that."

So I wouldn't be a piece of bloody meat hanging from a metal pole.

Small favors.

"I want you to keep in mind how I would prefer to introduce this to you," Sebastian said quietly, speaking as he walked around my body so his voice skimmed over my shoulder. "Your legs spread with a bar between them, strapped to a vibrator, orgasms in between every time I take my tools to you. You claim I like pain, and I do. But remember what I told you? I *love* taking people to the place where they can no longer distinguish between pleasure and pain and it's all an overwhelming, intense, euphoric experience for everyone.

"But we can't do that now."

I pulled against my cuffs, struggling. "Don't pretend I chose this."

An arm came around my waist and yanked me back against his body. He was hard against my ass, mouth pressed to my ear. "Didn't you?"

"*No.*"

"We laid out the rules, princess. You're the one who chose to break them. And in every world, there are consequences for breaking the rules. But in this one, they're immediate and painful. Try not to brace yourself. It makes it worse."

Why do you care?

I flinched away from the words even as I thought them, because they didn't ring true. He was the one who held me and praised me after yesterday's test, and for the rest of the day, they'd kept me close and simply let me be with them. No training and no punishments. Either sitting at their feet, or occasionally on their lap, and it was comforting.

But today felt different, and I didn't know why. I didn't know anything. I was losing myself. It was a hard thing to accept, but more than all the other shitty choices I didn't have in this situation, that was the one which was the most difficult to accept.

My own soul was untethering itself, and I didn't know where it would end up. Adrift on the sea of these Alphas and the whims of their world.

The sound registered before the feeling.

Crack!

A line of fire across my upper shoulder that somehow felt right. Not like a punishment, but like an external validation of the confusion and swirling uncertainty inside. It was pain, and yet it wasn't painful. Not truly.

Somehow, it was a relief.

Because I *had* chosen it. In spite of my genuine fear, I knew telling them no would result in action, and I wanted to do something. I'd chosen this when I didn't think there was a way to choose anymore.

So every stripe of pain was a reminder that I still had choices in the fog of gray uncertainty and confusion.

The implements changed. Varying degrees of intensity and sensation. All over my back, my ass, even over my breasts. I savored the bite and the familiar floating place it took my mind to. Here, there was an impossible, strange sense of joy and synergy between Sebastian and me. Before the hits landed I could almost sense them, and I felt connected to him. There was no anger in his energy, and though this was meant to be a punishment, it didn't feel that way.

My body wilted, hanging from my restraints when my knees could no longer support me, and the blows finally stopped. My skin was warm and extra sensitive as Seb wrapped his arm around me and unhooked my wrists, taking my weight and lowering me to the floor.

In front of me, I saw Derek and Nick talking to Delano. I didn't want to see him. He could go fuck himself. He made everything worse. He was the reason things were bad. I felt it in my gut.

Sebastian picked me up and carried me away. I stayed limp, my brain so much happier than it had been. It didn't make sense, but the way he held me, what he'd done...

I chose not to question. Being in his arms was a miracle in itself, and I curled deeper into them, burrowing into scent and warmth. His fingers curled around me with nothing but tenderness. "I have to put you down for a second, princess. I'll be right back."

Softness pressed against my skin. Some sort of blanket, and I was on a couch. A couch? Blinking my eyes open, I found myself in a small corner of the club. Near the elevator to go upstairs. The door to the kitchen was right there, and through it, the door to the storage room. We'd walked through it several times now. I knew where it was.

I closed my eyes again, resting.

"You seem like you need a companion." An unfamiliar voice said. I dragged my eyes open and found a pair of jeans in front of my eyes.

I didn't know who he was, the cloying, *blazing* scent of burnt lavender coming off him. "No."

He laughed. "I wasn't asking."

The blanket was pulled off me, and he stroked a hand down my back. I moved, trying to wiggle away, but there wasn't really room on the couch, and I was still cloudy enough I didn't know if I could stand and run. "Don't touch me."

"You'll have a good time with me... and my friend." This wasn't Delano, but he was an Alpha, and I didn't want him near me any more than I wanted the other snake. His touch felt like poison.

"Stop."

He pulled on me, and I fell to the floor, pain radiating through my knees, hips, and elbows.

The man was ripped off me and shoved against the wall, a hand at his throat, squeezing. Sebastian was there like a dark avenging angel made of fury. "Did I say you could touch my slave?"

The Alpha's voice choked out. "I didn't know she was yours."

"Oh, I see. But being inside *my* club, you surely recognize what those cuffs mean, don't you?"

No answer.

"Don't you?"

"Yes." The word was weak as Seb choked the life out of him.

"So you didn't know she belonged to me, but you knew she belonged to someone and chose to touch her anyway," Sebastian mused. "I've killed men for less."

The man could no longer speak, struggling to get my Alpha's hands off him. A small crowd was gathering in the nearby hall, staring.

"The only reason you're not dead on the floor right now is because there are people watching—members of the public —and you're not worth whatever lawsuit or fine killing you would bring. Not to mention our reputation. I don't care who the fuck you are, whose son or cousin or whoever let you in here. No matter which side of *Catena* you're on. When you're in my domain, you follow my rules."

He dropped him, and the man sputtered, hauling in a breath. "Fuck," he groaned. "Overreacting much over some bitch?"

Metal flashed, and though it wasn't visible to anyone else in the room, I saw the blade not pressing against the Alpha's throat. "If you touch her again, I will kill you," Sebastian said. "I can't bar you from this club on a first offense, but if you touch anyone else who doesn't belong to you, you're out on your ass if I don't get to you first. If I do?"

He let the threat hang in the air.

"Understood?"

"Understood."

The knife disappeared and Sebastian picked me up off the floor, cradling me. I looked up at him, reaching up to touch his face as he strode with me to the elevator. "You saved me."

The briefest touches of his lips on my temple. "No one touches what's *mine*."

The crowd watched us as the elevator doors closed, Christopher Delano among them.

CHAPTER TWENTY-ONE

SELENA

*S*ebastian strode into their apartment and didn't stop. Where before there was no anger in him, now it poured off him in waves. Not at me, but at the man he nearly killed for touching me. We didn't stop until we reached a room I assumed was his. Dark burgundy walls and rich wood furniture. A bed that went on for a thousand miles.

He laid me down on the bed and tore himself away from me before stripping his clothes off with a force that was beautiful to watch. Prowling to the bed, he spread himself over me, dark eyes fiery with a thing I couldn't name.

Mine.

My soul recognized his in spite of everything.

He saved me when I needed it most, and right now, he needed me. There weren't any words for him to say.

Seb grabbed my hips and flipped me over flat onto the bed. Shoving my thighs apart with his knee, he was there, cock pressing into me. So fucking big, and from this angle it felt even larger.

There was no mercy in him now. What little he had, he used to let the Alpha who touched me live. His fingers wove through mine, gripping my hands and pinning them to the bed as he began to move, fucking me with everything he had.

Rutting me.

Oh *god*. My eyes rolled back in my head, the way he moved, taking me with brutal instinct. He was in rut. Taking me back from that Alpha had sent him over the edge, and here we were.

His low growl sent arousal tearing through me. My pussy

gushed wetness around his cock, only making it so much easier for him to fuck me like the world was ending. Did he expect me not to come? That wasn't going to happen. When I did come, it was going to be an explosion like no other and there would be absolutely no stopping it.

Seb's mouth was on my neck and shoulder, biting and licking before he spoke. "You say you don't want to be a slave, princess. But every time we put you in your place, you surrender so fucking beautifully I can't believe you're telling the truth."

"I—"

"Be quiet," he growled, the Alpha command rolling through me, making me pant with need. He was already taking me hard, and the way he said it, pushing my hands into the comforter, made me need him to take me harder. "I'm going to speak and you're going to listen while I fuck you, Selena."

"Yes, Master."

At this moment there was no doubt about who my Master was. It was him, and every piece of me believed it.

He growled again, melting the last flimsy veil of resistance. Seb's knees pushed my legs wider, allowing him to fuck every thick, hard inch of him into my cunt with each thrust. His hips slammed into mine, and I truly, totally surrendered.

"You were made for us, little mate," he said. "And we are who we are. I'm always going to be the man who likes to spank your swollen cunt while you're tied up and helpless. Who wants to watch you lick up his cum like it's desert and see it shine on your lips, and watch my brothers fuck you while you're unconscious so your body gets pleasure even if your mind doesn't."

I moaned into the blankets. Everything he painted in my mind added to the pleasure he forced into my body. Because

I already knew what it felt like, I couldn't even breathe because I was reliving it all.

"And you love it," he said. "The deepest part of your mind accepts that you need this. To be dominated in ways that aren't acceptable and aren't accepted by everyone else. That you feel fucking safe kneeling at our feet, knowing we'll protect you from *anything*. And you hate that you love it, but you do."

Fuck.

A bubble of bliss popped open in my chest, the tiniest of orgasms making way for a larger one. Sebastian's body moved, and his skin brushed mine. The heated sensitivity of where he punished me made everything feel *more* and *bigger* and fuck me he was going to send me into oblivion.

"You think you can't want this because of who you are. But there's a difference between wanting something and needing it, Omega. You need to be owned, and we need to own you. Because someone else making those decisions for you is what you've always wanted."

I shook my head. That was impossible. He wasn't wrong that I liked pieces of it—I'd fantasized about some of these things for years. But the rest? Being owned? He was wrong. No one could choose that. Right? You didn't just decide to hand over the entire control of your life to someone else forever. It wasn't a thing.

"Resist it all you want," he growled the words in my ear. "But you'll figure out the truth. I think you're terrified of the truth of how deeply you need it, princess. Because I could tell you that the three of us were never going to let you come again in your life. That this fuck here would be the last orgasm you'd ever have, and they would back me up. We could decide that for you, and you would fight us, but in a place you can't even sense you crave that level of control. And the fact that I'm the one that can give or take away that pleasure is the thing that makes you come."

A fucking supernova burned across my vision. A meteor so bright everything in my body locked up, arched, rigid, helpless to the most powerful orgasm I'd ever had in my life.

It was a living thing inside me, writhing and bucking, carrying pleasure to every fractured corner and every last cell. I screamed, voice ragged, the pleasure going on for what seemed like forever until it finally let me go. It dropped me, limp and spent while my Alpha continued to fuck me in the aftershocks.

"See?" He kissed my neck, biting hard enough to bruise, and came. Heat filled me, spilling around the size of him, his knot swelling and locking us together.

Without releasing my hands, he moved us, rolling to the side and curling around me so I was the little spoon and he surrounded me entirely. I was so tired, and he was too, the brush of his lips still warming my shoulder. "You're mine, little slave," he whispered. "And we both know it."

Sleep pulled me down. I fought it, but the tide was too strong. There were so many questions, but how did I ask them when I was desperately afraid he was right?

CHAPTER TWENTY-TWO

SELENA

Sebastian was asleep. His arm flung over my hip, the blankets scrunched around our waists. But more importantly, I wasn't chained. Because of the rut, and passing out so quickly, he forgot. And at this point they trusted me.

We weren't knotted together anymore. Frankly, it was incredible I was awake, but at the moment I was crystal clear. Like something from beyond myself tapped me on the shoulder and told me this was the moment I needed.

What I was about to do would ruin what little trust we had entirely, but Anna's life was still on the line. As with so many things in my life since I was taken, I didn't have a choice.

It was a long shot, going off the conversation from the dining room, but it was the only shot I had. I knew the shipment had come in, and I knew where it was. In the storage room by the kitchen. This was my chance to find out who was selling the hormones to them, or at least an address the syndicate could track down.

More importantly, it was the only chance I'd had this entire time. The days passed so quickly and equally here that I didn't know how much time had passed, but I knew time was running out. It was now or never.

During my heat they woke in an instant. But the way Seb had unleashed himself tonight, he was exhausted. I moved with aching slowness, inching out from beneath his arm and slipping off the bed silently. One thing my training—especially with Seb—had taught me? How to be quiet.

I picked up his t-shirt he wore beneath his suit and slipped it on. He was so tall it fell around my thighs. I was already risking everything. I wasn't foolish enough to go walking around *Catena* naked.

Likewise, even though it was probably twenty floors, I couldn't take the elevator. It would make sound. So I went to the hidden fire exit and slipped into the cold concrete stairs. They didn't know I knew where this was, but I saw it when we passed through the living room and kitchen. And I knew enough about doors like these at the hospital to know it didn't have an alarm.

If I was lucky, I could get the information, get it to the Syndicate through the phone, and get back to Seb's bed before any of them knew I was gone.

Granted, I hadn't been lucky in years, but I was still hoping for some kind of break. The stairs were chilly and drafty, and by the time I reached the floor I needed, the soles of my feet were scraped and aching from twenty floors of concrete steps.

The club was empty. I honestly wasn't sure what time it was. The windows upstairs had been dark, so I guessed it was the early hours of the morning but still before dawn. All the staff had gone home. Not even the thumping bass came through the walls right now. It was good—I didn't have the layout memorized yet. It took me a while to poke around to find the kitchen and the right door, which wasn't locked. Why would it be? There was nothing in here but liquor and napkins, or so most people thought. And no one who wasn't supposed to be in the club could even get this far.

Except for me.

The door swung open into the darkness, the room in front of me looking like a gaping maw ready to swallow me up.

Thankfully, the light switch was easy to find. Stacks of boxes created a maze for me to walk through. This part, at least, was familiar. I knew what the hormones looked like from the hospital. But I also knew where to find them because of that day in the dining room. Thank you, Steve.

Stacks and stacks of boxes in the back corner that clearly hadn't been there long, haphazard as they were. All of them were labeled. Except for—

There. A smaller stack of boxes on a shelf, tucked in between what looked like vodka, and drinking straws. It made sense—they wouldn't want to draw extra attention to these.

The shipping labels didn't have a name. I didn't think they would. But they *did* have a company name. *Normality, Inc*. The address was halfway across the country. I should have gone and gotten the Syndicate's phone first. That way I could have taken a picture of the information instead of having to commit it to memory. But I did. I repeated the name and address until I could say it back to myself and not forget it.

Another nursing trick coming in handy. We needed to memorize things quickly in order to take care of patients. One address wasn't difficult.

Just to be sure, I opened one of the boxes. The blue plastic cases filled with vials were achingly familiar. My heart sank. Part of me had hoped it wasn't real, and they weren't actually using these hormones. They had real uses. Injecting them to make people smell more appealing in order to *sell* them was not only unethical, it was dangerous. I'd seen the effects of these overdoses firsthand. They weren't good.

I shut the box. I had what I needed, and so far, so good. Now I just had to get the phone and get back upstairs. If the Syndicate was true to their word, they could get me out of here tomorrow.

Despite everything, I wasn't going to pretend the thought didn't make me sad. The Alphas upstairs were… they were everything I wanted, if things were different. They drove my body crazy, and in the small moments, I thought I imagined something more in the way they looked at me than what they claimed I was.

No matter what Seb had said in the middle of the incredible sex, and no matter how much I loved the submission he talked about, this was real life. I couldn't be a slave in the real world. I needed to be home and have my friends and my life and make sure my sister was okay.

Turning, I froze.

The three Alphas I'd just been thinking about stood at the door, watching me. They hadn't made a sound, and on all their faces, was bitter disappointment.

"Hello, Selena."

CHAPTER TWENTY-THREE

___

SEBASTIAN

J surfaced from sleep, sensing something different. After taking Selena like that, I hadn't been able to keep my eyes open. The little Omega had taken everything I gave her and loved it. Just a little longer, and we could make her ours in the way that really mattered.

Reaching across the bed for her, my hand felt nothing but cold sheets. I opened my eyes, and she was nowhere in the room. But I'd fallen asleep so quickly I hadn't attached her cuffs to the bed. It was possible she was in the bathroom.

"Selena?"

No answer.

Sleep still tugged at my consciousness, but I dragged myself out of bed and went to the bathroom, flipping the light on. No Selena.

Strange, but I wasn't panicking yet. Tugging on a pair of sweats, I went down the hall to the cage room. "Little one?"

Sometimes Omegas needed familiarity and comfort. But she wasn't in the cage, and she wasn't in the nest. She wasn't anywhere I saw in our apartment. Going back to my room, I grabbed my phone before going to Nick's room.

He looked up when I knocked and opened the door, eyes bleary. "Yeah?"

"Selena's gone."

That got him moving. "What do you mean she's *gone*?"

"I just woke up, and she's not here."

He jumped out of bed, scrambling to follow me as I pushed into Derek's room. "How the hell did you lose her, Seb?"

151

"When we fell asleep she was beside me. Hell, I was knotted in her. When I woke up just now, she wasn't in the bathroom, the cage, or the nest. She's nowhere I've found."

Derek swore. "The cuffs?"

I sighed. "We both passed out. It was intense. Short, but a full rut. It's not like I expected her to get up and walk out. Where is she going to go?"

With my phone, I opened the app to our security cameras in the building and started clicking through them for anything that looked out of place. At least it was the time of night when there were the fewest people in the building. But with Delano still here, I was going to tan her ass if she'd gone exploring.

There. There was a light on in the storage room that shouldn't be there. "Got it." I jogged to my room and grabbed a shirt from a drawer, even as disappointment echoed in my chest. After everything, we'd begun to think we were wrong, and Selena was somehow simply in the wrong place at the wrong time, somehow.

This proved differently.

"Where is she?"

"The storage room by the kitchen."

Nick sighed. "Fuck."

We all headed to the elevator. "Don't let her know we're there. Maybe we can find something out," I said.

"I hoped it wouldn't come to this," Derek said. "I really —*fuck.*"

I shook my head because I knew exactly what he was feeling. Strange, considering we'd been expecting to be stabbed in the back, but hoping it wouldn't happen.

The elevator opened on the kitchen floor, and we all moved silently through the room toward storage. No sounds let us know what she was doing, and for a brief shining moment, I hoped that someone on the staff had simply left the light on, and she wasn't inside.

But there she was, wearing my shirt.

Back to us, in the corner where our shipment of Omega hormones was being stored. That was what she was after? Not exactly the worst thing we were involved in at the moment. I heard her muttering under her breath, and it sounded like she was repeating something over and over.

I slipped my phone into my pocket, and together we watched as she opened a box and checked it thoroughly. Selena sighed, and even the soft sigh was sexy, because I knew how it sounded when I pushed my cock into her and she wasn't completely ready.

She turned and froze, seeing the three of us waiting. "Hello, Selena."

Her tan skin went pale, and I hated it. She was afraid of us. The citrus in her scent went rancid with terror. "Hi."

"What are you doing down here, little one?"

"Nothing." The word was rote and without emotion. Clearly a lie.

Derek scrubbed a hand over his face. "We've asked you before who sent you, and you told us no one did."

"I was just exploring. I didn't really know my way around—"

Nick stepped forward quickly, invading her space. "You're already in enough trouble, sweetheart. Let's not add blatant lies to it."

She didn't contradict him, instead casting her eyes to the floor.

"I guess it's time to get the truth out of her," I said to Derek. "Have any ideas?"

His mouth was a firm line. He didn't want to do this any more than I did, but it had to be done. "Black room?"

Nick turned. "That could be interesting."

Grabbing Selena's wrist, he pulled her toward us. She dug her feet in and resisted. "I'm sorry," she said. "I was just exploring. Please."

153

I took her from Nick and pressed her against the wall so fast her breath left her. "We've given you so much time, little one, to tell us the truth. We don't want to interrogate you, but you've given us no choice, and we *will* get it out of you one way or another."

"Please," she whispered, and I closed my eyes, desperately trying to block out the aching of my own heart. Especially after the experience we just shared. I felt more connected to her than ever, and this was like shoving a knife into myself.

"You know very well that we can inflict pain without permanent damage, princess. We're going to go to the Black Room, and you won't be leaving that room until you tell us the truth. So think carefully about how much your boss's secret is worth to you. We'll still be lenient if you tell us now."

Her tiny whine cracked my soul, and I shoved myself away from her. I couldn't be near her and hear those sounds and do what I needed to do. Of the three of us, the bulk of this punishment and interrogation would fall on me. I was the sadist. I was the one who knew how to bring someone to their knees with pain and still keep them whole.

In the past I'd done it to some truly evil people. Selena wasn't someone I wanted to apply those talents to. Even earlier tonight, when I whipped her, I hadn't tried to cause her pain. It was a show for Delano. But we would do this. And she would finally tell us the truth.

I guess this was always coming from the first day she walked out into the theatre.

The Black Room had plenty of things to use, all of them harsher than Selena could take. She was a masochist, but not a deep one. She liked an edge of pain—and enough of one that it satisfied me and made my cock hard at the thought of whipping her ass or spanking her pussy till she screamed.

This wouldn't be the pleasurable pain. The real kind I'd already done everything to avoid.

"Strip her," I said, not looking back. Every step closer to the room allowed me to sink into the place I needed to be. I would do this. I would hurt my Omega to protect every other Omega in the world, and I could only hope I would be whole at the end of it.

CHAPTER TWENTY-FOUR

SELENA

*N*ick's arms were unyielding as they pulled me into the empty club. I yanked against his hold, but I already knew too well there wasn't anything I could do to overcome their strength.

We went into a room I hadn't visited before.

Thank god, because it looked like a torture chamber.

Oh.

Shit.

Sebastian looked at me. "Sure you don't want to tell us?"

God, if only it were as simple as *wanting* to tell them something. If it were the only thing that mattered I would have spilled my guts when I'd first been on my knees in the theatre, sucking Derek's cock. The only thing I knew was Anna was relying on me, and I only had so much time.

Nick guided me toward the back of the room, toward something I didn't recognize. Somewhere between a sawhorse and a triangle. The legs were adjustable.

"Do you know what this is?" Nick asked as Seb glanced at me and went about lowering the wooden triangle thing.

"No."

His hand tightened on the back of my neck. "Now is *really* not the time to forget your manners, Selena."

I shuddered. "No, Master. I don't know what it is."

"This," Derek said, "is a pony board."

The name didn't give me any clues to what it did or what it had to do with me. The three of them seemed to think it was going to open my mouth. And maybe it would. I knew there was only so long I could withstand actual torture. But I had to try.

For Anna.

Nick moved me, arranging me to stand over the triangle they'd lowered nearly to the ground. "I've never heard of a pony board, Master."

"Well," Nick said. "You're about to get an up close and personal lesson about what they're like."

He attached my cuffs to a dangling chain, and Seb pulled on it, yanking my arms over my head. The chains pulled my hands higher, raising me on my toes. High enough that I had to focus to balance, not high enough to take any of my weight.

Seb's eyes were cold as he secured the chain there. Already my legs were shaking. I wouldn't last long in this position, which was what they were hoping for, of course. That coldness took on a feral gleam as he bent down and raised the skinny wooden triangle between my legs. The edge of it was rounded, not sharp. But it was still thin enough that it looked painful.

He raised it until the thin edge of wood rested directly on my clit, and locked it. I still wasn't sure what this was supposed to do, but the way they were looking at me right now—like I was the enemy—I didn't like it. Even being their... slave, I missed the tender moments and amusement in their eyes. The small signs that showed me they were human and not just monsters.

"Why do you think it's called a pony board?" Seb asked. "You may answer."

He went to the wall, where a frightening amount of things were displayed, from canes to whips and sharper things I could *never* imagine anyone could ever use for pleasure. Picking up a cane so thin I could barely see it, he walked around me so I couldn't see him.

"I honestly have no idea, master."

Fire erupted in the sole of my left foot, where he let the

cane fall across it. My balance was gone, and the inch of give the chain had…

Oh fuck.

All my weight was now on that thin, blunt line of wood. It was a different kind of pain than the cane. That was already fading. This was deep, dark, and *pressure*. Right on my clit too, because that was where he placed me.

I found my footing and lifted myself up on the balls of my feet, suddenly realizing the predicament I was in. If I didn't want the harsh pain between my legs, I had to keep standing exactly like this. But the strength in my legs would fail, and I would be stuck with the sharp, painful pressure, or worse, trying to keep myself up and repeatedly failing, falling onto the wood over and over again.

"It's called a pony board because you ride it," he said.

More than anything, I hated what they'd done to me. Because if they weren't trying to get information out of me, if this were about pleasure instead of my role in this ridiculous plot, I might enjoy it, knowing I was submitting to it for them and I could be rewarded. I already knew how much Sebastian liked his predicaments.

There was no reward for this.

Still, my nipples hardened into points, and I knew the wood beneath me would soon be wet.

"Perfect," Derek said, looking at my breasts. "Makes it easier." He quickly grabbed clamps and attached them. They hadn't used them on me yet, but the pain was familiar. This, at least, I knew. I could bear it.

Until he had more chains and small, dark balls in his hand. I'd seen the weights before in porn, but they'd never used them on me. He attached one to the center of the chain between my breasts, and the pain stole my breath. "This can stop, *gattina*. You have to talk to us. You have to tell us the truth."

"I *can't*," I moaned. "I can't."

The way he looked at me, startled, I realized I fucked up. It was the first time I'd even admitted there was something for me to tell.

"I'm sorry to hear that," he said softly. "In that case, you're going to stay here until you change your mind."

Nick grabbed my hips and tilted them back, exposing me just a little more.

"Still can't damage our property," he said. "So we'll only clamp you for fifteen minutes at a time. But it's not going to be fun."

I realized what they were doing a second before the pain hit. The clamp bit down on my clit, sending shudders of pain and pleasure through me. God, no.

The soft tinkle of chains reached me. And it got worse. Two weights—one on either side of the board, pulled on me. Pain was everywhere now.

"Please," I begged. "Please, don't do this. I promise I'm not a bad person. I'm not trying to do anything to hurt you. Please."

The fact that I saw both regret and agony in their eyes didn't make the pain any better. Because they were still going to do it.

Sebastian stood by the chain. "Last chance, Selena."

I couldn't do it. I couldn't give in and let Anna die. She was all I had left, and they'd already taken me from her for far too long.

He sighed. "All right."

One more inch of slack in the chain, and everything was harder. I really had to balance now, calves straining.

Nick came over with a gag. "They'll be back to take things off in fifteen minutes. But we'll talk in an hour, slave. And just because those are coming off doesn't mean other things won't go on."

"Please—" He used the word to shove the ball in my mouth and connect it behind my head. My mind was going to a place I could no longer control. Pain—even the good kind of pain—took me to vulnerability and openness. I wasn't strong. I wasn't made for this.

I wasn't who the Syndicate said I was, and I needed to get them to believe me while still protecting Anna. If she was blacklisted...

Tears welled in my eyes and overflowed.

"Seb," Nick spanked my ass, jostling the chains and weights, causing fiery sparks to go everywhere. I whimpered. "Maybe an anal hook for the next round?"

"That's a good idea."

They walked toward the door, and everything inside me crumbled. I couldn't do this. I couldn't watch them walk away. I was fucked up with some kind of Stockholm syndrome, but they were mine. My Alphas. It didn't matter that they were bad men, they were still mine.

My right leg failed, and I fell onto the board, pain splitting me open. I screamed, and sudden fury and fear tore through me. With how tight it was, I shouldn't have been able to shove the gag out of my mouth, but I did it.

"They're going to kill my sister."

Tears flowed down my face, and I leaned into the pain, not bothering to right myself. Because if I was giving in, I deserved the pain. This could be the thing that killed her.

All three Alphas were looking at me now, and they came back. "Please." My voice shook. I sniffed, trying to get control, and I couldn't. "If I tell you, they're going to kill my sister."

Derek stepped close to me, fire in his eyes. "Who? Who is going to kill your sister?"

I pressed my lips together. They hadn't said they would do anything, and the Syndicate said they were always watching. Was this a trap?

He cupped my face with a hand, voice low. "I promise,

Selena. I will not let anything happen to your sister. I swear it, no matter what happens, we will keep her safe."

I wilted in the chains, fully resting on the board. One more sob, and I finally let it go. "The Syndicate. The Underground Omega Syndicate. I can prove it. I swear. Please, Masters." It wasn't even a conscious decision to call them that.

The weights disappeared, and Nick took Derek's place, keeping my face close to his, lips at my ear. "Breathe with me, sweetheart. It's going to hurt."

"It can't hurt anymore," I murmured. "It already hurts too much."

He swore under his breath. "Get her the fuck down."

The board beneath me disappeared and I could stand on my own again. The sharp pains in my nipples and clit barely phased me. My knees gave way, and one of them caught me before I sprained my shoulders falling into the chains.

Sobs still fell out of me, and I recognized the scent of sweet mountain air in the chest I was pressed against. A blanket wrapped around my shoulders. "Talk to me, *gattina*."

Kitten.

I pressed my face harder into his chest. "The theatre. The room with the cages. I promise. I can prove it."

Something rumbled beneath my ear, and I went still. He was purring. None of them had purred for me since my heat, and it made everything come to the surface.

"Hold on, Selena," Derek whispered. "We're going to fix it. I promise."

We were moving, but my face was still so buried in his chest I didn't know where. Even if it hadn't been, the tears that wouldn't stop wouldn't let me see anything.

"We're here, Selena," Sebastian said, voice uncharacteristically gentle. "Show us where."

Derek helped me as I lifted my head, wiping my face with

the blanket. I was a fucking mess. "Back there," I pointed. "Behind that curtain."

Not much had changed since I woke up in this room. There hadn't been any more auctions. We walked over to the cage, and I started to get down. "No, you don't," Derek said, tightening his hold. "Just tell us. I can't put you down right now."

I cleared my throat, my voice raw. Quiet tears still spilled over, saved up from all this time. "There's a loose floorboard. Underneath it is the phone that was with me when I woke up in there."

Derek's body went entirely still.

Nick was the one who opened the door and felt along the boards. "Holy shit," he said, finding the board and the phone right where I left them. "Is there anything else here?"

I shook my head.

"Good," Seb said. "We shouldn't do the rest of this here."

The others didn't say anything, but they agreed. We were suddenly moving quickly, until we were inside the elevator that took us to their private floors.

They took me straight into the living room, and Nick pulled out the big, comfy pillow Sebastian had put me on the first day. Derek set me gently on it, and they sat on the couch in front of me. "Okay, Selena. Tell us."

My body ached, my head ached, my heart ached. Everything ached. "I told you the truth the first day," I said quietly. "Or the simple version of it. I went to sleep in my bed, ready to be on vacation for my heat. I woke up to someone in my house. They drugged me, and I woke up in the cage, hearing Derek tell all those women to serve and keep their eyes on the floor. That," I pointed to the phone in Nick's hand. "That was all that was with me, except the nightgown. I don't even know who changed me."

I still didn't like to think about that.

"I'm not what they say I am," I said, voice quivering again

and tears rising. "I don't know how this happened, or why I'm here. I'm not supposed to be here."

Seb held out his hand in a familiar gesture, and I found myself leaning into his touch, shifting to rest against his knee. His hand stayed on the back of my head. This was the only place I'd really found peace. I didn't know if that was the most fucked thing in the universe, but right now? I didn't care.

"What's on the phone, sweetheart?"

"Their instructions," I mumbled.

I heard the phone unlock, and the deathly silence as they read through the letter. No need to read it out loud. The words were burned in my brain.

"Fucking hell," Derek said. "Did you know anything about these people?"

The question wasn't directed at me.

"No," Seb said. "But I'd like to give them a piece of my fucking mind."

"Are the jammers on?" Nick asked.

"Always. But I'll double check." Sebastian stood and gently pulled away.

Derek came down on his knees in front of me, pulling me up into his arms. "I am so sorry, *gattina*. Nothing is going to happen to Anna, baby. I promise."

I melted into his arms, even though I knew I shouldn't. "How can you be sure?"

"Because we're going to take care of it," Nick said. "We have all the information they want, and it's nothing like they think."

Lifting me off the ground, Derek settled back on the couch with me on his lap. "We have some truth to tell you too, and I'm so sorry we couldn't tell you sooner. We're not who you think we are."

I looked up at him as Sebastian returned and sat. Nick's hand soothed up and down my arm from where he sat behind me, and then he stood, moving to perch on the coffee table so I could see all three of them. "What do you mean?"

"I mean," Derek said. "Our names are the same, but we're not... we don't sell people, Selena. Or own people. We're trying to *take down* those people. All the women at the auction? They were Betas. Specially trained and *wearing* Omega hormones in order to pass so they could trace the people who bought them. We're close to having all the major players within reach, and then we're going to arrest all of them. Including Delano."

His words sank in, and I couldn't wrap my head around them. "What?"

Sebastian reached out and put his hand on my ankle, rubbing slowly. "We work for the government and have been undercover for three years trying to take this trafficking network down."

Derek held me closer. "So when you walked out into the middle of the auction smelling like you did, we didn't know what to do. Delano offered to pay an unlimited amount of money for you. And he isn't like us. He would torture you for sport. Make you a real slave. He would have broken and killed you. And I..." He shuddered. "I couldn't let that happen. Because as soon as I scented you, I knew, *gattina*. I knew that you were mine."

I pushed up away from him, and he let me go. My body needed to move. Clutching the blanket around my chest, I started to pace. "So the Syndicate sent me in here to find the hormones, and you're not even the people who are making them?" Rage flowed through me. "This was all for nothing? Everything I did—"

"No," Nick stood and came to me. "We know who makes them and harvests them. That's a separate operation, and we couldn't shut it down until ours goes first because they're so tangled together. But I promise, the hormones we use... they don't inject them. That's not what you're supposed to do with them. The ones who are injecting them are looking for the high, and you know firsthand how that can work out."

My mind whirled, and I didn't know how to think or feel. "So all of this? Everything... You don't really like this? You don't..."

"I wouldn't say that," Sebastian said. "There's a reason we were chosen for this mission. But in our own lives, you would be a willing slave, Selena."

"There's no such thing."

He raised an eyebrow. "Isn't there? Come here."

Everything was out in the open now. I didn't have to obey him, but I still did, and I didn't resist him when he pulled me down to straddle his lap. "Will you let me paint a picture for you?"

"Okay..."

Slowly, he lifted his hand and slid it behind my neck. His touch felt different now. It was just as possessive, but there was less expectation there.

"You're a nurse?" He asked.

"Yeah."

A rare smile that did things to my stomach which were confusing given the circumstances.

"Imagine a normal day at work," he said, voice lowering near a whisper. "Doing what you do. And coming home to us. Kneeling at our feet. Letting us take over and allowing you to breathe."

I did imagine it, and my cheeks heated, because when he said it like that, it didn't sound bad. It sounded close to what I'd imagined with them countless times in the past weeks. Close to what I wanted to experience before I was taken.

"The word *slave* is just a word, baby. A role to play. In our world, you'd still be on your knees, but you would be treasured there. Exactly the way we've felt this whole time and been unable to show."

"All the time?" I asked, unsure if he knew what I meant.

166

Seb shook his head. "No. Not all the time. All the time in the bedroom. The rest of it is negotiable. Because that's how this is truly done." He brought my face closer to his. "Everyone agrees to it. And you'll never be able to understand how sorry I am we that couldn't offer that to you. We didn't have a choice if we wanted to save both the mission and you."

I placed my hands on his shoulders, unsure how to feel. Logically, everything told me I *should* be angry beyond belief. That they forced me into everything. But they hadn't, had they?

"You did offer me a choice," I said. "In a way."

"Not the right one," Nick said. "And it was desperation."

Turning to look behind me, I studied him. He looked... distraught. "Why desperation?"

"Can I—" he dropped his face into his hands. "Can I still touch you?"

I stood off Seb's lap and went to him, letting him wrap his arms around me and my blanket. "You want to know the truth?"

"Yes."

"Because we wouldn't force you," he said. "I couldn't... none of us would be able to live with ourselves if we did that. And if you'd tried to walk away, I would have followed you and blown this entire operation to save you." He pulled me closer, burying his face in my stomach. "I don't know if that makes me good or bad. But there were no *good* choices, and you were, you *are* everything."

I sank down into his lap. "You're so sure I wouldn't be safe?"

"Delano still wants you," Derek said. "His eyes never fucking leave you when we have you with us. To him, you're a toy he wants to break. He told me as much. So yes, I'm sure. If he'd even suspected you were alone and unprotected, you would be gone."

A shiver ran down my spine.

I felt strangely blank. All of this was... a lot to process. What I felt, and what I thought I *should* feel. The reality of all of this. The Syndicate, my sister. "Why not just keep me out of sight until he's gone? Why train me?"

"We've done our job well," Sebastian said. "Though we've never touched the women we sell, we've crafted the reputation of being the best of the best. Selling perfectly obedient Omegas. Having you and not training you would raise more flags than it would lower."

"What happened to them?"

"The Betas?" Nick asked.

I nodded, and he tightened his hands around my waist. "They go in and do what they need to. Everyone is a volunteer. There are protocols to get out. Another medical marvel. They can seem dead, and we get them out. Some of them have gone in a number of times."

It wasn't something I could imagine.

"I... need to think."

"Of course," Derek said.

They didn't stop me as I stood and walked through the living room and toward mine. I hadn't stopped until I was in my bed, curled up. Inside the giant steel cage with the door open.

Why was it that of all the places in the world I could feel safe, I felt safest in a cage?

CHAPTER TWENTY-FIVE

SEBASTIAN

*W*e all watched Selena walk away, the blanket dragging around her like a cape.

"She told the truth," Derek said. "That first day. She's right. She told me she didn't know how she got here and I didn't fucking believe her."

"Of course you didn't," I said. "We haven't been able to trust anyone in three years. Why would you assume the one person out of place at the most important event we have was telling the truth?"

Still, my pack mate looked absolutely wrecked, and I knew how he felt. Because the Omega who just walked away from us was ours, and we might have destroyed everything before it even had a chance to start.

That was the price for saving the world though, right? You gave up everything of yourself in order to save everyone else. But it was different when you were sacrificing the woman who might be the love of your life.

Nick looked between us. "You would have done the same, right?"

He meant going after Selena even though it would have meant breaking our cover.

"Yes."

Derek nodded. "Fuck me, yes."

"How do we fix this?" I asked. "Not only between us, but the fuckers that took her."

Standing, Nick tossed the phone she'd hidden to me. "The letter says a month. It's been a little over two weeks. So we do have some time. But at this point, everything is in place. I don't mind burning those fuckers to the ground. Give them whatever they want to make sure Selena is out of it.

"What I'm more interested in is *why* they took Selena. One look at her, and anyone would know she's not a killer."

He wasn't wrong. Especially with what we'd been doing. We all could tell now if someone had it in themselves to kill. Our sweet Selena didn't. Her being a nurse made absolute sense.

"I want to find out," I said. "But we're flying a bit blind. We don't know how big their operation is, or how connected. Until we know more, I don't think we do anything. Because the sister is the priority here. We'll keep Selena safe. But I don't want our poking around to prompt these people to follow through on their threats."

Derek snorted. "You know me. I'm all for violent revolution if necessary. And I don't think the goal they stated is a bad one. But if you do things like this to achieve it, is it really possible to achieve those goals with any integrity?"

He had a point.

"And what about her?" I asked. "Did we fuck this up too badly?"

"I hope not," Nick whispered.

Every word he told her was the truth. We wouldn't have forced her. I would put a gun to my head before forcing myself on her. But we painted the picture otherwise. We gave her a choice, but it wasn't really a choice. It was the only option she had.

My heart ached because of it.

And I couldn't even tell her I felt bad about all of it, because I loved the things we'd done together, and she did too. Because Selena was *ours*. We were built to fit her needs exactly like she was meant to fit ours.

If things had been different, I would put her in the exact same position I had earlier tonight. Making sure she was *dripping* wet the entire time. Forcing orgasms out of her before leaving her to fight strength and gravity.

My little Omega liked pain and submission at the deepest levels of her soul, though I knew she hadn't accepted it. She thrived on her knees, blossoming in our control, and all I wanted in the world was to experience that the way it was *meant* to be. All parties agreeing and enjoying. Pushing and pulling, adapting because we're human.

"I love her," I said, the words springing from me suddenly. "I love her so fucking much."

Derek reached over and put a hand on my shoulder. "Me too."

"If the two of you didn't know that about me by now, we're not as close as I thought we were," Nick said.

We all chuckled, though nothing about any of this was remotely funny.

"God, I just want to go to her," I said. "I know I can't."

"No," Derek said. "We need to give her the space she asked for. She deserves that much."

I let my head fall into my hands. "I don't want to lose her."

"You haven't lost me," Selena's voice came from the hallway. She was still wrapped up in the blanket. "I was restless, and I realized I had more questions, nor was being alone great for my brain at the moment. But I would like some clothes, please."

Nick stood and left immediately. He came back from his bedroom with a t-shirt and sweatpants. Selena stepped around the corner to change, but didn't retreat entirely. It felt like a small victory. And honestly, seeing her clothed was refreshing. I loved the way Nick's clothes seemed to drown her.

When she came back into the living room, I saw her glance at the cushion at our feet before sitting in a chair across from us. That was for the best. This wasn't a conversation for power exchange.

"Why Betas?" She asked. "If you're using Omega hormones anyway, why not just train Omegas?"

Derek cleared his throat. "Well, taking down the manufacturer was on the list. But more because it's practical. Betas don't have heats, and they can't be bonded. It's safer for them. Sending in Omegas could end badly even with the precautions."

Selena nodded. Our cuffs were still on her wrists. God, I wanted to put real ones there. The three of us had had a permanent set designed a long time ago, in the hopes we would find someone exactly like her.

When we took her measurements I had them made. My cock sat up and paid attention to the mental image of Selena with our jewelry on her. Delicate white gold bands that didn't come off. Once they closed, the only way to remove them was by cutting them off or welding them open.

Wrists, ankles, neck. I wanted her underneath me with nothing but the symbols of our ownership of her. Our *willing* ownership.

My Omega looked at me like she could read my mind. "You have other questions?"

She looked so uncomfortable that it took everything in me not to go to her and take her in my arms again. "I don't know." Her voice was thin and emotional. "I'm so confused."

"By what, sweetheart?"

Selena's eyes filled with tears. Pulling her knees up onto the chair, she wrapped her arms around her knees. "I wish I had met you anywhere else," she said, and the way she said it shattered me. "Any other time. Because I feel like I should be so angry and betrayed and hate you, and I don't. I'm not sure if it's because we're scent matched, or because you gave me kindness when you could. But I don't know how to feel, and I hate it."

Standing, I went to the windows and stared out, unable to stay still without going for her. To her. Telling her the truth.

"And… I heard you," she whispered. "I heard you say you love me."

The air in the room went so still you could have heard our hearts beat. I turned to her, Derek and Nick already staring at her. Whatever she said next…

"And I want to say it back, but I feel like I shouldn't trust you, and yet I do, and that's why I'm confused. Because of *everything*."

I couldn't hold myself back anymore. Crossing over to her chair, I knelt in front of it. The reversal of roles wasn't lost on me. "May I touch you?" I breathed.

The look in her eyes broke what little was left of me. Because that look told me, truly, how much damage we had done. "You're asking?"

"I'm asking."

Her shoulders wilted. "Okay."

I rose up higher on my knees and gathered her to me. "I wish I could let you see into my mind right now," I said. "Nothing I can ever tell you will be enough to show you what I feel, and how much… *fucking regret* I have."

"We," Derek said. "We have."

"We have." I felt like I was cracking open. "And I wish we'd done what Nick said. I wish we'd walked out with you and never looked back. Maybe then it would be different. But I don't blame you, Selena. We don't deserve your trust, sweetheart."

She hiccuped a sob into my shoulder. "Would people have died? If you left?"

"Yes," Nick said quietly. "The women they're still selling. Maybe the Betas who we sent in, if their cover was broken."

Selena cried harder. The dam we broke by making her confess hadn't fully closed. "Then how can I be angry? It's selfish."

"Then be selfish," I said, squeezing her harder. "Be fucking selfish, because none of this is fair. You're innocent. Ripped out of your life and shoved into an impossible situation you didn't deserve. And even though we were trying to protect you, we still hurt you. Made you feel like you were nothing." I choked on the word. "I love you. You're my Omega, Selena Martin, no matter what. But I know there might not be any coming back from this. And if that's what you decide…" I forced myself to pull away from her and look at her face. "Then I accept that. And I'll treasure every moment I had with you, even when you didn't know how we felt."

I lifted my hand to her face, brushing away some of her tears with my thumb. "But if there's any way to make it right, we'll do it. Anything."

Moving away and releasing her felt like pain. And not the kind of pain we both enjoyed.

"My sister?"

Derek took the place I'd vacated. "We have to be very careful," he said. "We don't want to do anything that would accidentally make them follow through on their threats. While we still have a little time on your clock, we're going to do some very quiet digging. But Anna is going to be just fine. We promise. No matter what happens, you'll be free of them, and Anna will be safe."

"Okay."

We could offer her that relief, even if we couldn't offer her anything else.

CHAPTER TWENTY-SIX

SELENA

*N*ick stood and came over to where I sat. He reached down and took one of my hands. No, one of my *wrists*. His fingers went to the leather cuff on it, beginning to undo it.

No.

I yanked my hand away from his, and he looked startled. "You don't need to wear these right now," he said.

There was no explanation for the way that cracked me in two. The cuffs told people I was theirs. They just said they loved me. So why were they taking away the one thing that claimed me?

"Please talk to us, sweetheart. I wish I could read your mind and answer all your fears, but I can't if I don't know them."

I ran my finger along the inside of one cuff. "It's probably fucked up."

Derek huffed a laugh. "There's nothing about this situation that isn't."

Fixing my eyes on the floor, I shivered. Surrounded by Nick's scent on his clothes, it was even harder to admit, because saying it would hurt them, and I didn't want that. I didn't know what the fuck I wanted. "Taking them off makes me feel like you don't want me."

"Fuck, sweetheart." Nick reached for me and stopped. I didn't think there were any tears left in me, but I was wrong. When I held out my arms, he pulled me into his, lifting me off the chair and wrapping my legs around his hips. I clung to him like the anchor he was.

Derek was right. There wasn't anything about this that

wasn't fucked up. Because they were the source of the problem and the source of my comfort.

We were moving, and I didn't realize until the air grew quieter and darker that we were in the nest. We hadn't been here since my heat ended.

Nick laid me down on the dark velvet, looking down at me. "Cuffs or no cuffs, dynamic or not, no matter how we came to this point, there is *no* world where I wouldn't want you. You are *my* Omega, and always will be, no matter what happens."

Sebastian and Derek were at the edge of the nest. "Can we stay here tonight?" I asked. "I don't... I don't want to be alone."

Nick rolled to the side and cuddled me into his chest. "Of course we can."

Derek slid in behind me, and Sebastian sat at my feet, pulling them into his lap. I closed my eyes and breathed in the mixture of their scents I was so used to now. The idea of not having that—

"When this mission is over, what happens?"

"We haven't really thought that far ahead," Derek said. "It's hard when you're so deep in the middle of something, wishing you could be somewhere else."

Sebastian ran his hands over my legs and ankles, seeming like he needed to touch me. "But as far as the three of us? We're done. The agreement we made will take care of that. We knew going in, this assignment would take everything, and we agreed to do it, on the conditions that it would be the last mission we ever did, and that our every need and want would be taken care of for the rest of our lives."

Nick's lips brushed my temple. "We don't have a house yet, but we want one. And it can be wherever we want. If—" He blew out a shaky breath. "It can be near you if that's what you want. Or somewhere so far away that you never have to think about us again."

"Stop it," I hissed. "Stop talking like I—" My voice cracked, and I buried my face deeper in his shirt. Without looking at them, the words were easier. "How am I supposed to walk away from you when we're scent matched? *Everything* matched? You know, the night I was taken, my Beta friend tried to get me to come to *Catena* as a patron. He thought I would like it, and I told him no, not wanting to admit how right he was.

"But it's not just that it's... am I broken? Scent or no scent, falling in love with you while you trained me to be a slave. How do I explain it? How do I accept it? What kind of person likes that?" I shook my head. "You gave me the choice, and I took it. But everything still hurts." Then, quieter. "I am broken."

"No, *gattina*, you're not broken," Derek said, shifting and turning me so I faced him. "You are not broken. If anything, you're one of the strongest people I've ever met. You did all this for your sister, knowing you were innocent."

He pushed the hair off my face and ran his fingers through it. "There's no black and white here. That's why it's so hard. But whatever you want is what we'll do."

"Tell me what *you* want," I said. "I'm tired of thinking about me. I just want to listen to anything until I fall asleep and wake up feeling... not like this."

Derek stroked my hair again. "What do I want? All right. What I want is to finish the mission. We're no more than a few days away now. After everything is finished here, what I really want is to take you out of this place. Find a house the four of us love, or build it, if that's what we need. Or five, if Anna is able to stay with us. The rest of what I want is similar to what Seb described. I don't know what we'll do for ourselves, but I know I want you. I want our cuffs on you— real, permanent ones. I want you at my feet and on your knees because that's where you want to be and that's where you feel safest. I want to build a playroom that rivals this club so we can have our way with you in every way we've already taken you and more.

"I want to learn the *real* you, and I want to show you who we are and not who we're pretending to be. What I want, Selena, is to love you for the rest of my life. And spend all of it making sure you know how fucking *precious* you are. Most of all, that even though you're on your knees, wearing our cuffs, we're the ones owned by you."

There wasn't anything I could say to that. I slipped an arm around his waist and held him closer, letting the purr in his chest lull me down into sleep, where, for a little while, I could forget everything.

CHAPTER TWENTY-SEVEN

SELENA

*W*hen I woke, I felt fuzzy. The amount of crying and revelations before I fell asleep took everything out of me. Absolutely fucking everything.

Derek wasn't holding me now. Instead, I was curled into Nick's chest. The spicy scent of his peppermint helped bring me fully to consciousness. Warm skin, and the soft, subtle sound of his purr beneath my ear. His tattoos stretched over his chest and shoulder. A giant tree, the trunk stretching down his ribs; the branches holding different symbols I hadn't dared to ask him about.

I didn't know if I would now.

Because I was still conflicted and confused.

Mostly because what they said *made sense*.

Every interaction they had with me, from the very first time Derek took me away from Delano, he'd protected me. Harshly, but it was still protection. Everything we'd done together, even the harshest things, they had been with me. In spite of their words making me an object, and their punishments, it never *felt like the truth*.

And the heat?

If they'd been like some of the monsters I'd encountered, they never would have done that. They would have tied me up in the club downstairs, gagged me, and declared me open for free use. That's what the others would have done.

But these Alphas had abandoned everything they had to do, and now I knew, put their entire reason for being here at risk, in order to give me a good heat. Because they loved me.

I wished they'd been able to tell me the truth—I never would have given them away. If anything, I would have

179

played along. But in the same way I couldn't trust them because of how we met, they couldn't trust me. I didn't blame them for being suspicious. The Syndicate had made me suspicious, and there was no way around that.

Because of who we were and the way we'd been pushed together, there had been no way for us to trust each other. But in a strange sense, we'd found our way to each other anyway. Was it fucked up and totally not black and white? Yes.

Were the four of us going to have to make up a different story to tell people who we met? Absolutely. But…

I wanted them.

As soon as they told me the truth, everything clicked in my chest. Who I felt they were instead of who they claimed to be. Like all of us had been fighting our way to the truth through impossible circumstances.

Derek was right when he risked telling me that not everything was the way it seemed. And so was Nick, when he told me he needed me to fail their punishment. To keep their reputation with Delano.

It wouldn't be easy, and there would be plenty of missteps. But I didn't think I could walk away from them now. They were my Alphas. They knew how to make my body sing, and when I gave them what they asked for, the submission was beautiful. But I didn't want to be a slave. Not like this.

"Your head seems like it's going a million miles a minute, sweetheart."

"I didn't know you were awake," I said.

His purr grew stronger. "I'll be honest. I don't think any of us slept very much."

"Why not?"

"Guilt," he said. "Trying to figure out how to do this with you, and undo the damage we've done. Just watching you sleep because you're so fucking beautiful, and when you're sleeping, you're not in pain."

I tucked my face into his chest.

His hand came up behind my head, holding me closer, and his voice was ragged. "I need to ask you, Selena. Is there any chance? Did we..." The pause was agony. "Did we ruin everything?"

A whine slipped out of me. "No. I won't pretend that I don't want you. I do. But it's hard. You weren't able to trust me, and I wasn't able to trust you. Still, with all of that, last night excluded, I liked everything you did to me. I can lie and say I didn't, but clearly a part of me needs this kind of submission. As much as you need the other side of it."

Nick rolled us so he was pressing me into the cushions. "I'm glad to hear that, sweetheart."

"But I am not a slave," I said, tone final. "And after this is over, and all the bad guys are in jail, you are never going to call me that again. I know it's a word and a role, and if all of this had never happened, maybe I'd enjoy playing around with it. Not now."

"Agreed." Sebastian's voice came from the door, and both my other Alphas appeared. "I don't know that any of us could truly call anyone a slave after the last few years."

Nick sat up and pulled me with him, revealing that my other Alphas had brought us breakfast. It smelled amazing. Eggs and bacon. Some kind of juice I couldn't identify, and biscuits with honey. I would give them that. The food had been good my entire time here.

"Thank you," I said. Both for the food and the acknowledgment that I wasn't a slave.

Derek set my tray down beside me and kissed my hair. "You don't even know the relief it is to treat you the way we've wanted to this whole time."

I began to eat, suddenly ravenous. "Will this put you in danger? Of taking them all down?"

"So long as we only act like this here, no," Nick said. "We will have to keep up appearances."

"I can do that. I would have done that from the beginning if I'd known."

Sebastian reached out and touched my knee. "We know."

The juice was delicious. Maybe mango? Mixed with something else. "You thought I was a spy?"

"Something like that." Nick began to eat his own food. "It's not the first time someone's tried to plant someone within our organization. As disgusting as it is, this market is… competitive."

We all ate quietly after that, enjoying each other's company in easy silence. There was so much we had to figure out, and yet, it was nice to exist in this space where we didn't acknowledge all the difficulties we'd have to overcome.

When we finished, Sebastian took the trays and disappeared. When he came back, there was a black velvet box in his hands that looked like one that might hold a necklace.

"What's that?"

He smiled, and it was a beautiful sight. How much had these men been able to smile in their time here? Or smile genuinely? "Something that I'm not sure you'll like, but I still want to show you."

I looked at the box warily.

Derek laughed and pulled me across the cushions so I was sitting between his legs. "Don't be nervous, Selena. We're never going to force something on you again."

Sebastian knelt in front of me. "Do you remember what Derek said last night?"

"Which part?"

"That we wanted our cuffs on you, but real and permanent ones."

"Oh." I leaned back into Derek as he slipped his arms around my waist. His hands teased the soft roundness of my stomach beneath Nick's t-shirt—something I didn't normally like. But at the moment I just liked him touching me. "Yes, I remember."

Placing one hand on the top of the box, Sebastian took a deep breath. "When we took your measurements that first night, we already knew we wanted you to be ours. A long time ago we had these designed, but not made, because we hoped we would find our person—our Omega—who would want to belong to us just as much as we would belong to her."

He opened the box.

Nestled inside looked like metal concentric circles. Or almost circles. None of them were closed. The pale metal looked delicate, and I saw tiny, swirling designs across the outside of the metal. "What are they?"

Sebastian picked up one of the smallest ones and held it out on the palm of his hand. "They're cuffs and a collar." I reached out, and he stopped me. "Be careful. The thing about these cuffs is that once they are closed, they cannot be opened."

My stomach swirled at the same time that my skin heated. "Ever?"

"They can be cut off," Nick said. "But no, not ever. The way they're designed, they are permanent."

I picked up the cuff from Sebastian's hand. It was just as light and delicate as it looked. I held it up beside my wrist. This wouldn't look like anything more than a bracelet or a necklace. But to us, it would mean everything.

"You want me to wear these?"

"Do we *want* you to?" Derek asked, whispering into my neck. "*Fuck*, yes. But if you don't want to, we'll have a set made that open. If you don't want to wear them at all outside of the bedroom, we can do that too. But if we move forward, we want cuffs on you in the bedroom."

I didn't mind that. The idea of being cuffed for them and *wanting* to be there? It was so hot, my scent whirled around us. "I know we're not there yet, but what about a bond?"

"Yes," Nick said. "But we won't bond until everything with our mission and the Syndicate is over. We're prepared, and there shouldn't be any problems, but it's still dangerous. We're not willing to bond you and have you in total pain because of us if something happens."

It made sense, but hollowed out my gut. "You're sure it'll be okay?"

"Yes, *gattina*. A precaution."

"If I put these on, will Delano know there's something different?" I asked.

Derek took one of my wrists and held it out. It was still wrapped in the leather cuff. "He might. But if you'd be willing, we would cover them with these still. The addition of a leather collar wouldn't be that strange."

I looked at the jewelry box and the delicate cuff I still held. What would people think if they found out I'd accepted a permanent gift from men who'd done this?

The deeper part of myself rose up and smacked me. What would people think of me giving myself to men who were so selfless they spent three years of their life living in the darkest situations humanity had to offer in order to protect the innocent and vulnerable?

There was no right or wrong in this. The second the Syndicate chose me, they changed the course of everything. And I wasn't going to decide the rest of my life on what-ifs. What if it didn't work out? What if I had regrets? What if something else bad happened?

What-ifs got you nowhere. All you could do was deal with the events in your life as they occurred. And for better or for worse, these men were mine. We had a rocky road ahead of us no matter what. But I wanted us to be on the road together.

"I'm scared," I said. "But I want to."

Derek went stiff around me, and then I was on my back and he was kissing me hard. "Really?"

"Really," I said. "I could go through the entire thought process if you want me to."

Nick playfully shoved Derek off me and took his place. "Sweetheart, we want to know everything about you. Every thought and every word you want to tell us. And as soon as I can bite this gorgeous neck of yours, I want to feel everything emotion you have. But seeing our cuffs on you? I've only imagined it and I'm hard."

Yes, he was. I felt it where his hips rested between my legs.

Sebastian took his turn, dark eyes searching my face. "You're scared, princess. Are you sure?"

I blew out a shaky breath. "I know I want you. All the rest of it makes me nervous, and it's going to take time."

"For me too," he said, dropping his lips to mine. "What I did to you last night—"

"We don't have to talk about it."

"Yes we do," he said. "Because I don't want it between us. I'm sorry, Selena. I'm sorry we didn't believe you, and I'm sorry I hurt you. It doesn't matter that I didn't want to, and it made me sick. I still did it."

Reaching up, I took his face in my hands. "One thing I do know is that the four of us will never get anywhere if we keep blaming ourselves for choices we were forced into making. If I wasn't afraid for my sister's life, I would have told you everything the second I walked into the theatre. If you weren't trying to protect vulnerable Omegas, you never would have been here at all."

Sebastian kissed me, far more gently than I was used to with him.

"I know for a fucking fact," I said. "All of us are going to struggle with this. It's not going to be easy, and it's not going to be simple. But for now, let's be grateful that in all the bullshit, we still found our matches."

"God, I love you so much," he breathed the words against my skin. "If you're sure, I want to put them on you."

"I'm sure."

Sebastian reached over and retrieved the cuff that had been knocked out of my hand when Derek tackled me to the cushions. Then he took my wrist, and this time when the leather cuff was unbuckled, I didn't panic. He set the leather one aside and lifted my wrist to his mouth, kissing the inside of it.

"I love you, Selena Martin. And from now until I bond you and forever, I'm going to make sure you never fucking doubt it." He opened the cuff and put it around my wrist. I already felt how perfectly it fit, lightly resting against my skin. Sebastian locked eyes with me as he clicked the metal closed.

The thin cuff melded seamlessly together. Where the opening had been, there was no trace of it. "That's amazing," I said.

"There's a small mechanism inside that locks together," he said quietly. "It will never come apart unless we cut it off."

My stomach flipped. It felt *right* as much as it was terrifying. "I don't plan on cutting it off."

He kissed me again, before backing up, allowing Derek to take my ankle in his hands and undo the leather cuff. Kissing up my leg, he took one of those cuffs and clicked it into place. "You are everything," he said. "I love you."

Nick couldn't even speak, but he didn't need to. Everything he felt was so clear in his eyes, it was like he spoke it out loud. Sheer joy and love. He ran his hands up and down my leg before attaching the thin metal circle. Derek locked my other wrist, and finally, Sebastian took out the collar and knelt behind me. He brushed my hair off of my skin and kissed me there. "Thank you for trusting us, princess, in spite of everything."

The metal closed around my neck, the fit perfect enough

to stay where it needed to be, and not too tight to be uncomfortable. If anything, it felt like it was *meant* to be there. The *click* resonated through me like a physical force. I was theirs, and they were mine.

"*Fuck* I love the way this looks, *gattina*," Derek said.

So did I. The pale metal—what looked like white gold and not silver—complimented my skin. It looked like high end jewelry and not a symbol of the relationship between us.

I grinned. "Is this where we talk about the *actual* rules?"

Seb pulled me back against him, purring loudly. "Right now there are no rules, princess. I don't know that hashing out our dynamic right now is the best idea. When we're in the club, it's the old rules, and you know why. When this is over? We can talk about all the rules you want."

I nodded. "Fair enough. But I'm not agreeing to never come. Just throwing that out there."

Derek burst out laughing. "No worries there, Selena. I love watching you come too much to deprive you of that. Though I can't say the same for the other two."

Seb laughed in my ear. "Oh, I'll like denying you, sweetheart, but definitely not all the time." Then his voice lowered. "Though you can't lie to me. You like the threat of never getting to come again. The idea that I can take it away from you forever turns you on."

My face flushed, and I couldn't tell him he was wrong. When he threatened to give me the last orgasm of my life, I had the *hardest* orgasm of my life.

"What do we do now?" I asked.

The three of them sighed. "Now, we need to make an appearance downstairs. But this time, you'll be in on the training. Is there anything in particular you *want* to do?"

I thought about it, shame and arousal washing through me. Nick grabbed my foot and locked eyes with me. "Nope. Don't second guess yourself, and don't be embarrassed by anything. I promise, there's nothing you can say that will make us feel differently or make us look at you differently."

"I'm claustrophobic," I said. "That's what happened with the gas mask. But for everything else?" Swallowing, I looked between Derek and Nick. "I know what I just said, but speaking of denial..."

CHAPTER TWENTY-EIGHT

───────────

SELENA

*M*y brand new metal accessories were covered in leather to hide them, but I loved knowing they were there.

The club was pretty much empty right now, as it was during the day. But I saw the people I now recognized as the staff and also Delano's men.

But it was getting late. I spent most of the day at their feet in their office, plainly visible as men came in and out. A couple of times they put me in the cage in the office, but it was entirely different now. Now the cage felt comforting and safe because we were both choosing it. They wanted me to go in so I could rest my knees and take a nap, as well as being less exposed.

What they were going to do this evening was going to be delicious torture, and I knew it was my idea, which made it both better and worse. I was going to struggle and probably be punished. But this time I'd asked for it. Because I'd wanted to try something like it, and they'd eagerly agreed.

In fact, Sebastian hardened instantly where he'd been pressed against me.

"Where should we display you?" Nick asked. "For your little show."

He wasn't really asking, moving me with a hand on the back of my neck. Over to one of the stages. A main one. This wasn't the part of the club where only *Catena's* darker patrons could go. It would be everyone. Up until now, the training had been more private. "Master," I said quietly.

"Yes, slave?" The way he said it now had an entirely different meaning, and I sank into him and his strength.

"There's someone I know who frequents this club. His name is Kyle Forsyth. Also a nurse."

I didn't have to explain to him why I told him that. Kyle coming in and seeing me being fucked, teased, and tortured wouldn't be good for anyone, and would cause questions and a scene.

"Thank you," he said quietly and pointed to a spot on the floor. "Sit there and don't move. You may sit casually." He hooked my leather cuffs together in front of me before striding over to some of the staff and speaking to them. Shortly after, they began to move, putting things onto the stage. Two wooden posts, screwing them down. Metal rings on the floor. A *big* dildo attached to the top of one of the posts, and a chain above it. A sybian in between them.

When they asked me, I hadn't specified exactly what I wanted, just gave them an idea. The three of them had lit up with excitement and spoke about it out of earshot, deciding what they wanted to do with me.

Now that we were on the same page, there was something unspeakably hot about it.

It took a while for the stagehands to set everything up, and by the time they were done, people were beginning to arrive and were interested in what was clearly going to be some kind of display. A few even wandered over to me before they saw my collar and backed off.

Clearly, the collar did what my cuffs had not when that man tried to take me off the couch.

If only something so simple would be a deterrent for someone like Delano.

One of my Alphas was never out of sight, though they weren't next to me. I wasn't worried. But I was nervous. Anticipating. Eager. Because there was so much play at stake here. I could play the role of their slave and embrace it because I knew I wasn't, and that was true freedom.

Derek came and sat down, pulling me between his legs. "Ready?"

I didn't answer. He didn't expect one. My role wasn't to speak. My role was to keep my mouth shut and take what they gave me. Which tonight? Was a lot.

"Time to put on a show," Derek said. "Let's go. It will take time to set you up."

Pulling me onto the stage, he pushed me to my knees over the sybian, making sure my clit was *directly* on the vibrator. "Put your toes on the floor," he instructed.

Doing that pushed my weight into my knees and took away any leverage I had. Leverage that was taken away further with the rubber belts he wrapped around my legs, strapping my shin to my thigh and tying me to the floor.

My eyes went wide when I saw the drill. I thought they were done with that?

Nope.

He unlocked my cuffs and pulled one hand behind me. "Don't move." Sebastian's voice was there, his hand holding my arm against the post. The sound of the drill was loud, and when it ceased, I couldn't move my hand. Thick, hard metal trapped it against the wooden post, stretching it backward. And then the other one.

I groaned. This was going to be hell. But I also knew they would be so hard watching that it would be hell for them too, unable to take me the way they wanted.

Finally, the dildo was in front of me.

Sebastian smirked, and I saw the hard edge of the man he played, along with my real Alpha, who still liked the bite of pain. "It's tempting to pierce your nose for this so we can do it more often. But this will have to do."

The chain the stagehands attached to the post had a clip. And Seb pulled my head forward, straight into the dildo. I had to take it into my mouth, just like he planned, before he clipped the chain to my nose.

191

I realized with sudden clarity that I couldn't move back. My entire body was immobilized, mouth wrapped around the dildo, clit pressed against one of the most powerful vibrators in existence.

Fuck, they really outdid themselves.

"Remember," Nick appeared in front of me. "Every time you come without permission adds to your punishment. So don't come unless you ask." Then he smirked. "But you can't exactly ask right now, can you?"

I moaned, and he laughed, the three of them retreating to the chairs in the audience. Between my legs, the sybian sprang to life. I was done for. Whichever of them held the controls to the device pleasuring me wouldn't matter. They liked this part. They *wanted* to see me scream.

This time I had no idea what the punishment was. But I didn't plan on holding myself back very long.

The vibrations sprang to life, and I closed my eyes.

CHAPTER TWENTY-NINE

NICHOLAS

*D*erek held the remote to the vibrator beneath Selena, and the way she stiffened as it turned on, parts of me stiffened too. Our Omega looked fucking stunning, and she was *our* Omega. The fact that she wore our cuffs and collar against her skin was so distracting, I could barely keep my head on straight, and it was a struggle not to smile like the sun was coming out of my ass.

My pack mates felt the same.

Selena pulled against the metal restraints that held her arms, arching her back, but there was no way she was getting out of those. The only thing that would make this better is if there was a dildo on the sybian.

It wasn't dissimilar to the previous denial scene we'd put her through, but this time, it was something she truly wanted.

A crowd was gathering to watch behind us. How long we'd be able to take watching her writhe and come, I wasn't sure, but we would try.

"The shipment is ready." Delano's voice swept under the music, stealing the joy out from underneath me like finding coal in a Christmas stocking. "Would you like it to come here?"

"When would it be delivered?"

"We could have it here tomorrow."

I nodded. "How many?"

"Three, to start. I thought that would be enough to judge."

"Fine. Make it happen."

He stepped closer. "I do have one question."

I looked over at him, adopting Seb's style of strength and letting nothing color my tone. "What?"

"Have you been stringing me along?"

"What the hell is that supposed to mean?" I turned to face him, giving him my full presence.

He looked to the stage, where Selena moaned, and I could scent her floral sweetness from here as she succumbed to Derek's toying and came. "I've made it clear I want her, but the way Sebastian fought my man for her last night and carried her away, it doesn't seem like you're going to follow through."

Ice flowed through my veins. "That was your man?"

He was wise enough not to confirm it.

"Let me make myself clear, Christopher. We never offered her for sale. You have made your interest clear, and we told you a decision would be made if she was for sale after her training was complete. It isn't. And we are under no obligation to sell her to you or anyone else if we don't want to.

"Further," I glared at him. "If this is how you behave with business partners, and attempt to circumvent them by taking things that don't belong to you, we'll have to reconsider our agreement."

His glare was just as strong. "I hoped, given us going into business together, you might consider her a goodwill gift or a bonus."

"We don't give bonuses people haven't earned. You're valuable, Delano, and you know it, but don't overstep. And you know us well enough to know you'll only get one warning. Take something from us we haven't offered or you haven't paid for again, and you're done. You don't want to be on our bad side. Now leave. I'm done seeing you for the night."

The only reaction he showed was a tic in his jaw, but I knew the signs of fury well enough to know he was fucking pissed. I didn't care. He had sent someone to touch my property, and that wouldn't stand. But tomorrow? It was over. Getting my phone out, I did the hardest thing in the world and turned away from Selena long enough to send a text to headquarters.

> Shipment of new merchandise incoming tomorrow. Go for TD?

It had to be enough. Between everything we'd collected and observed, everything the Betas had gone through and gathered, with the added on-hand evidence of stolen Omegas? Delano was going down for a long fucking time.

My phone buzzed.

> Go.

Thank fuck.

This time tomorrow, it would all be over, and we could leave this hell hole behind with Selena and never look back. I sent them back the confirmation code that would have everyone scrambling and getting ready. We were the leads of this operation, but we were also external to it.

We weren't a part of the takedown. Delano still needed to think we were real, at least until we sent him to a prison so dark he never came back out again.

Turning back to the stage and our Omega, I saw Seb approaching her with a sadistic gleam in his eye. This would be good.

CHAPTER THIRTY

SELENA

The floor beneath me was a puddle of slick and cum. Already Derek had made me orgasm twice by toying with the vibrator, and I wasn't resisting. They could punish me all they wanted, but I was going to come.

But when Sebastian stepped onto the stage, I froze. What was he going to do? My sadist Alpha was unpredictable.

He unhooked the chain from my nose and got rid of the big dildo, allowing me to heave in big breaths. Fuck. Saliva ran down my body, and from the way his eyes followed it, I knew he thought it was hot. But I still didn't know what he was going to do.

The vibrator soared upward, and I threw my head back, crying out to the ceiling. He was aiming to make me come again. But I managed not to. For the moment.

"Master," I gasped.

"Slave."

"What's the punishment?"

One raised eyebrow. "The punishment?"

"For coming. What is it?"

"We haven't decided yet." The side of his mouth quirked up into a smirk. "Guess you'll have to be a good girl and do as you're told."

His eyes moved briefly to the left of us, and his face turned stern, and I recognized the coldness of the Master. We were being watched, and now that I understood—now that I could play the game with him—I loved it.

Sebastian undid his belt. "Open your mouth."

My stomach curled with nerves and arousal. I hadn't

197

taken Seb in my mouth yet because he was so fucking big. Not like I thought it would never happen, but my body could barely fit him as it was. There was no chance he made it down my throat.

But I opened my mouth and closed my eyes.

The sound of his belt whipping out of his pants cracked beside me, and the stiff leather came behind my head, pulling me to his cock, stretching me into the predicament even as Derek turned the vibrator up again. I fought the urge to moan. The hardest part of this ruse now wasn't playing with them. It was pretending not to be aroused by the men I was falling in love with.

When I had doubts, it was easy to pretend.

Now I wanted to consume Sebastian like an apple pie.

His cock slipped past my lips, stretching my mouth open and filling me before I'd even taken half of him. "Good girl," he muttered under his breath. The pretending was killing them too, and maybe this wasn't a good idea. If we were being watched, I was about to come, and I loved it.

"Don't you dare," Sebastian said, pulling on the belt. I was stretched in every direction, impossibly immobile. "Don't you dare come, slave."

A shudder of pleasure ran through me, and I held the orgasm back despite my promise not to. "You'll swallow me without any pleasure for yourself. Or didn't you learn your lesson last time?"

The sybian *surged* beneath me, sending my head into the stratosphere. I froze, mouth open, letting Seb fuck me. It was so intense, somehow it was easier to resist. My jaw ached from his cock, and he groaned before pulling back, coming all over my face.

"I changed my mind." The words were a grunt through his orgasm. "You'll wear my cum. Today you don't deserve to swallow it."

198

Suddenly the sybian turned off, and they were extracting me from the position I was in. I hadn't even realized how hard it was on my body until they released an arm and my shoulders groaned in protest.

"You sure, Seb?" Derek joked. "I wanted a chance to fuck her throat like that. I would have let you control the toy."

"He's sure," Nick said.

Something about the way Nick said it made my other Alphas pause, and they moved faster.

Nick clipped my leather cuffs in front of me and walked me to the elevator, Sebastian's cum still dripping down my face and chest.

They left the set-up behind for the staff to break down.

"Let's take a shower," Nick said, pulling me out of the elevator into the apartment and unhooking the leather accessories as we went.

"What's going on?" I asked.

"Not until we're in the shower."

"But—"

"Selena." His voice lowered. "Please."

He held my hand all the way to the shower and stripped before taking me inside. The others were just behind us, and suddenly I was under deliciously hot water and surrounded by Alphas, cum melting off my skin.

"We're good to go," Nick said. "It's happening tomorrow."

"You're serious?" Sebastian asked.

Nick snorted a laugh. "Trust me, this isn't something I would joke about."

"What?"

Seb pulled me into his arms. "Delano, and everything else. We'll be able to take him down tomorrow."

I looked over my shoulder at Nick. "Why did you have to wait until we were in here to tell me?"

"Besides the fact that I like you naked and wet?" He

smirked. "Our apartment doesn't have any bugs, and there are frequency jammers, but we don't take chances about something like this. A shower is loud and obviously immune to most electronic things."

Sebastian tilted my face up to his. "Did I hurt your jaw?"

"I mean, that will take getting used to," I admitted. "But no. You could have left me there and had the others fuck me, too."

"No. Something wasn't right. Delano wasn't there, but his men were. I needed to be more alert than having my cock in your throat, though don't ever doubt it loves to be there."

"That's because I kicked him out for the night," Nick said.

Derek stole me from Seb and pressed me against the tile wall while the others talked. I tried to listen, but it was hard when he was *kissing* me like this. Nothing more than kissing like teenagers, his body roaming down my skin and finding the metal cuffs where they lay against my skin. He traced the collar when he reached my neck again.

Between us, he was as hard as a rock.

"I'm not sure you understand what seeing you in these pieces does to me."

"I'm pretty sure I can feel what it does to you."

"Cheeky Omega."

"You like that," I pointed out.

Derek grinned. "I do. But I still need you to know how much I love it and you. And I will gladly put you in that exact same position again for the chance to fuck your throat like that. If I had my way I'd be in your throat every damn morning."

My memories flashed back to his 'breakfast.' The way he fucked my throat so easily and the sounds he made when he came. I was suddenly perfuming in the middle of the shower.

"Damn, baby," Nick said, leaning against the wall beside me. "I'm pretty sure you smell even better in here and I didn't even know that was possible."

"What are you going to do about it?" I teased.

"Right now?" He turned my head toward him and took my mouth in a searing kiss. "I'm just happy to have you here."

Something in his eyes told me it wasn't the whole truth. "What did I miss?"

"Nothing," he said. "Delano still wants you, and I told him in no uncertain terms that he can't have you and to fuck off. He wasn't pleased about that."

Sebastian joined on my right, and now all three Alphas were crowding me into the wall. "We don't have to do anything more in public, right? He scares me."

"No, princess. We're done with that. Anything we do now will just be you and us." He lifted my wrist to his lips, kissing the slender cuff.

"Good."

Drying me off, Derek wrapped me in a fluffy towel before giving me one of his shirts. "Believe me when I say I wish we could spend the night in the nest fucking you. But it's almost over now. We have a lot to do before the takedown tomorrow."

"Like what?"

"Like things that are boring as fuck," Nick said. "But you can stay with us. Especially since we need to feed you."

"Where will you be?" I asked.

Sebastian swept me off my feet and carried me toward the kitchen. "Our office downstairs, for the most part. But when we're finished, I plan on sleeping in the nest with you."

Words nearly poured from my lips, and I held them back. But my Alpha saw and pinned me with a stare. "What was the thought, little one?"

My whole body flushed pink with embarrassment, and I already knew this was part of the confusion I'd been telling him about. "Can I sit at your feet?"

He stopped in the middle of the hallway and stared at me until he lifted me up higher in his arms and kissed the hell out of me. "You don't have to sit at my feet, Selena. But if that's something you want, and it makes you feel safe, you never have to fucking ask."

CHAPTER THIRTY-ONE

DEREK

Selena's head rested on my shoulder as I cradled her in my lap in our office. The last few hours had been nothing but communication between us and headquarters. Raids would be conducted across the country, all at the same time, or within minutes of each other.

It needed to be as coordinated as possible in order to take down as many pieces of the network as we could. Everything we'd done, and everything the Betas and other undercover agents had gathered, had been translated into a sprawling plan with more arms than a centipede.

We were all glad it was coming to an end, and we didn't have to do much. In fact, it was to our benefit to stay out of the spotlight.

Our Omega had spent some time at our feet, something I would never fucking take for granted, and something we could now allow her to do comfortably and gently. But she was tired after everything she'd been through in the last two weeks—everything we put her through. And when her head began to droop, I picked her up and cradled her as we listened to the plans and communicated anything else that was needed. More than anything, we were live sources of information.

Sebastian was in the middle of cleaning his gun, making sure it was ready for anything, because we would be back up. Three blocks away, the strike team that would hit *Catena* was getting ready in the same way.

Nick watched behind the big screens while I held our girl. Her fingers curled into my shirt, pulling me closer even while sleeping.

"That's all, everyone. Use the chains of command and keep your lines as clear and open as possible."

"Jensen," Nick said. "Stay back?"

"Yeah."

Seb paused in his polishing, and we all waited until there was a heavy sigh from the screen. "In case no one has already told you this, we owe you guys a hell of a lot. And if anyone —*anyone*—tries to give you shit about getting anything you want, even if it's the most ridiculous flamingo colored car, for the rest of your lives, you send them to me."

Nick chuckled. "We appreciate that. You're on with Derek and Seb, and one very sleepy Omega."

I heard a sound of surprise. "Is there a story there?"

"There is, but not for a night before this is finished. Or at least not completely."

"What can I do for you?"

Nick paused, his eyes falling on Selena. "We need some information, but it is incredibly delicate because, as usual, there could be lives at stake. I need your promise that you'll handle this with absolute discretion."

"You have it," Jensen said.

"Have you ever heard of the Underground Omega Syndicate?"

I wished I could see his face, but Selena was still only wearing one of my shirts, and I was done showing her body to anyone she didn't choose to. If I had it my way, we'd be the only three who ever saw it again.

"I've heard of them. Bunch of misguided Omegas trying to do some good and going about it all the wrong way. Usually get themselves and the people they recruit into more trouble than it's worth."

"Sounds familiar," Sebastian said, words dripping with sarcasm and rage.

"They're after the hormones," Nick said. "From Normality—"

"Yeah. I can see why." Jensen didn't even let him finish. "We've been getting reports that Normality is trying to use high doses to force a change in designation. So far though, it hasn't worked. The people just die. It's being written off as some weird overdose, but that's not what it is. What does this have to do with you, though?"

"That's what they're doing?" Selena asked.

Her eyes were bleary, and her face still tucked into my chest, but she was now awake and listening.

"Are the designation changes voluntary?" Nick asked.

Jensen laughed. "No. Not as far as I know."

"Last question," Nick scrubbed his hand over his face, "and I promise I'll clarify. Do we have any way to identify who Normality is using to do these tests?"

"I don't personally, but I'm sure the squad tracking Normality does. As soon as we're done with the network, it's their turn. So they're running on borrowed time, anyway."

Nick nodded. "The Syndicate sent someone to find Normality through us because I'm guessing they don't have any of that information. But the person they sent in was innocent and is being blackmailed. We'd like to give them what they asked for and make sure the correct person gets what's coming to them."

Selena reached up and touched my cheek. I looked down at her, momentarily getting lost in those big green eyes. "I work at Saint Mercy's," she said quietly. "Or at least I did before I was taken. I don't know if they've fired me yet after not showing up to work for a week. The Syndicate said they made an excuse, but I don't know what it would be."

I lifted her higher and kissed her forehead. "Jensen," I raised my voice so he could hear me. "Check the overdose deaths from the last two weeks at Saint Mercy's here in the city. It will be a good place to start. If you can give us a name connected with the deaths, and before that, we'll be grateful."

"I can do that," Jensen said. "I'll be very interested in

hearing whatever story you have. I'm sure you've got a hell of a lot of them."

"Most of them don't bear repeating," Sebastian said. "But thank you."

"The four of you keep your heads down," Jensen said. "This will all be over soon."

Nick ended the call, and I pulled Selena upward and closer, cradling her more thoroughly to my chest. "We're going to find out who it was, *gattina*."

"Thank you." She sighed and snuggled down into me. "I love you."

My heart stuttered. Until now, she hadn't said it, and my guilt still ran deep enough that I didn't believe we deserved it. I met my pack mates' eyes and knew they felt the same.

"Let's go upstairs," I whispered. "You're exhausted, and everything will be over soon."

"Mmmk." She was fading down again, and I couldn't keep the smile off my face.

Standing, we gathered our things, and Sebastian opened the office door for me. We all froze, suddenly on alert. Christopher Delano and his entire group of men stood there with guns trained on us.

CHAPTER THIRTY-TWO

SELENA

*T*he shift in the air brought me fully awake, along with the change in my Alphas' scents.

Not to mention the very distinct sound of guns being cocked. I didn't dare look toward the door, but I looked up at Derek, and he was pale. His throat worked as he swallowed. "Delano."

"I told you I didn't want to see you until the shipment arrived," Nick said.

"And I decided I wasn't going to take orders from you," Delano said. "Not after what I found out."

The sound made me look. Stumbling and shuffling, one of his men brought someone forward and tossed him at our feet. He was so bloodied and bruised he was barely recognizable, and where he fell, he didn't move.

"Steve," Sebastian said. "Can you hear me?"

Steve. The man who had come into the dining room and told them about the shipment. He must have been in on everything. And told Delano. I cringed away from the sight. With how he looked, I didn't blame him for telling them everything.

I broke after two minutes of torture. That would have taken hours.

Sebastian didn't get a response.

"I should have listened to my gut when the three of you popped up out of nowhere," Delano said. "But everything checked out. Everyone talked about how good you were, and none of your clients had anything bad to say about your business practices. However, I'm sure you know by now you can't live long in this business without your instincts, and mine have been screaming about you ever since that bitch showed up."

Derek's hands tightened on me, but he said nothing. There wasn't anything to say, and right now they had the upper hand. What could we do?

In the corner of my eye, Delano shook his head. "I do have to hand it to you. You played your roles well. And if you hadn't been so fucking protective of some Omega cunt, you would have gotten away with it. Too many things didn't add up, especially when you told me to fuck off. So I decided to ask some questions. And if you think my network will go down so easily, you don't know me well."

"I think we know you just fine," Nick said.

"If you know me so well, you know I don't leave anyone alive."

A gunshot rang out, and I yelped, curling into Derek. The air was entirely still, and when I peeked out from my hiding place, Delano's gun pointed at where Steve had lain. He wasn't alive anymore. And part of me wondered if that was for the best, given the condition he was in. But the nurse in me grieved.

"Put her down," Delano said.

"No."

Another shot rang out, and Derek and I went down to the floor together. He grunted in pain, and I saw blood leaking from his shoulder. "Derek."

"I'm all right," he said quietly.

"Stand up, bitch."

Derek tried to stop me, but he couldn't with the bullet wound. I scrambled to my feet, incredibly conscious of the fact that I was only wearing Derek's shirt and their cuffs.

"Come over here."

Sebastian growled, the sound ripping through the air like a living thing. "I already told your man once. If you touch her, I will fucking kill you. That goes for you, and anyone who works for you."

The smug smile on Delano's face made my skin crawl. "Oh, I'm going to do a lot more than touch her. And the fact that you want her so fucking much is going to make this so much sweeter."

Nick lunged for me, and all the guns came up. He wrapped himself around me protectively, but I recognized he wasn't truly holding me.

"Don't think I won't kill her here," Delano said. "Much as I want to play with her, watching you suffer would be just as fun. Take your hands off her."

Looking down at me, Nick dropped his hand to my arm, sliding it down to the inside of my wrist. He pressed his thumb intentionally several times before stepping back, his eyes full of anguish.

What—

The tracker.

Nick was telling me they could find me. That they weren't just letting Delano take me. And I already knew if there was any way for them to win this fight, they would. But anything they did would only end up with all four of us dead.

It wasn't that they weren't fighting for me. It was that they needed to wait until they could win. I already knew they would fight for me. *Had* been fighting for me even when I hadn't known it.

I love you.

He mouthed the words.

A retching sound came from behind me. "Take her before I have to see more of this disgusting sentimentality."

Hands closed down on my arms, pulling me roughly backwards. I looked at each of them, memorizing their faces and the looks they gave me now. Just because they could find me didn't mean this wouldn't be the last time I would see them.

"It was a good try," Delano said to them. "Best of luck to the next group that gives it a go."

Some of the men stayed behind to hold my Alphas at gunpoint, and they dragged me through the empty club and down the stairs toward the outside world. I hadn't been outside in over two weeks, and it was terrifying. But I wasn't going to show these assholes any weakness.

We entered the lobby, and Delano lifted a walkie-talkie to his mouth. "Kill them."

"*No.*"

Gunshots rang out through the radio, and I fought them. I needed to get back to my Alphas. But there wasn't anything I could do. There were too many of them, and I wasn't strong enough to fight. Something slammed into my head, and there was only darkness.

CHAPTER THIRTY-THREE

SEBASTIAN

They dragged Selena out of sight, and I memorized the faces of the men who were touching her.

Because they were going to die.

Christopher Delano was going to die.

My mind sank into the deep place beyond panic and beyond fear. Panic led to mistakes, and we couldn't make any mistakes. Our Omega's life was at stake.

The men Delano left with us, we could take, but we needed to wait until they were distracted enough to do so. Christopher didn't leave anyone alive, so they were here to kill us. That was good, because it gave us the freedom to kill without mercy.

One of them had my gun, where they took it after finding us here. I grit my teeth. Had we let this happen? Should we have noticed Steve was missing? How long did it take them to torture everything out of him?

Derek still crouched on the floor, putting pressure on his shoulder. Thankfully, it looked like a place that would heal and hadn't hit anything. He was lucky, because I doubted Delano was that good a shot.

A radio crackled. "Kill them."

The three of us moved. I slammed into the nearest man and shoved the gun toward the ceiling as he fired, yanking the gun from him and striking him across the face before shooting him in the head.

And then the next one.

Five men, and we were faster. There were now six dead bodies on the floor.

"Derek?"

"I'm fine," he grunted.

Nick was already at the desk, calling. "Jensen."

"What?"

"Go. It has to be now. Everything is a go."

"*What?*"

Nick shook his head. "They took Steve and tortured him. Delano knows everything and is on the run. We don't know who he's told, but if you want any shot of this happening, send people in *right the fuck now*. The *Catena* team isn't needed here. Send them elsewhere."

Jensen swore and started shouting orders. I grabbed the first aid kit and bandaged Derek's wound while Nick typed furiously. I already knew what he was doing, and I could barely make myself stand still.

Delano wasn't stupid, and if he knew everything about us, he knew that we were the best. The men he left were disposable. He knew we would likely come out of this alive, which meant he waited until he was almost clear of the building to give the order.

Selena was already gone.

The tracker we put in her was going to save her life if we could make it in time. And the only thing keeping me from losing my absolute shit was the fact that Delano wouldn't do anything to her until he got where he was going. The bastard liked to take his time, and that didn't mean taking her in whatever vehicle he shoved her into.

"It's live," Nick said.

"Direction?"

"East."

Derek groaned as I pushed against the wound. "Okay, just wrap me up."

Jensen's voice came through. "Underway. Where's Delano?"

"On the run. With our Omega," Nick growled. "But we

know where he's going. We've got a tracker on her. Forwarding the signal to you now."

"You need support?"

"Yes," I said. "But we're not waiting. Send people to follow, but we're going to be en route. Don't tell us to take him alive."

He laughed, low and vicious. "Didn't even cross my mind."

"Jensen, we have six bodies here. Tell whoever you send that if anything happens to our Omega in the course of her rescue, we won't be held responsible for what we do. She's our scent match."

"Fuck," the man swore. "Do you have enough in case we can't get there?"

"It'll have to be," I said.

"Keep me posted."

Nick ended the call, and we moved as one, going to the elevator and up.

"You going to be okay?" I asked Derek. The shot was through and through, but it still hurt like a bitch.

He glared at me. "I'm fine. I'd take more if it meant she's safe."

I knew the feeling.

Nick tapped on his phone, forwarding the signal from the tracker to ours. "Fuck, I'm glad we're suspicious bastards," he said.

Putting the tracker in had worked to our advantage. We did it because we thought she might be a spy, but this? Maybe deep down we knew we'd need to protect her like this.

Derek entered the code on the door we never opened. Guns, vests, explosives. Enough firepower for a small army. There was no telling what we would face when we found her, and if we would survive the attempt. This was why we hadn't bonded her, because if one of us died, the pain of that would destroy her further, and we couldn't do it.

But even if we all died trying to get her back, we sure as fuck were going to try, and we weren't going to stop fighting until our last breath.

We all strapped on vests and took more guns than were strictly reasonable. "Ready," I said.

"Let's go."

There weren't any words needed.

We took the elevator straight down to the garage and got into the fastest car we owned, Nick already loading up the signal from the tracker into the GPS.

It was moving East, faster than I thought possible. But it didn't matter. No matter how far he took her, we would be there.

We were going to get our Omega.

CHAPTER THIRTY-FOUR

SELENA

*T*he position I was in was familiar. Strapped down, and unable to move. I knew before I even opened my eyes that's what had happened. It felt like I was in some kind of chair—maybe like a dentist's chair.

I always hated going to the dentist.

Where was I? How long had I been asleep?

Pain scraped through me as something was shoved beneath the cuff on my ankle. It was so sudden, I couldn't stop my sound of anger and surprise, my eyes flying open to find Delano with bolt cutters.

He heaved down, cutting through the delicate metal. "So glad you could join me."

"What are you doing?"

"That's a stupid question and you know it."

He was cutting off my cuffs. The permanent markers of my commitment to my Alphas. "Why?"

"Because I want to remind them that you don't belong to them anymore. Say hello." Delano nodded behind him to a camera set up on a tripod with a red light, telling me it was a recording.

I was naked, of course. He'd already seen me this way multiple times, but it meant something different now, and I tried to guide my mind away from the terror brewing like a storm.

"I thought you killed them," I said, swallowing. There had been gunshots through the radio.

"I hope I did," he admitted, coming around the chair and shoving the bolt cutters beneath the cuff on my other ankle. It was pure agony until he cut it off. "But those three Alphas are good at what they do, even if they were stupid enough to let a bitch like you get in the way of their goal. So just in case they survived—and there's a good chance, considering none of my men have checked in—I decided to record our time together so they can enjoy it as well."

I braced myself as he approached my wrist and showed no mercy while he cut off my cuffs. The tinkling metal as they fell hurt my heart. I wanted to wear them forever, and I told them I wasn't planning on taking them off. But I wasn't going to cry in front of this man.

He would make me scream, I was sure. But I wouldn't show him how afraid I was or how the sound of their cuffs broke me.

Delano grabbed my hair and wrenched my head to the side. I cried out as the bolt cutters shove beneath my collar, strangling me. Fear went through me like lightning, and I wondered how I ever could have thought my Alphas were evil. Because every moment they were with me and every punishment they gave was tender in comparison to this, and he hadn't even started.

"Arrogant bastards," he muttered. "Cuffs that don't open? They thought they'd get to keep you forever, I guess."

I said nothing.

A metal clatter drew my eyes, and my breath froze in my chest. The long tray of implements I hadn't seen—

Oh my god.

"What should we start with?" He asked. "Should I warm you up or dive straight into the good stuff?"

My whole body shook. "What are you going to do to me?"

The man smirked. He *smirked*. "Normally I'd have cut out your tongue by now for asking so many questions, but since we're playing for the camera..." There was a knife in his hand and he dragged the tip of it down my arm. "I'm going to find the kind of pain you respond to most," he said. "And by pain, I don't mean the pansy ass beating Sebastian gave you. I mean *pain*. Whether it's burning you or cutting you open, which-ever one makes you scream the most? That's the one I'll use.

"And then I'll take you. Fuck you and make you bleed until your throat is raw with screaming, and there's nothing left of you."

I blinked at him. "You really are a monster."

"I would have thought you knew that by now," he shrugged. "I don't apologize for it. There's nothing quite like making an Omega scream in agony while knotted in her cunt. It makes your body squeeze down like a vise." He groaned and grabbed his dick through his pants. "You can't even help it, and it's the best fucking thing in the world."

Stripping his shirt over his head, he tossed it aside before doing the same to his pants and underwear. He was already hard. "I want you to see what's coming for you," he said. "But first, I think I'll try a few things."

Delano walked out of sight, and I fought against the restraints. The rubber straps holding me down were so tight they nearly cut into my skin. There was no way to move anything except for wiggling my fingers and toes and turning my head. No way out.

Please find me.

If they were alive, they were coming. The tracker in my arm was there for a reason. I hated it when they put it in me and now I was so fucking grateful.

A low hiss, and I had no warning. Blazing, fiery pain against my left arm. I screamed, the stench of burning flesh singing the air and the sizzle of my own body burning. Delano had a red-hot poker held against my skin, searing, ravaging. Already my throat felt scratched.

I sagged when he pulled the poker away. "That was very good. Promising. I've never had anyone take to burning before. That could be fun."

Heaving in breath, I tried to keep myself conscious. The pain…

Don't focus on it.

Sharp biting on my other shoulder, causing me to whimper. Delano drawing lines down my skin with a scalpel and gradually getting deeper. It hurt so fucking much. Not as much as being burned, but I—

A scream ripped out of me as he stabbed the blade straight into my skin, and he laughed. "There we go. I wonder what will happen if I do that in the burn."

"No," I moaned. "Please."

"Beg," he said. "I always like it when you beg, knowing nothing you ever say will make me change my mind."

His hand pulled back, and I flinched, ready for the pain to take me. A gunshot rang out, Delano suddenly screaming, Sebastian standing in the doorway to this room with the gun pointed.

Blood poured from the wound now in his hand.

Tears poured down my face. They were here. They found me.

"You *fuckers*," Delano swore. "How the fuck did you find this place?"

Nick was by my side in a second as Sebastian backed Delano up against the wall, gun pointed straight at his chest. Derek helped get my feet free. "Be careful of her arms," he said.

Seb just looked at Delano. "Sorry to disappoint. I won't be answering any of your questions. You, however, are going to have some fun. Well, as fun as what you were about to do to my Omega."

Delano stared at me as Nick carried me out of the room and up the stairs. A whole phalanx of people were here, cleaning things up. There were dead bodies, and I didn't know how they had done all this without us hearing.

At the ambulance, Nick put me down and kissed me

soundly. "Selena, will you be all right if Derek and I go help Seb? We'll be right back, sweetheart. Promise."

I nodded. "Okay."

My whole head floated, and I wasn't sure any of this was real, anyway. The paramedics wrapped a blanket around my chest while they worked on my arms, and I watched my Alphas retreat to deal with the man who'd put us through hell.

_____

CHAPTER THIRTY-FIVE

NICHOLAS

Seb still had him at gunpoint. Good. Though Delano was looking carefully around to see if there was anything he could do. There wasn't.

"Glad you're both here," he said. "Get him over to the chair."

Derek and I obliged. The men who'd dragged Selena away from us were already dead, and Delano would be the same. No one was going to say shit about what we were about to do. Was it right?

Probably not.

Did the fucker deserve a painful death for everything he'd done?

Yes.

Of all the bad things we'd done to save Omegas and take this fucker down, this was one I would never be sorry for.

Delano bolted, but I'd expected it. Throwing out my arm, I clotheslined him in the throat and he went down. "I don't think so. I'm glad you tried, though. It wouldn't be sporting if you didn't. But you're surrounded, your men are dead, and in spite of everything, you still thought you were beyond catching."

This place was in the middle of fucking nowhere, and admittedly, if we hadn't had the tracker in Selena's arm, we never would have found her. She would have died in this basement, and none of us would have ever been the same.

We were only a few hours outside the city.

Derek and I hauled him to the chair where he had our Omega tied down, and held him there, securing the straps.

Seb holstered the gun as we strapped him down. "Have anything to say for yourself?"

Delano seemed resigned to it. "No."

"Too bad."

I walked over to the camera and turned it off. We didn't need a record of this. "He burned her," I said. "And cut her, from the looks of it."

On the floor, there was a poker still glowing, and it sat next to the remnants of our Omega's cuffs. I spotted the bolt cutters on the table, and fury surged through me. Grabbing them, I handed them to Sebastian.

We wouldn't make Sebastian do everything, but there were some things he was better at.

"Everything that happens here is what you have coming, Delano. And frankly, you need a hell of a lot more than we can give you." We found gloves and put them on.

Sebastian put the bolt cutters between his legs, and we got started with a punishment that was a long time coming.

When he finally stopped moving, we all let out a breath. We hadn't taken as long as we could have drawing out Delano's death. But there were other, more important things, like going back to our Omega and making sure she was okay.

The three of us looked like we'd come out of a horror movie with the blood that was on us. I didn't know what it said about me that I didn't feel remotely bad about the damage we'd inflicted on him, but I didn't. I knew exactly what he'd done to countless women over the years, and what we gave him was nothing in comparison.

I retrieved the memory card from the camera before we left the basement. Things were far calmer than when we left, the bodies gone and our soldiers milling around. To my surprise, Jensen waited for us.

"Am I going to like what I find down there?"

"I don't imagine so." I gave him the memory card. "Selena is on there, and we found her naked. I don't doubt what he said on here is incriminating, but if anyone other than who is necessary sees it?"

He held up a hand. "I got it. Thank you. We weren't able to get everyone we planned, but it was enough."

"It's done?" Seb asked. He sounded exhausted. We all were.

"It's done," he said. "You guys are free. We'll need some debriefs from you, and testimony, when the time comes. But as far as I'm concerned, y'all are free to go."

I didn't even know how to react to that. After three years… it was hard to believe. Nothing was going to sink in until we'd been out of the club for a while. "We'll need a place to stay until we get on our feet."

Jensen held out a hand and shook mine before giving a card to each of us. "This is Roger Parker's number. Part of his job description is to give you whatever you need. Let him know, and he'll make it happen. Oh, and while you were down there… doing whatever, some of the information you asked for came through."

All three of us perked up. "Tell us."

"For a while, all the overdose deaths—especially the ones marked as hormone overdose—were connected to a Selena Martin."

I growled, and Jensen smirked. "Yeah, I thought that might be the reaction when I saw her staff picture and recognized your girl. She's asleep, by the way. My guys did some more digging. The reason they were connected to her was because a keycard registered to her accessed the medication storage at the right times. But it was a clone."

"A clone?" Derek asked. "What do you mean?"

"Meaning, it would register in the system as Selena's name, but it wasn't her actual staff card. The difference in the system was so small there would be no reason for the hospital to notice. But for the last two weeks, there's been another name. Kyle Forsyth."

"Selena mentioned he's her friend," I said.

Jensen nodded back toward there were now some computers set up. "I thought you'd want to see this. Because the first card was a clone, we checked this one too. Also a clone. Kyle's card was copied. Nothing truly suspicious popped up in these deaths, so they weren't investigated. But because the hormones are controlled substances—"

"There are security cameras," Sebastian finished for him.

"Indeed there are." Jensen tapped a few buttons and pulled up security footage of someone who was very much *not* Selena coming out of a door in the hospital. "This person, whose name is Gloria Parker, is connected with every swipe of the cloned cards. We dug into her financials, and she's being paid by one of the shell corporations Normality uses. This is her."

I grit my teeth. "Thank you, Jensen."

"They're probably going to make a move on Normality shortly, now that this is over."

Seb huffed a laugh. "We don't give a shit. As long as we have proof of this to get the Syndicate off Selena's back."

"You can have whatever you need."

Derek looked around. "Where is she?"

He nodded behind him to a door that was shut. "They treated her, and she's sleeping. One of the EMTs is with her."

"Thank you, Jensen."

"No," he said. "Thank you."

He handed us some wipes to clean off the blood, and we went to see our girl.

CHAPTER THIRTY-SIX

SELENA

The EMT thought I was sleeping. And I had a little. But now I was just resting with my eyes closed. I didn't want to talk to anyone but my Alphas, and they were dealing with Delano. However long it took, I didn't care.

My arms ached, but the bandages and painkillers they gave me were helping.

It could have been so much worse.

The door opened, and I kept my eyes closed. They gave me some loose scrubs that had been in the ambulance, but more than anything, I wanted my own clothes. Or some of my Alphas clothes. I just didn't want to be here.

"She's sleeping?" Derek asked.

"Yes," the EMT said. "Has been for a while."

I opened my eyes and found my Alphas there, all standing and looking at me. They had blood on them, and it looked like they tried to scrub off. "I'm not sleeping."

My voice sounded strange. A bit spacey. Probably because of the pain meds.

The EMT looked over at me, and then at my Alphas. "I'll give you guys some time." He slipped out of the door, and they came over to me. The tall ambulatory stretcher I was on wasn't exactly comfortable, but it was better than being in the actual ambulance.

Seb leaned down and buried his face in my hair. "Selena. Fuck, we shouldn't have spent so much time with him."

"Is he dead?"

"Very," Nick said.

I smiled in spite of myself. "Good."

Derek ran a hand gently over my arm where the bandage was. "We weren't fast enough."

"You saved me," I said. "He was going to kill me, and you saved me. I'll heal from this. How's your shoulder?"

"It will heal."

Sebastian ran a hand over my hair. "Will it hurt too much if I hold you, princess?"

"No." I wanted them to hold me.

He scooped me up off the gurney and pulled me close, taking me over to one of the chairs. Carefully, he made sure not to press too hard on the bandages. "I'm so sorry," he whispered. "He never should have been able to touch you."

"He's dead. He can't touch me anymore." Later the horror of it all would probably hit me, but at the moment I was content to be here, surrounded by the warm, sweet scent of baking apples, with traces of the others' peppermint and mountain air.

"We're going to go back to the city," Derek said. "And we're going to get the phone for the Syndicate. We can clear you."

My head snapped up and made me dizzy. "Really?"

"Yeah, baby," Nick said. "Someone cloned your keycard and made it look like you were the one taking the drugs from storage. After you were taken, they cloned the card of your friend Kyle."

"No," I said, my stomach dropping. Because I now had a memory that made sense, and it couldn't be true. "It's Gloria?"

Seb looked at me. "How did you know that?"

I shook my head, trying to pull myself upright, and he helped me, settling me on his lap so he could still hold me and also see the others. "The night I was taken, when I got home, Gloria's keycard was in my bag. She'd thrown her wallet in my purse at the bar and I thought it fell out. I remember thinking I would make her come get it, but I didn't think anything of it. But if it was the copy of my card... was that how they found me?"

My Alpha's arms tightened around me, and both Derek and Nick's eyes were filled with rage. "Probably," Derek said. "If she put the card in your bag, knowing the Syndicate might trace it? Having looked and seen your names in the logs?" He shook his head. "I don't know why they wouldn't just check the security footage like we did."

"Oh, they can't do that," I said. "To check the footage like that would require a court order. Because of potential patient information. Not that the Syndicate really cares about what's legal. But I'm guessing it's not as easy as just hacking in."

A flicker of a smile appeared on Derek's face. "No. Not quite that easy. Or simple. But it seems like she set you up."

Sadness welled in my chest. "She's my friend. Or I thought she was my friend. Could she really have done this?"

"She did do it, princess." Seb brushed my hair off my shoulder and brushed a kiss where my neck met my shoulder. "The company that harvests the hormones is paying her."

"Oh."

I pressed a hand to my chest. Somehow, that hurt more than anything else. I didn't know if Gloria had known what the Syndicate would do to me, but we'd been friends for years. Even if she hadn't known, her throwing me under the bus and giving me to them felt like a stab in the back.

"But once you give them the information, you're free, sweetheart," Nick said. "And we'll make sure your sister is okay."

"She's sick, right?" Sebastian asked. "What's wrong with her?"

I shook my head. "We don't know. We've never known. Still trying to figure that out, but she's nearly always in pain and can barely eat. It's some kind of auto-immune disease, and we've found enough treatments that work to keep her alive. But being blacklisted from all medical facilities would kill her."

"We're going to help her," he said. "Promise."

Sebastian kissed my neck again, right where the collar should have been. "He cut them off," I whispered. "I didn't want them gone."

Derek came over and crouched in front of me. "If you want them again, *gattina*, we'll make you another set. You're still ours, no matter the jewelry."

It hit me then. This was over. Really over. They were done. "You're free?"

Nick smiled. "Yeah. They're going to get us a hotel for now, but we'll figure out where we want to go. But personally, I think we need a few days just for the four of us. Lots of sleep. Lots of sex. Talking about the rules. And more, if you want to go to work again. Everything."

"That sounds perfect," I said.

Sebastian set my feet on the floor. "They know where to find us," he said. "Ready to go home?"

We didn't have a home yet, and he knew that, but it wasn't the point. The four of us were home. Against all odds, and through impossible circumstances. We were home.

"I'm ready." I reached out and caught Derek by the arm, and Nick came to me too. Pulling them in, they surrounded me on every side. "I love you. Before we leave, I just need you to know it."

All three of them began to purr, and we didn't leave the room right away, because kissing them was more important than anything else, and now?

We had all the time in the world.

CHAPTER THIRTY-SEVEN

DEREK

I took the new box of cuffs from the delivery man. So far Jensen was correct—they were bending over backwards to give us everything we wanted. And that included expedited creation of things which were destroyed, like our previous order for Selena's cuffs and collar.

They didn't ask questions either, which was just fine with me.

Retreating into our hotel suite, I put the cuffs and collar away. Today wasn't about them. We would get to that. Today was about Selena getting her life back. She was sitting between Seb and Nick, looking down at the phone which had taken everything from her.

We checked and triple checked the information and helped her type it out. Now we just had to hit send.

She was leaning with her hands on her knees, a hand over her mouth. "What if they decide it's not enough? That I'm not done?"

Nick took her hand and kissed the back of it. "Then we'll deal with it. And they won't like being on that end of things."

My Omega let out a shaky breath. "Okay."

She pressed the button and sagged back onto the couch. There was still a week on her clock for the Syndicate, so in theory, there shouldn't be any problems.

Seb purred, following her back on the couch. "Good girl. You're going to be okay, princess."

"Especially after tomorrow," I said.

"If I don't throw up in the middle of that."

Tomorrow we were going to confront her friend. And have her arrested for murder. Not exactly an easy thing to do, but Selena needed it. Just like she needed to submit more deeply than she would ever admit.

"So," I said, sitting down across from her. "Now that you're done and need a distraction, you want to talk about rules?"

Her eyes met mine with a sudden gleam. "All right."

"And remember that these can change. Because we're all agreeing to them. And we already know the first one. No calling you a slave."

"Correct," she said. "And the next one is that I don't want to do this all the time."

"In the bedroom," Nick said. "Always. I don't think you're going to talk us out of that one, sweetheart."

"I don't want to talk you out of it." Her breath went short, and we all scented her arousal. "We could do agreed upon times outside the bedroom. Like a weekend occasionally."

I chuckled. "No arguments from me."

She pulled her knees up to her chest. "I might want to sit at your feet sometimes. As weird as it is."

"It's not weird," Seb said and kissed her cheek. "It helps you. Don't question it."

"Okay."

"Now." I couldn't stop my smile. "For some real and actual rules."

Selena raised an eyebrow. "What did you have in mind?"

"Wherever we move, you'll have a bedroom, and so will we. But when you're in one of our beds, I want you chained to it for the night."

Her eyes went wide, and her scent strengthened again. "Why?"

"Why not?"

"I—" She thought about it. Our little Omega struggled with what things *should* be. It took her time to realize this was just the four of us, and we could do whatever we wanted. "We can try that."

"Good."

Looking between the three of us, her shoulders strengthened. She was beginning to enjoy this. "I want an orgasm every day."

"With occasional exceptions for long term games of denial, I agree," Nick said. "But we'll discuss those."

Selena nodded, and Seb grinned. "Before you leave bed in the morning, your mouth touches our cocks. Whoever's bed you're in. Not necessarily a full blow job or throat fucking, but at least one touch."

I watched her hands tighten where she held her knees. She was keeping herself still on purpose, trying not to let us know how much she liked that idea. But after weeks of watching her every reaction and learning her scent, she wasn't able to.

"All right," she whispered. "I can do that."

"You'll fucking enjoy it, princess," Sebastian said.

Nick stood and crossed to the kitchen of the massive suite and poured himself a glass of water. "You sleep naked. I want to see and touch what belongs to me."

"Not like the clothes would last long anyway," I muttered, and we all laughed.

"We'll choose safe words," I said. "Several different ones. Because for the three of us, 'in the bedroom' means anything sexual. And you're more than aware that we can make anything sexual. So we'll need some signals in case you're not okay with it."

"Yeah, that's good."

I stretched, leaning back on the couch. "This one isn't sexual, but it is necessary. We never go to bed angry. What we're doing takes communication, even when it's not full time. We either talk it out, scream it out, or fuck it out, but letting hurt fester overnight is a recipe for disaster."

"I definitely agree with that one."

"That's all I can think of. For now," Seb said. "I'm sure I'll have more ideas."

The phone chimed on the table, and all of us looked at it. Selena whined, and Seb picked her up to sit her between his knees. "It's okay, princess. No matter what happens, we've got you."

She picked up the phone and clicked it. "Hello, Selena Martin. You have fulfilled the terms of your assignment and have earned your freedom. Please respond with your current location so you can be retrieved. Good," her body melted back into Seb. "They don't know I told you. And I don't want to be retrieved."

"Then tell them that," I said. "Tell them retrieval isn't necessary. And add on that you expect to never fucking hear from them again."

Slowly, she typed out the message and tossed the phone back onto the table. "I'm glad that's over."

"Me too. Just one more thing to do," I said. "And then it's *all* over."

"I don't even want to think about that," Selena whispered.

"Well," Nick shrugged his shirt over his head. "We happened to have a very big bedroom here, so I think we can take care of any thoughts you have. We'll fuck them out of you."

Sebastian had her up and into the master bedroom in a second, and I followed Selena's laughter. I would never get tired of that sound, and as much as the Syndicate could go fuck itself, I supposed I should be grateful. Without her, we never would have found her.

I walked into the bedroom to find our Omega already pinned down to the bed and being stripped naked. We weren't letting her out of here until we absolutely had to.

CHAPTER THIRTY-EIGHT

SELENA

Derek held my hand as we walked into the emergency room. It felt so alien that I wasn't sure what to do with myself. Did I want to come back here? I hadn't decided yet. My Alphas told me I didn't have to work anymore if I didn't want to, but I wasn't sure I was ready for that either.

"Selena?" A voice gasped.

Kyle came rushing over and drew me into a hug. "Holy shit, it's good to see you. How was Africa?"

"Africa?" I looked at him. "That's what they told you?"

His face was instantly wary. "Yeah. An email let us know that you'd gotten accepted to an emergency residency in Africa and had to leave right away after your heat. They didn't say how long you'd be gone or anything, but whatever it said, they made sure to hold your job."

"That is… very much not what happened," I said quietly. "I'll tell you everything, but I can't tell you right now."

Kyle's eyes shot to Derek and my other two Alphas behind me. "Yeah, I think you have some things to tell me."

"I do," I smiled. "This part I can. This is Derek. The two behind me are Sebastian and Nick. We're scent matched."

"Holy shit." His smile was huge. "Congratulations."

Derek squeezed my hand, and I nodded. We needed to move quickly. The police were outside and making their way through the other entrance of the hospital, and we didn't want Gloria to find out before we confronted her. "Where's Gloria?"

"She's with a patient in room seven."

"Thanks."

"What—"

I touched him on the arm. "Like I said. I'll tell you everything. Just hold tight for now."

Kyle blinked. "Okay."

Derek allowed me to lead him deeper into the ER, and people waved to me, not at all bothered that I was here and back. It was almost like I never left. If they thought I went on some kind of travel nursing adventure, it made sense. It had happened before.

"Selena," a deep voice. "It's good to see you back."

I turned and found Dr. Avila—the very same Alpha both Gloria and Kyle had teased me about. And now that I had my match… his voice didn't hit me the same way. It was rich and deep and good enough for the fantasies I'd been trying to hide, but it was nothing compared with the reality of *my* Alphas.

"Thank you," I said. "I don't know for how long, but it's good to see everyone."

I didn't give him a chance to trap me in conversation. This thing needed to be over.

We stood outside the room where Gloria was and waited.

"You okay?" Derek asked.

"No. But I have to be."

The door opened and Gloria came out, stopping short when she almost ran into us. "Oh, sorry. Excuse—" Words died on her lips and she went pale. "Selena."

"Hi, Gloria. Surprised to see me?"

"Of course I am. I thought you were in Africa."

I looked at the woman who I thought was my friend. Did I ever really know her? Apparently not. She'd killed at least eight people trying to force them to be Omegas against their will. She wasn't any better than Delano or the people who had been taken down.

"Did you think that? Or did you know I'd been taken by

the people you sold me out to in order to save your own skin?"

"What are you talking about?" Anger shone on her face. "Sell you out? Selena, how long have we been friends?"

"Apparently not long enough to keep you from throwing me to the dogs." I held up the keycard she'd thrown in my purse. My apartment was exactly the way I left it three weeks ago, and we'd retrieved the card before coming here. Later, I would move my things to whatever house the four of us moved to. "Recognize this?"

"What the hell? Where did you get that? I had to get mine replaced."

I sighed, suddenly exhausted and not wanting to play this game. "We know, Gloria. You really didn't think you'd get caught? You're on fucking camera when this card and the one you're using to impersonate Kyle were used."

"No one can access that footage," she snapped and went rigid, realizing she just incriminated herself.

Derek chuckled. "I assure you, it can be accessed."

She only hesitated a second before turning to run, but it was too late. Straight into the arms of the officers who were waiting. "I don't know what you people are *talking about*," she shouted. "I didn't do anything wrong."

The officer spoke her rights as he walked her through the ER toward the outside, everyone gaping as they went. Kyle looked at me, stunned. "What the fuck?"

"I know, and I'm sorry. Can you do lunch soon?"

He shook his head. "Girl, for this? I'm free any time. Call me and tell me when. Preferably as soon as fucking possible."

"I will. I really need to go see Anna right now, but I'll call you. Tomorrow, maybe the day after, okay?"

"Okay." He pulled me into a hug. "It's really good to see you, and based on that... I'm glad you're safe."

"I'm very safe now." I glanced back at my Alphas. "You're not going to believe half of it."

Someone called his name across the ER, and he needed to go, but he gave me a long, disbelieving look. Frankly, everything that happened? I wasn't sure he *would* believe me.

"Do we have to do anything for her?" I asked.

"Not at the moment," Nick said, pulling me to him. "Once she's charged, maybe. But that's later."

I wanted to stay in his arms, but I forced myself to step away and make my way through the hospital to the wing where my sister was a near-permanent resident.

Saint Mercy's was one of the best hospitals in the country for mysterious illnesses like hers. My Alphas said she could move in with us, and she could be taken care of wherever, but I wanted it to be her choice. Almost like someone who needed to move schools, it was the same. She had friends here and trusted her doctors. I wasn't going to pull her away from all those things for purely selfish reasons. I of all people understood the comfort of familiarity.

Her door was open, and the nurse at the station, Jessica, waved to me. "I need to go in first," I said.

"We're here if you need us," Sebastian said. "Love you."

"I love you."

My sister slept. She looked a lot like me when I was younger. Dark hair, tan skin, though hers was paler because of her illness. I glanced at her vitals. She was doing fine.

I smoothed her hair back from her face, and she stirred, sighing. "I know, I know, I need to work on actually sleeping at night," she mumbled.

"Yes, you do."

Her eyes flew open. "Sel? Oh my god, what are you doing here? They told me you got some kind of amazing internship or some shit and couldn't even say goodbye."

My eyes filled with tears, and I leaned down to kiss her on the forehead. "That didn't happen, but I'm here now, and I'll tell you everything. A lot of things are going to change."

"In a bad way?"

"No," I laughed. "In a very, very good way. At least I hope so. And the first thing I have to do is introduce you to some people."

Anna raised an eyebrow. "People?"

"Alphas."

She gasped. "Oh my god."

I squeezed her hand. "I hope you have time for a long story, little sis, because it's going to take a while."

"Where exactly am I going to go?"

We laughed together, and god it felt good. "I'll be right back, okay?"

"Okay." Her eyes sparkled, and I went to get my Alphas, happy that the worst of everything was finally, finally behind us.

EPILOGUE

SELENA

ONE WEEK LATER

"This is…" I turned around and looked at the space which had been empty two days ago. "How are you doing this?"

Nick leaned against the door to my new nest, smirking. "When we told you we hammered out an ironclad contract for *everything* in our lives? We meant it. Negotiating that thing took weeks, but we knew if we were going to give up years of our lives, it was going to be worth it. The government will probably curse our names for how much we mean to take advantage of it. But then again, we did help them take down the biggest trafficking network in the world and saved countless Omega lives. So there is that."

"There is that," I said in wonder.

The nest reminded me a little of the one we spent my heat in, but barely. The colors alone were enough to make my mouth drop. Rich emeralds with touches of gold, this one was about a hundred times more opulent than the one in their apartment.

"It's so beautiful," I said, the awe in my voice clear.

Derek stepped into the room. "Not nearly as beautiful as you."

My whole body flushed.

The house we now stood in was on the outskirts of the city, with a huge amount of land for us. It was close enough I could still work at the hospital if I wanted to, but I hadn't decided yet. The most important part was being able to visit Anna.

She decided to stay at the hospital with her friends and her team, telling me she didn't want to be bored while I got fucked all day. After I finished scolding her for language, I realized she had a point.

But with the resources we now had at our disposal, everyone was hopeful her treatment would progress, and maybe she wouldn't have to be in the hospital forever.

The rest of it... Gloria was in jail, and the guys kept getting calls to have meetings. It would happen for a while as everything settled. We *were* free, but we were still needed.

At least the Syndicate had fucked off, and my Alphas were going to make very, *very* sure we never heard from them again. They didn't tell me the plan, and I didn't ask. I didn't want to know.

While we were furnishing the house, we hadn't started with our official *rules*. But now that there was a nest, I imagined we would.

"We had some adjustments added," Nick said. "Just for us."

"Oh?"

Stepping onto the cushions, he knelt and spread two of them apart, showing me a thick loop of metal bolted to the floor. Something that rope or chain could easily be attached to.

Heat dropped through me, my body flushing harder.

"They're everywhere," Sebastian said from the doorway. "Even on the ceiling, so if we want to suspend you, we can."

"Is that a plan you have?" My voice sounded husky to my own ears. Fuck, there was no way we were walking out of here with our clothes on. And I didn't care. We were still in the phase where we were fucking each other every chance we got, and I didn't think it was going to stop anytime soon.

Derek pulled his shirt over his head, confirming my theory. "Yes," he said simply. "I want to suspend you in my ropes and fuck the shit out of you, Omega. In fact—" He stepped over to what I'd thought was a blank wall and pressed a button next to the lighting panel. The wall opened silently, and an entire *closet* of kinky things was revealed. Things all of them liked, and things I already knew I loved. Holy shit.

"They let you put that in here?"

"Oh, sweetheart," Nick said. "That's nothing compared to the playroom they're installing downstairs."

"What?"

Sebastian lowered himself, and I only had a second to prepare. He launched himself at me, catching me around the waist and twisting so I landed on top of him in the nest. "It's huge," he said. "And it has everything we could ever want."

"Does it have a cage?" I asked.

Derek laughed. "Of course it does. A big one *and* a little one. We've got a Saint Andrew's cross, a spanking bench, one of the chairs we used for you, and plenty of free space for whatever else we want."

Pure heat dropped over me, slow and thorough, as my mind painted images of what could be done in the basement now that we were all together and I knew everything.

"But," Sebastian said, rolling us over so I was pinned against the emerald cushions. "It's not ready yet. And we don't want to wait, if you're ready."

"Ready for what?"

He pulled back, letting me see that Derek had a box in his hand. A black velvet box. "Are those them?" I asked, scrambling toward him.

"They are. We've had them for a little while, but we wanted everything to settle, and even more importantly, we wanted to combine it with something else."

Nick pushed off the door. "We're free now. There's no reason not to bond with you, sweetheart."

My heart stuttered. *Bonding.* Both exhilarating and terrifying. It wasn't something we could take back. But then again, we weren't taking anything back, were we?

"Selena?" Sebastian curled himself around me from behind. "Did we shock you into an early grave?"

I laughed once. "No. I just… it feels so big." He snickered, and I turned and slapped his arm. "That is *not* what I meant, and you know it."

"I know, Princess. But it is big, and your pussy likes trying to fit all of me inside you."

My skin was hot with the intensity of my blush.

Nick came to his knees in front of me, and his shirt was already gone. "Using your naked chest isn't fair."

"We never said we were going to play fair," he said, taking my hand and lifting it. "But what do you say? Will you be ours?"

My eyes teared, and I couldn't do anything more than whisper. "Yes. I'm already yours."

He slipped a hand behind my neck and kissed me, gathering me close. "I love you," he whispered against my lips. "I know we still have a long way to go because of everything that happened and what we did. But even if it takes the rest of our lives, I want to go through it with you."

I wrapped my arms around his neck. "You saved me. More than once. All of you saved me."

"It doesn't mean we didn't do damage, princess," Sebastian pulled me back into his body. "And we have some damage too."

Derek came down into the nest. He was naked now, and suddenly I had too many clothes on. They couldn't get me naked fast enough, and I wanted their skin on my skin. They spread me out on the pillows, dropping their mouths to my skin.

"I want to give you a choice, *gattina*," Derek whispered.

I smirked at him. "A choice? How generous."

A hand turned my face so I was eye to eye with Sebastian. "You're not a slave, princess, but you *will* call us Master."

The shudder that ran through me was so deep that I gasped. "Yes, Master."

"Good girl," he purred the words.

"Yes, a choice." Derek laughed, hiding his smile in my skin. "Occasionally we might give you one when we're in charge."

"What's the choice?"

"Do you want to be tied up before or after?"

I blinked, noting the fact that I was getting tied up regardless, and this was one of the last times they wouldn't be able to tell that it made me wet. But I wanted to be free while we bonded. "After."

"After it is." He reached to the edge of the nest and grabbed the box with the cuffs and collar inside. "There's something a little different about these."

"What?" I asked.

Opening the box, he held it out to me. I picked up one of the wrist cuffs and examined it. The beautiful, swirling designs on the outside were the same. But on the inside...

Gattina.

The next one was *Princess.*

Sweetheart.

Baby.

All the things they called me. On each of the four cuffs meant for my wrists and ankles. And on the inside of the collar, their names.

My Alphas would forever rest against my skin.

Because I belonged to them.

"I love them," I whispered.

"Yeah?"

I was already nodding, and it was hard not to lock them around my limbs myself. But they were already ahead of me. Sebastian took the ones I had and laid them out on the cushions.

"Because of everything, we wanted this to have a little bit

of symbolism," he said, handing me the cuff for my ankle that said *baby*. "The first one for you to put on yourself. Because it's your choice."

I took it from him, heart pounding.

It was my choice. No matter that the Syndicate had brought us together, we were *meant* to be here. And I would always choose them.

Slipping the cuff around my ankle, I clicked it shut, savoring the familiar feeling. It wasn't ever coming off. I ran one finger over the thin band, my stomach swooping.

My choice.

I had to place my hand on my chest because it was so full. One cuff alone would be enough, but I wanted all of them.

Seb picked up the one labeled *princess* and took my hand in his. He locked his eyes with mine and grinned. "Did you think you were getting this right away? Come here."

I went, ending up straddling his lap.

"Hands on my shoulders," he said. "Don't fucking move them."

"Okay."

Sebastian looked at me. "What did you say?"

The flush rolled up my chest and into my cheeks. "Yes, Master."

"Better," he murmured. "Looks like we still have some training to do with you."

One hand slid down my stomach, turning to stroke my clit before he slipped a single finger inside me and left his thumb on my clit. "You know what I want to train you for, princess?"

A whimper came out of me as he added another finger. "What, Master?"

He slipped a third finger inside me, causing me to gasp. Circling his thumb on my clit, I dug my fingers into his shoulders, trying not to move them.

"My fist," he said softly, fucking me slowly and steadily

with his hand. "I want my whole hand in this pussy, with you coming all over it. I want my arm covered in your cum, princess."

The way he curled his fingers inside me, I had to close my eyes. "I don't know if I'll ever be able to do that."

"You will," he leaned in and whispered. "You will, and I'm going to strap you down to the chair in the playroom, fuck you and fist you until you're a writhing mess. But you won't be able to do anything about it because you won't be able to move."

"Fuck." His words sent fiery lust straight through me, and he wasn't slowing down. Now he was working me, forcing my body toward its first orgasm exactly like he knew how. "I—"

"Give me the orgasm, princess. It's mine."

Five more seconds, and I did. I shuddered on his fingers, pleasure spreading through me in desperate, delicate ripples.

Sebastian bent me back. "And so when I use anything on these, you remember who owns you."

He bit down on my nipple, breaking the skin. It was a world of pain swirling into warmth and pleasure and *love*. Sebastian was in my chest, his emotions humming beneath my skin. I felt the way he felt when he looked at me, and it leveled me. The depth and conviction of it—if I had any doubts left, those feelings were gone. "Oh my god."

Lifting my wrist, he closed the cuff around it and clicked it shut. I was his, and he was mine. "I love you," he said. "Forever."

I wrapped my arms around his neck and kissed him. Got lost in the feeling of his lust and love and everything else swirling between us.

"My turn," Nick said, tugging on my ankle.

A laugh burst out of me as he tugged me across the cushions on my stomach after he pulled me out of Seb's arms. "Present, sweetheart."

I lifted my ass in the air, baring all of myself so his hands could land on my hips and then— "Oh my fuck."

His mouth was on me, tongue delving deep, driving me back up into pleasure. And now I could feel the way Sebastian was turned on by watching us, and that fed my pleasure even more. Made it intense. What the hell was it going to be with all three of them?

Nick dragged his tongue up and licked my ass. Consuming it and reminding me what it was like to be fucked by all of them at once. And with that memory, the next swipe of his tongue over my clit sent me over.

I moaned into the cushions, and I felt his teeth just before he bit. Right below my ass. Pain and heat and Nick's presence forming into a bond I could feel.

He turned me over, lifting my leg and kissing my ankle before locking the *sweetheart* cuff around me.

His feelings were just as deep. Just as strong. Just as incredibly overwhelming. He dropped down onto me, kissing me hard and telling me without words how much he was in love with me. It rang between us, clear as a bell.

When he rolled away, Derek took his place. His cock rested between us, resting perfectly against my clit. He could so easily slip inside me, but he didn't. Instead, he rocked against me, teasing yet relentless.

Derek didn't stop, dragging me up to pleasure using nothing but his hips and his cock and that damn rhythm I couldn't resist. He had me panting and shuddering beneath him, nearly begging for him to just fuck me.

I arched beneath him, my vision going white and a cry flying from my lips before he leaned into my neck and bit into my shoulder. All three of them were with me, and the addition of Derek brought tears to my eyes. Beneath all the arousal and the love, I felt the truth of our whole ordeal. How much regret and guilt they held about what they'd had to do. They wanted to tell me from the second they met me.

Clinging to Derek, I let the joy and grief of everything wash over me. Wishing things had gone differently wouldn't change them. And in the end, there were so many lives saved and the world was better. The four of us could bear the pain for those reasons.

Derek kissed me. "You're fucking incredible, *gattina*." He placed the final cuff around my wrist, the one with his pet name, and clicked it closed. "I hope that even if nothing had happened the way it did, we still would have found you. Because I can't imagine going through life and not feeling this. Sit up for me."

He helped me up to sit between the three of them, and together they fit the collar around my neck and closed it. It rested perfectly against my skin, and I leaned into them. "I love you," I said. "So much."

Leaning in, Derek kissed his bite, and I shuddered with pleasure. "I love you, too. I'll be right back."

"Now I know why none of you bit my neck." Having a bite mark beneath the collar would be too much.

Seb laughed. "Don't worry, princess. We'll use our bites plenty." Reaching forward, he pinched my nipple right where he'd bitten, and it was like a heat-seeking missile aimed straight at my clit.

Derek returned with rope, looping my hands behind my back and tying them quickly. Then pulling my arms closer and tying them together above my elbows. It shoved my chest out, presenting my tits to my other Alphas. And then he pulled me down onto my back, my arms trapped underneath me.

Already, the heady, floaty feeling was sinking into me, and I loved feeling both their amusement at my reactions, and their own instincts and needs flaring to life. It was so much *more*.

One of my legs was pulled to the side, and Derek slipped some rope around it. "Might as well try the new features of the nest," he said. "Suspension can come later."

I pulled on my leg, and it didn't move. He'd tied it down to one of the metal loops, and he was already moving to take the other one so I was completely tied open for them.

Exactly where I wanted to be.

"Your pussy's gonna be so tight like this, princess," Sebastian said, fitting himself against me and stretching me open. I moaned, unable to speak, and he smiled, feeling how much I loved it. And I now understood exactly how he savored that delicate edge of pain.

Nick knelt over my chest. "Anything to say before I fuck your throat? Don't worry," he glanced over at Derek, who was already stroking his cock. "I'll share while Seb knots that delicious cunt."

Leaning down close to my lips, he kissed me gently. "But we're spending some time in here today, sweetheart. And there's nothing you can do about it."

My mind opened up as I dropped down into that place of complete submission, exactly where I wanted to be. They were mine. I owned them and they owned me.

"Any last words?" He asked again.

I smiled up at him. "Fuck me, Master."

Nick smirked down at me, and all I could feel was their happiness and love in my chest. He fit his cock to my lips. "As you wish."

EPILOGUE II

SELENA

SIX MONTHS LATER

A soothing hand on the skin of my back woke me, drawing me to the surface slowly, like being pulled up from the bottom of a well. My body was fine with waking up, but my mind liked the comforting dark and I groaned, curling further into the pillow.

The movement pulled on my cuffs, and the length of chain which somehow had worked its way around my ankle was suddenly too tight. And that damned hand was still touching my skin, waking me—and my body—up.

Derek's scent wrapped around me. That intangible sweetness of mountain air I couldn't get enough of. Lips brushed the back of my shoulder, then my spine. The back of my hair.

"I will have you know I was sleeping very deeply, and I'm annoyed you woke me up," I said, but there wasn't any venom in the words.

"Mmm," Derek hummed against my skin. "And here I was thinking I would reward you this morning before Seb gets to play with you."

Pushing off my pillow, I rolled straight into his arms. "Reward me for what?"

He smiled and kissed my forehead. "Do I need a reason to reward my Omega?"

"Usually," I muttered, causing him to laugh.

Derek ran his fingers along my collar and then down my side, purr rising to life inside him. The last six months had been a delirious, delicious dream. With the guys free of duty, we'd spent most of the time getting to know each other and doing... whatever the fuck we wanted. Which, a good portion of the time, was fucking.

Sebastian hadn't lied. The playroom in our basement rivaled *Catena* for all the space and equipment it had. And they'd made it comfortable and cozy at the same time.

It was one of my favorite places in the house.

Tracing his fingers over my bare hip, Derek smirked. "God, I hope Seb lets me help him today. Even if he doesn't, I'm going to watch."

I swallowed. "Why?"

Sebastian hadn't told me about what he planned for today. I had a suspicion, but the three of them were keeping it annoyingly under wraps.

"And ruin the fun?" he teased.

I made a face and groaned, and Derek lifted his hand gently to my throat, smile still on his lips. "Get it out now, *Gattina*. I don't think Sebastian is in the mood to be a brat tamer today."

"I'm never a brat," I scoffed.

He laughed, the sudden loud sound echoing off the windows. "Never a brat, my ass." As if to prove the point, he released my throat and smacked my ass, smoothing over the sting with his palm.

"Will you unchain me, Master?"

The rules we'd set in place in the hotel six months ago still stood. Whenever I slept in one of their beds, I was chained to it. I liked it more than I would ever let on. And they left the chains long enough to reach the bathroom with ease, so there was never a problem.

Derek took one hand in his, uncuffing me from the chain. And in the next moment he had me pushed flat down into the mattress, re-chaining me, but this time with my hands behind my back.

My heart started to pound. "Master?"

"I'll unchain you, *Gattina*. After. You know the rules."

I did know the rules. Could still hear Sebastian's voice as he laid this one down.

Before you leave bed in the morning, your mouth touches our cocks.

"I didn't forget," I whispered.

"No?"

I fought the urge to roll my eyes, and Derek grinned, knowing I was struggling with the sass. The nights I'd slept alone in the last six months were so few I could count them on one hand. I couldn't forget the rule even if I wanted to.

Which I didn't.

"No," I repeated. "And the rule requires my hands behind my back?"

Derek smirked. "No, that's just what I want today."

Leaning back against the headboard, he threw off the covers, revealing his cock, already hard with his morning erection.

Struggling to my knees, I bent over his cock, hair curtaining around my face, and kissed the tip of it. There. The rule had been satisfied.

But Derek hadn't.

His hand fisted in my hair, allowing me to see him as he guided my face lower, pushing his cock between my lips and deeper into my mouth. The way he looked at me set me on fire. As long as I lived, I would never get tired of that look. Like I was absolutely everything. The best thing he'd ever seen. Like he wanted to *consume* me.

I savored the taste of his skin and the feeling of him sliding across my tongue. Into my throat. I couldn't imagine a time when I'd ever had enough of them.

"All the way down, *Gattina*." His fist held me there when my lips reached the skin of his stomach. "*Fuck*, I love your throat, Selena."

I hummed around him, which I knew he loved, and his eyes went hot. He pulled me off him and up his body, arranging me to straddle his hips, but not pushing into me. "Soon I'm going to plan a scene with you. Nothing but you, bound, *worshipping* my cock."

My mouth went dry as his hands slid up my ribs, uncuffing my hands from behind my back. "Not now?"

A smirk played on his lips. "Not now. Though the fact that you want it might make it happen sooner."

My whole face and chest flushed with heat. "Can't help it, Master. I like the taste of you too much."

One hand slipped behind my neck, pulling me in for a kiss. "I *love* the way you taste," he murmured against my lips. "Now get downstairs and get ready so Seb doesn't kill me for ruining you before all of his devious plans."

"Tell me," I whined.

He kissed me one more time. "Nope."

Flopping off him onto the bed, I rolled away from him and off the bed, exaggerating the movement of my hips as I walked, knowing he loved to watch me walk away.

"Selena," he growled.

I smirked over my shoulder. "You said you were going to watch. I thought you might want some practice."

"You're walking a fine line, Omega."

Slipping into my room, I grabbed a robe and wrapped it around myself before getting ready. My morning routine, minus the shower. I'd showered before bed, and Sebastian was probably going to make me very messy today, no matter what he had planned. We'd shower after. Or take a bath.

I hummed to myself as I sat at the vanity and brushed my hair, just enjoying the simplicity of it. Life had been like that lately. It was nice to enjoy things for the sake of them while not having to worry.

A quiet knock, and I saw Nick leaning in the doorway. "Hi."

Coming up behind me, he dropped a kiss on the top of my head. "Morning, sweetheart." He set the coffee in his down on the vanity. "Breakfast is downstairs. You need to eat before you go to the playroom."

"I suppose you won't tell me what he has planned either?"

"Nope." Nick took the brush out of my hand and set it aside, instead sinking his fingers into my hair and giving me the kind of scalp massage that made me groan with pleasure. "But I think you'll enjoy it."

I narrowed my eyes at him in the mirror, and he smiled. In my chest I felt his amusement, along with Derek's. They liked teasing me and hiding things from me far too much.

"I just have one question."

"What's that?"

"Is this going to be like an all day thing? Or will we have a chance to do something else later. I'm in the mood to snuggle. With movies."

His fingers dug into my scalp again. "I think we'll be able to make that happen."

"Are you going to be there?"

"Absolutely."

"Will—"

One hand slipped to gently hold the back of my neck. "Stop. Come downstairs and eat something. Then go to the playroom. No detours."

"Yes, Master."

Leaning down, he kissed my cheek. "Good girl."

I wrapped my hands around the mug of coffee and took a sip. Nick always made it perfectly. The way I loved it.

Breakfast was cheesy eggs and bacon, which told me the scene wouldn't be easy. They always gave me protein before the more difficult scenes. But I didn't need it to be easy. I trusted them. They wouldn't do anything I couldn't handle, and they would stop if I asked them to.

I'd used my safe words before, and the way they cared for me only made me love them more.

Putting my dishes in the sink, I stretched, cracking my

back before going downstairs to the playroom. It was warm in here. The rich burgundy walls glowing with the soft lights that were hidden everywhere.

Sebastian stood with his back to me, preparing something. "May I come in?"

It wasn't something I needed to ask permission for, but I wanted to know if he was ready for me. He turned, smiling at me. "Yes, princess. Take off your robe and wait for me by the couch."

I obeyed, draping my robe over the arm of the couch before kneeling on the cushion in front of it. Here, in this room only, we observed more rules and protocols than in the rest of the house. Here, I knelt unless they told me otherwise.

Even after six months, I couldn't fully explain the comfort it brought me, and I'd let go of the need to understand. It worked for us. That's all that mattered.

Sebastian had dressed up. Black slacks and a black button-down shirt rolled to the elbows. A leather harness wrapped around his chest and back. Power rolled off him, and I loved it. Our bond told me he knew it, too.

Finally, he strode over and sat in front of me. I leaned in against his knee, his hand on my hair. He purred. "Did you sleep okay?"

"Yes, Master."

"Are you ready for this?"

I looked up at him. "It's hard to be ready when I don't know what's coming, Master."

Sebastian searched my face, and I knew from experience he was listening to our bond for how I was feeling. How nervous I was. I trusted him, but not knowing what he was going to do also tied my stomach into knots. It was something we were working on.

"What's your safe word?"

"Red."

He nodded. "Thank you. And the others?"

"Green if I'm good. Yellow to check in. Orange is 'I'm panicking or need something to change but don't want everything to stop.'"

Pulling the cushion between his knees, Seb tilted my chin up so I met his gaze. "I won't be gagging you, so you can use them if you need them. You also don't need to ask permission to come."

I blinked. "I don't?"

A devious smirk appeared on his lips. "You don't. I think you'll probably beg me to stop having them."

"That hasn't happened so far."

Sebastian leaned down and kissed me slowly before he spoke. "Do you remember when we bonded? What I told you?"

I remembered a lot about that day, but it was fuzzy with pleasure and the overwhelm of finally feeling them and how deeply they loved me. But exact words? Not all of them. "I don't think so," I admitted. "Sorry."

He chuckled. "That's fine. I told you I was going to train you for something."

My eyes widened. I *did* remember that. "Your fist."

Things suddenly clicked into place. Seb had been using larger and larger toys on me. Fingering me with three fingers and then four. At one point I think he even got his thumb inside me, but by that time I was so blissed out I barely noticed.

"I told you I was going to strap you down, fuck you and fist you until you couldn't come anymore."

A shudder rolled through my body, along with the tiniest bit of fear. Was I ready for that?

His hand tightened on my jaw, that sharp look in his eyes betraying his excitement. "I'm going to force as many orgasms as I can out of you, princess. You'll take my fist. My cock. Your other Alpha's cocks. Any way I can make you come, I will. Until I decide you're finished, you safe word, or pass out."

My stomach tumbled through my toes, dizzy, heady arousal and fear dropping through me. When he laid things out for me like this, I couldn't even breathe.

"Do you trust me?" He asked.

"Yes, Master."

"Any objections?"

I shook my head.

"Questions?"

"Will there be pain?" I wasn't a masochist. Sebastian could hurt me and I loved when he did, because he knew how to give it to me in a way I could handle. But if I was already being pushed, I wasn't sure I wanted to combine the two.

"There might," he said. "But not because I'll be hurting you. Because your orgasms might become painful."

"Oh."

He winked. "Go hop on the table."

The table wasn't really a table, but a device that had so many moving pieces I couldn't keep track. It let them create ways to restrain me. Right now it was set up almost like a medical chair, with a split between my legs where he could stand. I sat where he wanted me, not realizing he was right behind me.

"Are you comfortable?"

"Yes, Master."

He started strapping me down, and I started to float. My body recognized the feeling of being bound and knew what came next. Straps down my legs, over my stomach and arms. One across my forehead. I couldn't move a single inch, and I smiled. "This feels familiar."

I hadn't been in this position since the club.

"I thought you might say that. You want to warm her up, Nick?"

The others were standing behind him, and I hadn't even

noticed them come in while he was making sure I couldn't move. Nick grinned. "Yes I do."

My Alpha dropped to his knees in front of me and drove his tongue straight into my pussy. My hips arched, but they couldn't, flaring heat through the rest of me. "Oh, fuck."

Not having to hold myself back made everything different. Nick knew exactly how to drive me over the edge—they all did—and he swirled his tongue around my clit, lifting up underneath it just the way I liked.

"Hmm," Sebastian pulled one leg wider. "I think Nick needs access to more of you."

Derek pulled my other leg wide, exposing me further to Nick's mouth and his wicked tongue. Being tied down made everything so much more intense. I couldn't move to mitigate any sensation, pleasure building under lips and fingers and tongue. "Fuck."

"Don't hold it back, princess."

"I—"

He stepped up beside me, whispering in my ear. "Let go, Omega."

Pleasure crashed over me in a shuddering wave. A fast orgasm, just passing through.

"That's one," Sebastian said. "Derek?"

Nick switched places with him, and suddenly I was full of Derek's cock. On the heels of pleasure, I was already sensitive, and I suddenly realized exactly how hard this might be.

Laughing in my ear, Sebastian removed the strap from my forehead. "I want you to be able to look around. Look at me while he fucks you."

I turned my head to him, my eyes fluttering closed. Pleasure like this was gorgeous, and the fact that it was normal and commonplace for me wasn't something I took for granted.

"Look at me, Selena."

My eyes had fallen closed. I forced them open and found

him smiling. Fingers drifted over my cheek. "You look good while you're getting fucked, princess."

Sebastian kissed me, stealing all my air, deepening until I couldn't tell if he was kissing me or consuming me. One hand fisted in my hair, turning my face back to Derek, who leaned over me to kiss me too. His tongue danced with mine, in time with his cock, and I relaxed into their control.

It always took a minute for my brain and body to catch up to the truth. I belonged to them, and they would take me where I desperately needed to go.

Derek's thumb found my clit, and he smiled against my lips. "You like the way this feels? Being tied up and forced to come?"

I groaned into his mouth. "Yes, Master."

"Noted, *gattina*. This gives me all kinds of ideas."

Changing the angle of his hips, Derek drove into me exactly where I needed it. He captured the moan on my lips with his, fucking me through my orgasm and into his.

Seb chuckled. "All those ideas will have to wait."

Derek pulled out, staring at me with a gaze full of heat. "I'm a patient man. And I'm going to enjoy the show."

Across the room, Nick already had a seat. Derek joined them, both of them looking relaxed and easy instead of like they were about to watch me be absolutely fucking destroyed.

"How many times do you think I can make you come before you beg me to stop?" Sebastian asked.

I shook my head. I had no idea. They regularly made me come more than I ever thought I could, and it wasn't the entire *goal* of the scene. "I don't know, Master."

"What do you guys think?"

Nick stared at me, and in our bond, I felt his arousal as he watched me. Derek's too. They loved this. "Before she begs? I would say ten. I think you could probably get twenty out of her, though."

I gasped. "Twenty?"

"I'll go higher," Derek said with a chuckle. "Fifteen before she begs. Twenty-five until she's done."

"Derek." I stared at him.

He stared right back. "What did you call me?"

In the play room I didn't call them by their names. "Master. There's no way."

"Good luck," Nick said. "You just dared a sadist."

"I didn't."

"Oh," Sebastian said. "You did. We'll see how far we can get you."

Too late, I noticed the wand in his hand. The kind that plugged into the wall and had all the power. "I'm sorry," I said. "I didn't mean it as a dare."

"It's a dare you'll enjoy. No more talking unless it's our names or screaming from an orgasm."

The wand came straight down on my clit at full speed. I erupted, pleasure tearing through me like lightning. Already ragged and brutal and *fuck* it felt so good. My head dropped back, my eyes closed, and I sank fully into it.

"I think you're warmed up now," he laughed.

One finger slipped into me, feeling different. I opened my eyes and found my Alpha wearing gloves. With his sleeves rolled up, the harness, and now black plastic gloves…

It was the hottest thing I'd ever seen. I had no idea why the sight of him with plastic gloves on had my entire body tightening and need climbing once again, but he felt it and grinned. "That's good to know."

"Why the gloves, Master?"

"Because if my entire hand is going inside you, I want you to be safe. And now, because I know it turns you on. Quiet now."

The intensity on Sebastian's face had me quaking. It was only two fingers, but he was going to put his whole hand inside me. I knew how big his hands were. How big *every-thing* about him was.

A gentle smack on my inner thigh made me gasp. "You're tensing up, princess. Color?"

"A banana green," I admitted.

His mouth turned into a smirk. "So still green, but almost yellow?"

"Yes."

"I can work with that." He jerked his head at my other Alphas.

Derek kissed the side of my head when he reached me. "You're nervous?"

One nod.

"But you feel good?"

Another nod.

"Close your eyes," Nick told me from my other side.

Derek slid his hand around my throat, the gentle pressure emphasizing my collar. And between my legs, Sebastian sealed his mouth over my clit.

My hips bucked, but there was nowhere to go. One finger slid into me, and then another. Along with his tongue, it was nothing more than normal.

"Take a deep breath in," Nick said quietly. "And when you release it, relax everything."

One breath in, one breath out, and Sebastian had four fingers in me, filling me up. This was normal too. He'd been working me up to it when I hadn't even remembered it.

"Keep doing that," Derek whispered, brushing his lips over my ear. "Breathing in and out. Relaxing. Letting us take care of you."

Seb curled his fingers, and I shattered apart. The stretch and the fullness, the way he pressed against my G-spot... I panted, trying to keep breath in my lungs, but it was impossible with the way he fucked me. Deeper and deeper. Pleasure clawed at my insides, building up in every piece of me. Down to my *bones*.

He fucked me like his life depended on it, and those fingers felt so good. Another cresting wave caught me, and the fullness was too much. Unbearable because it was so *bright* with pleasure. I didn't think I could stop. My body was out of control and it made me panic as much as I craved every fucking second.

"There it is, princess."

My eyes flew open to meet Seb's. Only victory shone there. Between my legs, his hand wasn't visible. It was inside me, up to his wrist. I could just barely see the edge of his glove. A whine slipped out, and I caught myself before I spoke.

"Give me a color," Nick said.

He was *fisting* me. And even though I felt so fucking stuffed I couldn't take a full breath, it didn't hurt. I was on the edge of an orgasm so intense I didn't know if I'd be awake on the other side of it. "Physically green."

"And mentally?"

I shook my head.

"She's okay," Sebastian said, with his eyes on me. The steadiness in our bond steadied *me*. I was okay. "Give us some space."

They stepped back, leaving me trapped in Sebastian's gaze. "This is between you and me, princess. Just us. I've got you. Believe me?"

"Yes, Master."

"Good girl." Warm approval spread over his face. "I'm going to move now. I'm going to make you come. All you have to do is feel it. Keep your eyes on me."

Inside, it felt like he expanded. He was pressed against every part of me. Every place that they used to make me scream, *all at once*.

His fingers, I realized. He was opening his fist, and that's

261

why it felt bigger. It didn't take much with my body primed and ready to go over the edge. I tried to squeeze down on him. Utterly impossible. I could barely keep my eyes open and on him.

"Your pussy looks so good with my fist inside it, Selena. I knew you could do it."

Wetness and arousal slid around his hand, and he moved it again. Not it. His entire arm. Slowly. Fucking me with his whole hand and leaning down to taste my clit again.

I couldn't keep watching him. My eyes rolled back, the next orgasm coming in a wave. Pleasure had never felt like this before—a delicious enemy I couldn't get enough of and that might actually kill me.

Another orgasm as he moved.

And another one.

My mind turned to mush. I didn't know how many there'd been or how many I could take. Hell, I didn't know how to tell the difference between one and the other. It was all a golden cloud of sensation. A storm I couldn't escape from. Maybe a tornado?

No. I was too wet for a tornado. There needed to be some kind of rain.

"*Fuck,*" Sebastian's voice echoed through the room. "That's it, princess. Soak me."

Was I?

The next wave hurt in the best way. Like when my Alpha tied me up and used his floggers until I didn't know up from down.

Another wave, and it didn't feel like *I* was orgasming anymore. My body was, and I was just along for the ride. Not being able to move now made it better and worse. There was still nowhere for the pleasure to go, but now it kept me trapped in the complex tangle of agony and bliss.

"M-master." My lips felt numb. "I can't."

"You can, Princess." The wave came with his encouragement, and there was no way to keep quiet.

I shook my head. "Please?"

"Are you using your safe word?"

Did I want him to stop?

Yes. No. I didn't want it all to end. It would be too abrupt. "No."

"Take a breath for me, Omega."

I did, and it felt strange to not be full. Sebastian stood and crossed the room. I realized he'd pulled out of me. His fist wasn't in me anymore. A giggle burst out of me. I felt like I was floating and dizzy. Happy.

He grinned at me when he came back. "You feel good, Selena?"

"Yes, Master."

Standing between my legs, Sebastian was tall enough to lean over me and stroke my hair. His cock pushed into me, and I moaned. I was sore. It didn't hurt in a bad way. "We're not done?"

"I want you to give me one more, princess. Come all over my cock."

"I don't think I can."

He kissed me softly. "You can."

It wasn't gentle. Sebastian savored the bite of pain he felt in our bond. His pleasure fed mine, and mine his. I felt it building, even though it was impossible. There was no way to get there, except for him to push me over. I already knew it would ruin me.

And I trusted them to pick up the pieces.

Every muscle in my body locked, pain spiraling through me along with ecstasy so sharp and brutal, I screamed. Sebastian's warmth soothed the pain, and soft words of encouragement. I barely felt him come, but I knew he had. Knew the feeling.

I was delirious as he released me from the table. They

spoke among themselves, but I didn't absorb it. All I felt were warm arms around me, carrying me into the luxurious bathroom next to the playroom. One of my other Alphas had already run a bath, and Sebastian lowered me into the hot water carefully.

Then his chest was under my cheek, and I wasn't sure when he'd gotten in the bath. I was so drifty. Cloudy. It happened sometimes, and they didn't seem to mind.

"Do you have a color, princess?"

I lifted my hand out of the water, watching it drip off my skin and the metal cuff around my wrist. "I think I'm green."

"Do you have any pain? Sharpness?"

My body was sore, but nothing felt wrong. Nothing out of the ordinary. "No."

"Good."

Derek stood in the doorway, watching us. His shirt was off. When did his shirt come off? "We're getting the living room ready."

"Sounds good."

"For what?" I asked.

Sebastian moved me gently, leaning against the side of the tub before getting out and grabbing us towels. He helped me out and dried me off before wrapping myself in the fluffy robe I'd put on this morning. But it was *warm*. Like they'd put it in the drier.

"You told Derek you wanted to snuggle with a movie," Sebastian said. "So that's what we're going to do while you rest and come back."

"I didn't go anywhere."

He chuckled softly. "I know, pretty girl."

When he picked me up, his purr under my ear lulled me into perfect contentment. My Alphas had me. I was safe. Warm. Happy.

I blinked my eyes open into warm dimness.

The big screen television in our living room was on, and I

was lying on the couch, tucked in front of Sebastian. Derek sat on the floor near my hips, lightly holding my hand where it drooped off the cushion.

Nick was sprawled on some pillows, and it almost made me laugh. Normally I was the one on the floor.

"Did I fall asleep?"

Seb's purr rumbled against my spine, and a hand stroked over my hair. "For a little while."

"Sorry."

"Don't be." Derek squeezed my hand. "You needed it."

Nick smiled at me, and I looked between them. "Who was right?"

"Nick was closer," Seb whispered. "You gave me nineteen."

"That's a lot."

He kissed my hair. "Yes, it is."

Rolling over, I cuddled closer to his naked chest and inhaled, burrowing into his warm cinnamon apple scent.

"I'm proud of you," he whispered. "You did so well."

"I can't believe your hand was inside of me."

"It'll be inside of you again, princess. When you're recovered and ready."

My body felt wonderfully exhausted. All that pleasure and all that trust. They never pushed me beyond what I could take. "I'd do it again."

Sebastian chuckled. "Good."

"I love you," I whispered. "All three of you."

"We love you too, *gattina*. Do you want to keep watching? Or sleep."

I smiled into Sebastian's chest. "I'll watch. But I'm going to need a snack. And a drink. And a foot rub."

Laughter burst out all around me, and Sebastian sat up with me in his arms, kissing my cheek. "I think we can handle that, princess."

"So I'm in charge now?"

265

"Not a fucking chance." He dropped a kiss on my forehead.

Nick brought me chocolate, Derek brought me tea, and Sebastian got my favorite lotion, digging his fingers into my feet in the way only he could. The others sat on either side of me, and I settled down into pure comfort.

"What?" Nick asked.

"I can't believe this is our life," I said. "I'm so happy."

He picked up my hand and kissed the cuff on my wrist. "I'm glad, sweetheart. Because you're stuck with us."

"I never want to be anywhere else."

Derek started the movie again, and I fell asleep again, wrapped in their arms.

The End.

*H*ello beautiful readers!

I hope you enjoyed your journey into a darker Omegaverse with Selena!

It was definitely an experience to write something a little darker in this genre, and don't worry, there will be more to come in Omegaverse, both dark *and* sweet, in the near future.

In the meantime, I'd love to meet you! Sign up for my newsletter for updates and sneak peeks, and the occasional dessert recipe!

I also have a Facebook group where we share memes, I share snippets of works in progress, and everything in between. Come join the Delightful Deviants! I hope to see you there, and there will be more books very soon!

Devyn Sinclair

PLAYLIST

This is a playlist of some of the songs I listened to while writing *Seducing Selena*

I hope you enjoy this! Listen to the full on Spotify.

- **After All**— Culture Code, ARAYA, RUNN
- **Alive** — Zeds Dead MKLA
- **Altyn** — framed
- **Arres** — Serhat Durmus, Melanie Fontana
- **Beside Me** — Serhat Durmus
- **Control** — Zoe Wees
- **Chapter 54** — Kelsey Woods
- **Constance** — Spiritbox
- **Deepfake** — brakence
- **Distancing** — Juelz
- **Dumbledore's Farewell** — Nicholas Hooper
- **Drown** — HANDS
- **Excused** — Lowx
- **Going Insane** — SIPPY
- **Gris, Pt. 2** — Berlinist
- **If You Don't** — IMERIKA

- **JSYK** — Pauline Herr
- **Losing my mind** — Alter/Ego, enjoii, luna.moon
- **Lost** — Altare, Bafu
- **Lost It** — ZHU
- **Midnight in LA - Champagne Drip Remix** — BLACK NEON, Champagne Drip
- **Mom let me go - Veins Slowed Remix** — Masha Hima, Tokyo Tears
- **My Feelings** — Serhat Durmus, Georgia Ku
- **Outta Luck** — KATT
- **Rage** — Paaus, Lukrative
- **Red Eye (feat. TroyBoi)** — Justin Bieber, TroyBoi
- **Row** — sky fall beats
- **Tattoo** — Loreen
- **Truth Serum** — Joseph Trapanese

ABOUT THE AUTHOR

Devyn Sinclair writes steamy Reverse Harem romances for your wildest fantasies. Every sexy story is packed with the right amount of steam, hot men, and delicious happy endings.

She lives in the wilds of Montana in a small red house with a crazy orange cat. When Devyn's not writing, she spends time outside in big sky country, continues her quest to find the best lemon pastry there is, and buys too many books. (Of course!)

To connect with Devyn:

ALSO BY DEVYN SINCLAIR

For a complete list of Devyn's books, content warnings, bonuses and extras, please visit her website.

https://www.devynsinclair.com/books

Made in the USA
Middletown, DE
02 September 2024